THE RED RAIDER

THE RED RAIDER

A Western Duo

WILLIAM COLT MACDONALD

SAGEBRUSH
Large Print Westerns

Copyright © 2004, by Golden West Literacy Agency

First published in Great Britain by ISIS Publishing
First published in the United States by Five Star

Published in Large Print 2007 by ISIS Publishing Ltd.,
7 Centremead, Osney Mead, Oxford OX2 0ES
United Kingdom
by arrangement with
Golden West Literary Agency

British Library Cataloguing in Publication Data
MacDonald, William Colt, 1891–1968
    The red raider. – Large print ed. –
(Sagebrush western series)
1. Western stories
2. Large type books
I. Title II. MacDonald, William Colt, 1891–1968.
Gun fog
813.5'2 [F]

ISBN 978–0–7531–7755–6 (hb)

Printed and bound in Great Britain by
T. J. International Ltd., Padstow, Cornwall

Table of Contents

Foreword

by

Jon Tuska

Allan William Colt MacDonald was born in Detroit, Michigan, on December 2, 1891. In an early autobiographical sketch MacDonald had this to say: "I led the usual schoolboy's life and graduated from grammar school, after which I struggled through two years of high school. However, my animosity toward Latin verbs and a weakness for reading books aside from those prescribed by the high school course brought about a conference with my principal who suggested that I discontinue school. At this time an uncle, connected with a silk-importing firm, took me with him on a trip to China where I spent some weeks. Had I been less interested in reading I could have made more of the opportunities that colorful country affords, but in those days I noted only that China seemed crowded with half-starved coolies and had a rotten sewerage system." In 1907 at his father's urging he began attending night school and began working as a lathe operator for Dodge Brothers' Motor Company. He was promoted to an "efficiency engineer" (a job he hated) and finally, on the strength of a college extension course he took, began writing advertising copy and articles for trade publications. MacDonald married

Elizabeth Grace Brown, known as Betty, on June 5, 1920. One child was born as a result of this union, Wallace Allan MacDonald on March 20, 1926.

MacDonald began writing for the pulp magazines in the mid 1920s. "Romney Breaks In" in *Action Stories* (9/25) is typical of MacDonald's magazine fiction during this early period, relying heavily on vernacular parlance (which he later avoided) and with an emphasis on the kind of spectacular stunts Tom Mix liked to include in his Western films. "Cash" Romney rides into a saloon in Longhorn, Arizona, atop his horse and holds it up. " 'You all know me, leastwise most of you do, and you all know that Romney, of the Circle X, can throw lead accurate-like. Mebbe you're a bit surprised to witness me departin' from the straight and narrow thisaway, but punchin' cows gets plumb tiresome now and then.' " As it turns out, Romney only commits the robbery to get close to Scarface and his outlaw gang because he had been hired by the Secret Service to assist the government in capturing the bandit leader.

The first issue of Fiction House's *The Lariat Story Magazine* (8/24) contained the first installment of a four-part serial by MacDonald titled "The Red Raider". Harold Hersey, an editor for the Clayton magazines and later a pulp magazine publisher himself, claimed in his book, *Pulpwood Editor* (Stokes, 1937), that he had "bought Allan W. C. MacDonald's first Western novel" for *Ace-High Magazine*, a Clayton publication. Surely, here, he was mistaken, since the first Western novel by MacDonald serialized in *Ace-High* was "Don Gringo of the Rio Grande". It began with the 1st June Number in 1927, a full two years *after* MacDonald's Western serial in *Lariat*. The *Ace-High* serial was subsequently published in book form as *Don Gringo* (Chelsea House, 1930). MacDonald followed this second serial with a series of short novels for *Ace-High Magazine* that remain memorable for their sound characterization and extraordinary inventiveness. "The Outlaw Buster" in *Ace-High Magazine* (9/3/27) was the first of these, an off-beat story of pursuit following a daring robbery and contention over the ownership of a ranch after the owner's son and then the owner are both killed. This short novel definitely deserves to be reprinted along with other equally memorable magazine stories such as "The Son of the Wolf" in *Ace-High Magazine* (12/16/27), "The Gun-Slingin' Gringo" in *Ace-High Magazine* (3/18/28), and "Law Rides to Loboville" in *Ace-High Magazine* (3/3/29). MacDonald would later considerably expand and change "The Son of the Wolf" to form *Master of the Mesa* (Doubleday, 1947), but the short novel has many virtues not contained in the expansion. In Spring, 1928 *Ace-High Magazine* serialized "Gun Country" which would appear the next year in book form as *Gun Country* (Chelsea House, 1929).

Already by 1925 MacDonald had dropped "Allan" from his byline, but it was not till the end of the decade that he made the decision to depend exclusively on writing Western fiction for his livelihood. "I quit my job cold," MacDonald told a Pacific Grove reporter on the occasion of the appearance of his fiftieth book — *The*

Comache Scalp (Lippincott, 1955). "I said if I was going to be a writer, why wasn't I writing fiction. I had a lot of luck. My wife was pregnant. She said, go ahead and write. Lots of help, severest critic, and all that." From the time of that decision on, MacDonald's career became a long string of successes in pulp magazines, hardcover novels, films, and eventually original and reprint paperback editions.

MacDonald supplied an even more detailed portrait of himself for the American Fiction Guild that was printed in the bulletin for April 1, 1936. "Have called a lot of places home," he wrote in a rather laconic style, "but like best Chicago and San Antonio — so far. No telling where an itching foot will take a man. Living in Laguna Beach, California, at present. I like to poke around the Southwest border country, talk to old-timers, in search for story material, and such jaunts usually give a feller ideas about places he'd like to live. As to personal habits, hobbies, etc.: I smoke continually during waking hours, either Durham or ready-rolled; prefer Scotch to other whiskies; am essentially a beer drinker; like half a dozen cups of Java with a meal and my thick steaks rare; I'd be lost without a dog underfoot most of the time — the breed doesn't matter so long as it's a dog; get a big kick out of putting water colors on heavy white paper, but can't draw worth a damn; have also experimented (unsuccessfully) with oil colors, pen-and-ink, wood blocks; . . . my fiction reading runs to men like Hergesheimer, Faulkner, Clements Ripley, Rabelais, Powys; Thorne Smith can give me more chuckles and guffaws to the minute than any other writer I've found; I like autobiography and biography of the last century; Conrad Aiken's poetry strikes a high note in my make-up. Yeah, I read a lot. I like roses, tennis, chess, 'Scotch' jokes. Although I write about guns a good deal, I'm a rotten shot. Haven't done any shooting or fishing for a long time; mebbe I'm about due. Have a collection of first editions. Ambition? Someday I'd like to write a novel that could stand up with Frank Norris's *McTeague*, Mark Twain's *Mysterious Stranger*, and James Stephen's *Crock of Gold*. I don't suppose *I'll* ever do it. In fact, *I* wonder if it will ever be done."

Beginning in 1931, MacDonald began selling his literary properties to film companies. Several of his stories were used by Columbia Pictures as the basis for films in the studio's Tim McCoy series. "Dead Man's Return" in *Outlaws of the West* (1–2/32) was the source for *Texas Cyclone* (Columbia, 1932) as "Frontier Trails of Steel" in *Ace-High Magazine* (2nd March Number: 3/18/28) was for *Two-Fisted Law* (Columbia, 1932), both of which featured a young John Wayne as the second lead. Toward the end of the decade John Wayne would also be cast as Stony Brooke in eight films in Republic's Three Mesquiteers series. *The Riding Tornado* (Columbia, 1932), based on *Don Gringo*, and *Daring Danger* (Columbia, 1932), based on "Law Rides to Loboville" in *Ace-High Magazine* (1st March Number: 3/3/29), were other entries in the McCoy series. By the time *The Three Mesquiteers* (Republic, 1936) was released, this would actually mark the second time MacDonald's *Law of the Forty-Fives*

(Covici, Friede, 1933) was filmed, coming only a year after *Law of the .45's* (First Division, 1935). Over the years MacDonald would have well over sixty films to his credit, based either on his fiction or his characters. Only Clarence E. Mulford, who created Hopalong Cassidy, Max Brand, and Zane Grey among Western writers exceeded this record.

The Three Mesquiteers were certainly MacDonald's most famous characters and they were first united in *Law of The Forty-Fives*. While certainly not a new concept — Eugene Cunningham, for one, had anticipated him by calling three of his characters in *Riders of the Night* (Houghton Mifflin, 1932) by this same sobriquet, to say nothing of Alexandre Dumas's *trois mousquetaires* in the previous century — MacDonald's trio of traveling gunmen proved particularly enduring, characters that took on a life of their own for at least three decades in his series of Mesquiteer books and the concomitant series of Western films based on these characters. Tucson Smith serves as the informal leader of the group while Stony Brooke and Lullaby Joslin provide support with blazing six-guns as well as comic relief. *Law of the Forty-Fives* marked the initial appearance of Lullaby Joslin, a deputy sheriff when first encountered, while Tucson and Stony had actually made their debut four years earlier as the heroic duo in *Restless Guns* (Chelsea House, 1929).

One of the ingredients that usually came to be included in a Mesquiteer book is Tucson's capture by the villains. In *Law of the Forty-Fives* Smith is tied up and suspended over an open pit of rattlesnakes with the

xiv

hempen rope stretched across a sharp knife. He has to extricate himself from this insidious trap before he can take off after the villains. In *Riders of the Whistling Skull* (Covici, Friede, 1934) Tucson is left in the giant granite skull as dynamite charges begin exploding. In *The Singing Scorpion* (Covici, Friede, 1934) Tucson is tied up and left on a sacrificial altar in an ancient temple with dynamite beneath him. Another convention, both in the Mesquiteer novels and in MacDonald's other Western fiction, is the notion that the law more than otherwise frames the innocent and is in the employ of the guilty. In *Powdersmoke Range* (Covici, Friede, 1934) the reader is told that "Brooke and Joslin were about thirty years of age; Tucson a trifle older." In the fashion of Nueces and Shorty in Clarence E. Mulford's Corson of the JC saga, Stony and Lullaby engage in almost constant banter and wrangling that afford Tucson (and presumably the reader) with "considerable amusement". As many of the Mesquiteer novels, *Powdersmoke Range* opens on a scene featuring characters with whom the story will be most involved, in this instance the Guadalupe Kid, whose real name is Jeff Fergusson, and Caroline Sibley, the heroine who is being threatened by Big Steve Ogden. The Guadalupe Kid is framed on a murder charge, and the Mesquiteers have to expose the truth to exonerate him. A later novel in the series, *The Three Mesquiteers* (Doubleday, 1944), opens with Red Sherry's being kidnapped so he can witness the sale of the Horse-shoe N Ranch by Molly Norton. She has agreed to the sale because her father is held captive by the villains. Red winds up in jail, and he appeals to the Mesquiteers for help when they ride into Blue Cloud. By this time Jeff Fergusson works as the ramrod on the Mesquiteers' 3 Bar 0 Ranch. *The Gun Branders* (Berkley, 1960) would seem to be the final entry in the series in terms of its date of publication, but it was actually serialized in six parts as "The Gun Branders" in *Quick Trigger Stories of the West* (10/30-3/31), a magazine published and edited by Harold Hersey. Chronologically it is the second Mesquiteer book in terms of when it was written. Why MacDonald did not publish it in book form for thirty years is something of a mystery. It opens with the Mesquiteers, as always, "wandering rather aimlessly, hoping to find some excitement." They find it in the machinations of local gang boss, Matt Nirvan, who offers to buy ranches he wants to acquire. If the owner refuses, the owner shows up dead, and Nirvan has a bill of sale no one can prove was forged. Tucson, in a suspenseful scene, is left staked out over an ant hill from which he is able to free himself because Nirvan drove the stakes in vertically rather than at a slant.

For the most part MacDonald did not write Mesquiteer novels while the Republic film series was in production and only resumed doing so again in late 1943 when the series was ending. There is rather thin characterization in the early books, including the principals, but the events in the plots tend to be more spectacular than in the later books. Only in *Powdersmoke Range* (RKO, 1935) did the casting come close, at least in connection with Tucson Smith and Stony Brooke, to the physical descriptions

MacDonald supplied in the novels. *The Singing Scorpion*, with its story of unearthing the ancient city of the Scorpion People in the Valley of the Singing Scorpion, is arguably the most inventive and consistently interesting of all the novels in this series.

In the Mesquiteer books *who* is behind the trouble, if not always why, is apparent almost from the outset. Similarly, in non-series books and short novels, MacDonald would frequently introduce a genuine mystery into a rangeland drama. In "Skeleton's Gold" in *Western Story Magazine* (3/6/37), Jerry Cameron is a young Texas wrangler who buys an old .45 in Paso City and doesn't know that it contains a map to a hidden treasure. Solving the riddle of the murder that led to the treasure's being hidden in the first place is an integral part of the plot. *The Crimson Quirt* (Doubleday, 1942) finds range detective Peter Piper confronted in the middle of the desert by a dead man seated in a rocking chair with nothing else for miles around except a crimson-colored quirt that, ultimately, leads to the solution. MacDonald's son, Wallace, wrote in a letter dated May 19, 1991 that his father "had a lot of fun posing problems for himself and then facing the challenge of writing his way out of them . . . to make sense of this initial situation was the task of the rest of the story. Often Allan wouldn't know how it would all turn out till the very end." W. C. Tuttle in his stories about range detectives, especially those featuring Hashknife Hartley and Sleepy Stevens, pioneered the mixture of a murder mystery in a rangeland setting and surely influenced MacDonald in his own pursuit of such crossovers between the two categories. However, in addition to action and a mystery to be unraveled by delayed revelation, MacDonald's fiction is also notable for its humor. He had a gift for comic dialogue that compares well with that of both Tuttle and Mulford.

After years of depicting crooked lawmen Mac-Donald's officers of the law in the 1940s tended more often than not to be honest and, as characters, rather engaging. In *Rebel Ranger* (Doubleday, 1943) Johnny Auburn is a Texas Ranger assigned to investigate trouble between cattlemen and nesters. In a switch from the usual plot in which the nesters are innocent of wrongdoing, here they are actually hired thugs, part of a scheme to disenfranchise Alex Jenkins, a stubborn rancher, from his holdings. The friendship formed between Johnny and Deputy Sheriff Obie Grant is one of the most rewarding relationships to be found in MacDonald's fiction. Indeed, friendship is often a major theme in the novels from MacDonald's last two decades, and it is at the center of one of the most satisfying, *Powder Smoke* (Berkley, 1963), an expansion of the short novel, "Powder Smoke" in *West* (2/4/31). Powder Smoke Peters is Owen Thorpe's friend and is convinced that Owen has been framed for the murder of his brother. Sheriff Milt Lapps is not above bending the law a mite to help Owen's cause out of friendship, loyalty, and a desire to get at the truth. Miguel Cordano, a Mexican bandit, also helps Owen in his own way during a private conversation with Powder Smoke. " 'You're pretty decent, Miguel . . . ,' " Powder Smoke says. " ' . . . Decent,' " Cordano interrupts.

" 'No, I am Mike Cordane — bloodthirsty robber of banks and stages,' " In this novel, after having to use the euphemism "bustard" for nearly four decades, Mac-Donald was able to have one of Powder Smoke's hands refer to the real murderer as a "bastard". During banter out at Powder Smoke's ranch, a cowpuncher makes a disparaging comment about another's choice of reading matter. " 'You been readin' that *Her Cowboy Galahad* again . . . According to that author, all a cowhand does is ride to town for the mail, meet the pretty schoolmarm, rescue her from a rustlers' nest and ride off into the settin' sun with his arms around the gal. Not once did that hee-ro do any work around the outfit.' " There seems to be no such novel in actuality, but B. M. Bower came close to it in *Her Prairie Knight* (Dillingham, 1907).

Powder Smoke recalls for Owen how once as a young hellion a railroad detective named Quist interceded on his behalf. It was in *Thunderbird Trail* (Doubleday, 1946) that this new series character, railroad detective Gregory Quist, was first introduced. Quist represents a subtle shift for MacDonald in that this special operative for the T.N. & A.S. Railroad is not an altruistic "do-gooder", but rather a tough, arrogant, explosive type who specializes in solving murder mysteries. MacDonald must have found personal satisfaction as well as commercial success with this character for the Quist series of Western mysteries would continue through the 1960s. All the trappings of the Western at its most traditional are present in these tales, but the emphasis is obviously more on the murder mystery and commensurably less attention is paid to comic relief. In addition to the tighter, tougher tone of the Quist novels, MacDonald also managed to contrive more unusual mysteries for his hero to solve than had previously been the case in his Western fiction. For example, in *The Comanche Scalp* (Lippincott, 1955) Quist comes across a dead man seated in a rowboat in the middle of the desert. No matter that *The Comanche Scalp* borrows this initial situation from *The Crimson Quirt* (albeit in the former the corpse is seated, instead, in a rocking chair), MacDonald would frequently lift ideas and plot devices from earlier works and reuse them. This tendency to "borrow" has little impact upon the entertainment value of his generally well-constructed fiction and his colorful settings always manage somehow to carry the story in new directions in spite of any plot similarities to past tales. Allan William Colt MacDonald died on March 27, 1968 in Lakeport, California.

Having written nearly seventy entertaining Western novels in addition to a handful of short stories, MacDonald's stature as an author of Western fiction is secure. However, MacDonald himself was never fully satisfied with the quality of his output. One of his best efforts, *The Mad Marshal* (Pyramid 1958), received little attention and proved difficult for him to place with any publisher. This tale relates the misadventures of a corrupt town marshal who forms a partnership with a local brothel madam. Blackie Scarborough grows increasingly greedy in his quest for money and power while Arvila Priest, one of the author's most interesting female characters, warns her lover to proceed with caution. Blackie's rise and fall is portrayed with great skill in a subtle story of lust and greed. MacDonald certainly managed to stretch the limits of the traditional Western in this outing only to find his effort coldly received. No less impressive in retrospect is MacDonald's tribute to the trail drives of the Old West in *Stir Up the Dust* (Hodder and Stoughton, 1950). MacDonald spent a year in Austin, Texas, to pursue research at the University of Texas library to prepare for this book, but, as with *The Mad Marshal*, publishers showed little enthusiasm for it. MacDonald was so frustrated by these experiences that his son remembered him once declaring that "the world never wants the best that a person can give, but only the mediocre." Yet, this observation notwithstanding, Wallace MacDonald also pointed out that it was only when dwelling on this issue that his father "would grow black or [show] discontent . . . Even though Allan came to feel he'd been a failure because he'd never written more than 'bang bang' Westerns, in actual fact Allan had a lot of fun writing his stories." It is perhaps apt that William Colt MacDonald should have had so much fun writing them, since countless readers have enjoyed those same stories for almost three-quarters of a century.

Gun Fog

CHAPTER
ONE

Tobacco smoke hung thick in a haze near the low ceiling of the Topango Bar. Through the open windows of a side wall a faint dawn breeze filtered through, lifting the smoke in gentle swirls and making a trifle brighter the illumination spread by the shaded hanging lamp above the poker table. The low-burning wick, competing palely with the faint gray light entering the windows, showed five men seated around a table, their hands moving restlessly with cards or piled stacks of chips. Now and then, one of the players spoke in a monosyllable or grunted disgustedly, as the case might be. Few words were spoken. Play went on.

Beyond the circle of light, snoring placidly on a stool behind the bar, slouched Hippodrome Casey, better known as Hippo, proprietor of the saloon. The barkeeper and the poker players were the only occupants of the Topango Bar. Both front and rear doors had been closed and bolted hours before.

Gray dawn spread swiftly along the silent, deserted streets of Topango Wells. Along the eastern horizon there came a softness of rose-pink that blended with the mauve of early morning. Somewhere down the street, a block away from the Topango Bar, a window shutter made a sharp sound in the silence and fell to the earth, banging a man's shins in the descent. The man swore loudly and with sudden intensity. The shutter was picked up. Silence fell again.

One of the poker players in the Topango Bar spoke abruptly: "It's mornin'."

"But Knight's play," another put in, chuckling at the feeble joke.

"All-night play," another amended, then: "Well, what you doin', Knight?"

"Not so well." Jerry Knight smiled whimsically. He studied the cards in his bronzed fingers, a lean, red-haired individual still well under thirty. His smoke-gray eyes contemplated the pasteboards dubiously before he pushed his remaining two chips to the center of the table. "And raise it a mite," he advised.

"You're licked right now, cowboy." Kelt Flecker laughed. It wasn't a nice laugh. In fact, there weren't many people who liked anything about Kelt Flecker. But Flecker was a sort of boss in the Topango country and foreman of the Circle F outfit on top of that. His features were brutal, his eyes small and shrewd. He met Knight's raise and upped the pot another chip.

The other three players, Tim Beadle, George Corwin, and Herb Jacklin were Circle F cowpunchers, dressed like their boss in range togs — woolen shirts, sombreros, faded overalls, and high-heeled boots. Holstered six-shooters completed the costumes.

Play went around the table and returned to Jerry Knight. The other four waited for Knight to act. Jerry's good-natured features crinkled to a rueful smile. "That's all, there isn't any more," he drawled.

Kelt Flecker said: "You plumb cleaned?"

Knight smiled whimsically. "Two hundred dollars, horse, rig. I arrived yesterday evenin' a stranger in a strange land, and I been took in."

Tim Beadle frowned. "You claimin' our game ain't straight?"

"Now, I wouldn't go to say that," Knight replied gently. "The luck just ain't been runnin' my way. Usual, an all-night session like this one will bring a change of luck two or three times, but I been on the skids ever since the first hand was dealt."

Kelt Flecker mused: "Two hundred dollars is a heap of money to lose, cowboy. A savin' of several months' wages, I suppose." He watched Knight narrowly while speaking.

Jerry nodded, meeting the glance even-eyed. "Yeah . . . wages." There was just the barest pause between the uttering of the two words.

Flecker repeated — "Wages." — and laughed again, pure skepticism tingeing the tones. The three Circle F hands smiled.

"And so" — Knight yawned carelessly — "you *hombres* can finish the hand without me. I'm forced to drop out."

"Wait a minute," said Flecker. "Knight, you're a stranger in Topango Wells. We like to give you all the chance possible to win back what you've lost, just to show you we're square shooters. You ain't done yet."

"How you figurin'?" Knight took a new interest in the proceedings. "I got a bandanna and a sack of makin's left . . . that's all."

"Wrong," Flecker said promptly. "You got your guns yet."

Knight's brow wrinkled. "I sort of hate to part with my irons."

"You may not have to," said George Corwin.

"Good guns are security for chips with me any time," Flecker said smoothly.

"How much security?" Knight wanted to know.

"Enough to stay and raise . . . if you're game."

Knight smiled, drew his guns from holsters, placed them on the table before Kelt Flecker. "I always was a sucker for a gamble."

Kelt Flecker shoved some blue chips across the table. Jerry looked surprised, shrugged his shoulders, and accepted them. Play went on. Five minutes later, Knight said philosophically: "Easy come, easy go. Now I *am* finished, cleaned, done. Next thing I know, if I stick with you sharks, I'll be rollin' back to my home range in a barrel."

Flecker smiled genially. "You sure do have the breaks against you, Knight. Just where is your home range? You ain't said."

Jerry evaded that with: "I ain't intendin' to, neither. You *hombres* would be takin' that away, too, I reckon."

"We could try, leastwise." Flecker grinned widely. "What you aimin' to do now, Knight?"

"I been wonderin' about that myself." The red-haired cowboy chuckled. "Money, guns, horse, and rig gone. Well, I still got my ambition. Gents, you're lookin' at a cowboy for sale."

Herb Jacklin said: "Kelt, we're short a hand."

Flecker nodded thoughtfully. "But I don't think my bosses would let me take on another."

"I'm lookin' for a job," Jerry said, "though yesterday at this time I didn't think the cards would tell me to go to work again."

"Look here," Flecker said suddenly, "I'd like to help you out, Knight, but my bosses been after me to cut expenses. We do need another man, but I don't have the wages to pay one. At the same time, I hate to see the work get behind. Havin' the best interests in the Randall Land and Cattle Company at heart . . . which same is my boss . . . I aim to try and stake 'em to the help needed . . ."

"What's the point you're headin' for?" Knight wanted to know.

Flecker explained: "I'll stake you to eighty dollars' worth of chips. In return, Knight, you sign a paper consenting to work for me for two months. If you lose, I get a cowhand free of wages. If you win, you can buy the paper back."

Knight grinned broadly. "You can't tie that for big-heartedness, Flecker. Gimme them chips."

"As soon as you've signed said paper," Flecker returned. "I'll make it out . . ."

"Hey, wait a minute," Jerry interposed, "instead of takin' all chips, I would like my guns back."

"Forget it." Flecker waved one careless hand. "I'll give you the chips, like I said, and throw in the guns . . . and also your horse and rig. How's that for a proposition?"

"Not to mention the shirt offen your back, eh, if I ask for it?" Jerry chuckled. "You're sure too generous for your own good, Flecker."

"Kelt always was soft-hearted," George Corwin commented.

Flecker smiled good-naturedly, drew a small notebook from an inner vest pocket, tore off one sheet, and scribbled with a stub pencil for a few moments. Tossing the sheet and pencil across to Knight, he said: "Write your moniker, cowboy . . . and here's the chips. Now, with a new start, mebbe your luck will change."

"I'll bet you it will." Knight nodded.

But it didn't. Twenty minutes later, when the first rays of the morning sun threw a broad bar of light across the table, Jerry tossed his cards on the board, face up. "You win, Flecker. Three kings can top jacks and tens any time. When do I go to work?"

Flecker laughed. "I won't rush you, Knight. Anyway, you get grub and a bunk for two months. Here's your guns. And here" — in a sudden burst of generosity — "here's five dollars. I don't want to make it too tough."

"You've found one square rod, Knight," Jacklin said.

"Looks thataway," Jerry agreed. "But I don't want to sit in no more poker games with you *hombres*. You'd win my good reputation next."

For just a second Flecker's face hardened. "I reckon we got that already, Knight."

The eyes of the two men locked in a brief challenge. Jerry said easily after a moment: "Well, you had to get one some place, I suppose."

Flecker's face flushed. "Meanin' what?"

Jerry laughed suddenly, lounged back in his chair, stretching his arms, and yawning. "We were talkin' about my rep as a poker player, wa'n't we?"

"Oh," Flecker said, and relaxed, although it wasn't yet clear in his mind what Knight had meant. Before he had time for further thought on the subject, Jerry suddenly straightened in his chair, gathered up the scattered cards, and decked them. Rising from his seat he walked to the bar.

Flecker stiffened suddenly: "Where you goin' with them cards?"

Knight turned back, looked surprised. "Just givin' 'em back to the barkeep," he explained, tossing the deck down on the long counter. "They're his cards, ain't they?" Before Flecker or the others had an opportunity to reply, Jerry went on: "Hey, Hippo, wake up. We're through and cravin' an eye-opener. C'mon, Flecker, I'll buy a drink. Step up fellers. We'll drink success to the Circle F. I sure aim to do my share of the work."

The other four men strode to the bar. Hippodrome Casey slid his comfortably proportioned form off his stool, yawned widely.

"You gents through at last? My gosh, what a session. You got to be a hound for draw to stick it that long. Who's the heavy winner?"

"Kelt is." Knight grinned. "He got a top hand to help put the Circle F on a high-payin' basis. 'Course, I'm plumb cleaned out of money an' such material things, but I sure feel like I got a chance to get ahead in my new job."

9

"Cleaned out, eh?" mused Hippodrome. He shoved Jerry's money back across the bar. "That bein' the case, you'll need that money, cowboy. This one'll be on the house. Drink hearty, gents."

The liquor was downed, glasses clattered back to the bar. Corwin said: "If we get ridin', we can reach the ranch before breakfast is over."

"I'm ready to take on food." Herb Jacklin nodded.

"I ain't figurin' to make no hard ride on an empty stomach," Kelt Flecker grunted. "We'll eat at the Chinaman's where we had supper last night. Reckon our horses is still at the rack down there, anyway. We'd have to go get 'em. Anybody that craves to ride home before he eats is welcome to do it, but I'm payin' for the chow."

"Feelin' good this mornin', eh, Kelt," Tim Beadle said.

"Some," Flecker agreed. "C'mon, Knight."

Saying good bye to Hippodrome, the five men sauntered toward the door, unbolted it, and stepped outside.

CHAPTER
TWO

On the street, Jerry hesitated. "You fellers go ahead down to the restaurant," he suggested. "I'll be with you in a minute."

Flecker frowned suspiciously. "What you aimin' to do?"

"Get my horse," the new hand said promptly. "If you'll remember back to last night, I didn't leave my bronc' standin' in front of the Chinaman's place. He's around back of the saloon, under that horse shelter. I'll be right along as soon as I get him."

"Oh." Flecker's face cleared. "All right, Knight. We'll be looking for you."

Flecker and his three hands drifted off down the street, past various buildings with high, false fronts, the high heels on booted feet clumping loudly along the plank walks in the early morning silence. A few pedestrians had put in an appearance by this time.

Jerry rounded the corner of the saloon, passed between it and the neighboring buildings. At the rear of the Topango Bar he found and filled a water bucket, then proceeded on to the horse shelter where a wiry, black gelding whinnied at his approach. Watering the beast and filling a feed trough with food took only a few minutes. Leaving the horse, Jerry approached the rear door of the saloon that, by now, had been unbolted. Opening the door, he passed through into the bar.

Hippodrome Casey was yawning sleepily and polishing glasses when Knight entered. A look of surprise crossed his face. "Cripes! You back a'ready? Thought you was eatin' breakfast."

Jerry smiled, although an icy gleam brightened his smoke-gray eyes. "Figured you and I might as well get acquainted, Hippo. I won't keep you but a second."

Hippodrome looked uneasy. "What's on your mind?"

"I'm more interested in what's out of my pocket." Jerry smiled. "Hippo, Kelt Flecker is a right good poker player, ain't he?"

Hippodrome replied warily: "We-ell, I never knew him to lose with any regularity. He knows the cards . . ."

"In more ways than one." Jerry laughed. "Let me see that pack we were usin'."

"Oh, shucks, there ain't nothin' wrong with them cards," the barkeep protested. "Hell, I saw you break the seal on that deck yourself before you started to play. They're fairly expensive cards, too, made by a reliable company. Nothing wrong with them."

"Let me see 'em." Knight's voice was smooth.

Hippodrome hesitated, then reached to his backbar and tossed the cards in their cardboard case on the bar. Jerry examined the broken seal, then laughed shortly.

The barkeep said: "What's up? Ain't them cards all right?"

12

"I ain't looked at the cards yet. Yeah, Hippo, you're right about these cards bein' made by a reliable company. *But* whoever steamed this seal off the cover didn't replace it exactly as it was in the beginnin' . . ."

"Huh! What you talking about?" The barkeep's surprise was genuine, Jerry decided, after looking steadily into Hippo's wide-open eyes.

"All right, Slim, mebbe you ain't in on it," Jerry conceded. "We'll see what else we can learn." Sliding the cards out of their case, he scrutinized the backs of the pasteboards closely for several minutes.

Hippo said: "What you lookin' for?"

"Marked cards. And I've found 'em. Nice little example of block-out work, Hippo . . ."

"Block what . . . ?" The barkeep looked puzzled. "Hey, what you talkin' about?"

"Block-out work it's called. Look here. You see, the backs of these cards have got pictures of a little dog at either end. See? That dog's wearin' a collar. The cards are printed in red on the backs. Now, take a look at the dog collar on this ace of diamonds. Look close. See how someone has taken some red ink and filled in that white collar on the pup. It's right small. You'll have to look close. But if you know what to look for, you wouldn't have any trouble findin' it. Now take this king of clubs. Note how the dog's right forefoot has been blocked in with red. Now, here's a queen of spades . . ."

"The dirty, low-lifed scut!" Hippo exploded suddenly. He gazed unbelievingly at the cards. "Any more?"

"Sure." Jerry laughed. "Look 'em over. Here and here. Here's another . . ."

Hippo swore long and with considerable intensity. By now Jerry Knight was thoroughly convinced that the plump bartender had no part in the deception. "Where'd these cards come from?"

"Kelt Flecker!" Hippo exclaimed angrily. "He put one over on me."

"How come?"

"Couple of years back," Hippo explained, "Kelt started kicking about the cards I kept here. They were cheap makes, I admit that, but good enough. Kelt goes in for these all-night poker sessions now and then, and he complained that my cards didn't stand up under long handling. Well, inasmuch as I furnish cards free to anybody that wants to play, I wa'n't goin' to buy expensive decks."

"And so," Jerry put in shrewdly, "Kelt offered to furnish his own cards if you'd keep them here for him."

Hippo looked startled. "Now how in hell did you know that?"

"It's an old game, my fat one. It's been worked right often. Flecker simply bought new decks, steamed off the seals, changed the back markin's so he could recognize 'em, put 'em back in the case, and resealed . . ."

"My God! Was anybody ever so dumb as me? Say-y-y, I'll bet I tell that big crook a thing or two . . ."

"No, you won't. Listen, Hippo, you aren't to mention a thing about this. You just keep your eyes and ears open."

14

"Say" — Hippodrome Casey had a new thought — "did you know these cards were marked when you were playin' last night?"

"I suspected it. The only time I was allowed to win was on the small pots. When the kitty was plumb full, I lost."

"Why in time didn't you say somethin'?"

Jerry laughed softly. "And me a stranger on a strange range? Playin' against a foreman and three of his hands. Hippo, I put some value on my life."

"Guess you were wise at that," Hippo conceded. "It wouldn't do to buck the Randall Land and Cattle Company."

"I don't get you."

"That's the big company that is runnin' things around Topango Wells. Swallowin' up everythin' in sight . . . land and cattle. Owned by some old crook back East. Kelt Flecker rods the Circle F which is one of the company's largest properties. Feller named Bristol Capron lives here in town, calls hisself the resident manager. Between Capron and Flecker this range hereabouts is pretty well made to toe the mark. Me, I don't talk back so much my own self, but I'm damned if I'm going to let Kelt pull a slimy trick like this card deal in my barroom. I always run a pretty straight place. Live and let live is my motto, but . . ."

"I'm askin' you, Hippo, to keep your mouth shut . . . for a spell leastwise."

"But what you aimin' to do, Knight?" Hippo asked curiously.

"I ain't sure yet. I got a job with Flecker. Let's see what he aims to do first. For some reason he was plumb anxious that I take a job with him. His big-hearted talk didn't fool me none . . ."

A voice from outside intruded on the conversation. "Hey, Knight, what you doin'?" It was Tim Beadle's voice.

Like a flash, Jerry swept the cards off the bar to the floor back of the long counter. "You ain't seen me," he whispered swiftly. "And keep your mouth shut. I'll be in again one of these days."

Whirling, he moved quickly and silently through the rear entrance. The door closed softly on his exit. A moment later Tim Beadle strode into the saloon to find Hippo industriously sweeping the floor back of the bar.

"Hey, you fat slob," Beadle growled, "where'd Knight go?"

"Huh?" Hippo's mouth dropped open in apparent dumb amazement. "How in hell do I know? He left to get breakfast with you *hombres*. If you think I'm ridin' herd on all the strangers that come into this town, you got another guess comin'. What'd he do, run out on that agreement he made with Kelt?"

"That's what I'm wonderin'. He left us to get his horse which is supposed to be out back. Ain't turned up since. I figured he'd come in here again."

"Ain't seen him." Hippo resumed his sweeping. Muttering an oath, Beadle strode through the rear exit and found Jerry under the horse shelter just pulling tight his saddle cinch.

Beadle growled: "What in hell you been doin'?"

Jerry glanced back over his shoulder. "Oh, hello, Tim. Sorry if I kept you waiting. My pony was actin' like he had the heaves when I come out. Fooled around with him some, and he 'pears all right now."

"Oh, we was wonderin'." Beadle appeared placated. "Probably a lot of chaff and dust in that feed bin. I've seen horses act that way before. It comes, and then goes just as fast. Hurry up. Your nag will be all right."

"I reckon. You fellers through eatin'?"

"All but Kelt. He eats enough for two ordinary men. But he don't like to have his orders disobeyed. He expected you to come along at once."

"I didn't know I was under orders."

"You better find it out right *pronto*, Knight. Kelt is good-natured up to a certain point. After that, well, he'd just as soon lift your scalp as not."

"Is that so?" Jerry laughed shortly. "He won't be liftin' no scalp of mine."

"Don't get proddy, Knight. He'll lift it and make you like it, any time the idea hits him. Kelt is plumb bad medicine to cross, and in your position you better build your loops just as he tells you to."

Jerry swung up to the saddle. "What do you mean . . . in my position?"

Beadle laughed sarcastically. "All right, don't admit nothin' you don't have to. It ain't my business. But, cowpoke, if you don't play the game Kelt's way, it'll be played in a way not to your liking, *sabe?*"

"Damn'd if I do."

Beadle laughed shortly. "All right, I won't say no more, cowpoke. But you won't be able to run no bluff on Kelt."

In front of the Topango Bar, Beadle mounted his pony and the two men jogged down the street. Arriving at the restaurant, they found Herb Jacklin and George Corwin rolling cigarettes in the shade of the wooden awning that extended above the narrow sidewalk.

Beadle said: "Kelt still eatin'?"

Corwin shook his head, nodded toward a building on the opposite side of the street. "He's gone across to see Capron."

Jerry glanced across at the two-story brick building with its huge letters **RANDALL LAND & CATTLE COMPANY** painted across the front. Three windows were placed across the second floor that, no doubt, comprised the living quarters of Bristol Capron, the resident manager of the company. Below, on the ground floor, was the entrance flanked on each side by a large window on which was also painted, but in smaller letters, the name of the company.

"What kept you so long, Knight?" Jacklin asked.

"Horse bothered me a mite," Jerry explained easily. He added certain details to the story.

Jacklin nodded and said: "You better go grab your breakfast. Kelt will be ready to ride in a little while."

Jerry went in, ordered food and coffee, ate hurriedly. He had just emerged from the restaurant when a shout from across the street greeted his ears: "Hey, Knight, come over here."

Kelt Flecker was standing in the doorway of the building. As Jerry crossed over, Flecker advanced to meet him. Flecker growled: "What kept you so long? I was commencin' to think you'd gone back on your agreement."

Again Jerry explained glibly that he'd been bothered about his pony that had shown tendencies toward the heaves. Flecker's brow cleared as he cut short the explanations with: "Come on in and sign the payroll. Capron is sort of peeved at me gettin' him out of bed so early, so you better not say anythin'. Just leave things to me. No need to say anythin' about our agreement you signed. What Capron don't know won't hurt him."

Jerry nodded and followed Flecker into the office of the Randall Land & Cattle Company. The lower floor was a large room with not a great deal of furniture. A few chairs were arranged along one wall. In a corner stood a huge iron safe.

Near the window, seated at a desk, was a scowling-visaged individual with thin, sandy hair and grayish-appearing skin. His eyes were cruel and set deeply in sockets, his nose long and pointed. He was only partially dressed in dark trousers and a colorless shirt. His features still bore the marks of sleep.

"This is Knight," Flecker said, propelling the cowboy before him. "Where's your payroll list, Capron?"

"Dammit, Kelt," Bristol Capron snapped, "I don't like this. I told you not to sign on another man."

"Oh, hell," Flecker said wearily, "his wages won't break the company." It was evident the argument had been in progress before Jerry arrived. "After we got more time to talk, I think you'll see the wisdom of hirin' Knight."

Capron shrugged dubiously, reached into a desk drawer, and produced a small ledger, which he opened, and growled at Jerry: "Put your name down here."

He paid scarcely any attention to the cowboy while Jerry signed the book. When Jerry had straightened up from the desk, Flecker said: "Bris, I'll be back, in a day or so, to talk this over with you."

Bristol Capron nodded curtly. "Your talk better be damn' convincing," he snapped.

Flecker laughed. "C'mon, Knight," he said. "We'll be gettin' on." Taking Jerry's arm, as though in a hurry to leave, Flecker urged the cowboy through the doorway. Halfway across the street, Flecker chuckled. "No use givin' Capron time to ask questions. You've signed the payroll. I'll collect your money for you."

"And keep it, eh?" the cowpoke cut in.

"You ain't got no kick comin'," Flecker protested. "I staked you. You lost. If I get my money back, that's all you need to care."

"I reckon." Jerry nodded.

They joined Corwin, Jacklin, and Beadle in front of the restaurant. The three men looked rather curiously at Knight but didn't say anything. Horses were mounted and the five riders swept out of town, heading west along the trail that led to the Circle F.

CHAPTER
THREE

A trifle over an hour later, Jerry and the rest arrived at the Circle F Ranch. The buildings were large and in good condition, the huge, rambling ranch house being at present boarded up and not in use. Kelt Flecker lived with his crew in a long bunkhouse, one end of which was fitted up as an office. Besides Kelt and the hands who Jerry had met in Topango Wells, the crew contained a cook and three other cowpunchers who were at present engaged in various tasks about the barns and corrals.

Flecker led Knight into the bunkhouse, pointed out several vacant bunks. "Take your choice," he said.

Jerry threw his blanket roll over a lower bunk, then asked: "When do I go to work?"

"Tomorrow mornin'," Flecker replied. "We been up all night. I aim to take it easy today. You'll find I ain't hard on my men, Knight . . . providin' they always do as I tell 'em."

There was something ominous in the last words, but Knight paid no attention to the foreman's manner. He nodded shortly. "I've always been able to take instructions any place else I worked, Flecker."

"That's fine. Keep on doin' that and you and me won't have no trouble."

The day dragged along. Jerry talked to the other cowpunchers whose names were Steve Hackett, Shorty Wing, and Frank Reed. These three were men of his own age and lacked the hard-bitten look of Flecker and the hands with whom Jerry had played poker. They talked but little, although in the course of many careless conversations Jerry discovered that Hackett, Wing, and Reed knew very little of affairs concerning the Circle F. The three drew their pay and apparently did but little work for it — although that was, it appeared, Kelt Flecker's fault.

"Softest job I ever had," Shorty Wing told Jerry. "I ain't had to get into a saddle for nigh onto two weeks now. Kelt keeps us three at tinkerin' jobs, mendin' harness or fixin' corral posts and such. Him and the rest do what ridin's done. For all the cow work us three do, we might just as well be some of them damn' hoe men south of the river."

"What hoe men?" Jerry asked.

He and Wing were seated on a bench just outside a big hay barn door. Flecker and the other poker players were stretched, snoring, in the bunkhouse. Reed and Hackett were a short distance away, engaged in cutting circular strips from a cowhide with which to manufacture a rawhide rope. It was plain the two were just killing time.

Wing was explaining: "I mean them hoe men located south of Aliso Creek."

"I'm strange to this range," Jerry hinted.

22

"Sure enough, y'are." Shorty Wing showed a freckled grin. "I'd forgot that. Well, you see, the Randall Land and Cattle Company have a lot of small farms staked out to sell to suckers over that way. These poor benighted hoe men come out here from the Midwest to become dirt farmers. Cripes, they can't even raise enough to keep themselves from starvin'. When the creek's up, there's pretty good irrigation, but come hot weather the water peters out and the crops is ruined. Payments on the land can't be made, so the Randall Company takes back the farm and the following spring catches a new sucker with it."

"That," Jerry mused aloud, "is dirty."

"You think so too, eh?" Wing looked pleased. "That's the way it looks to Reed and Hackett, also. We mentioned the fact to Kelt once, but Kelt got sore. Told us to keep our mouths shut about what wasn't our business."

"Whose business is it?"

"Flecker says that's Bristol Capron's end of the game. Shucks! Knight, just as soon as I gather me a coupla months' more wages, I'm quittin'."

"Gettin' sick of your job?"

"Me and Reed and Hackett are plumb sick of loafin'. We ain't got enough to do. There's somethin' funny goin' on. I can't see what you was hired for . . ." Wing stopped abruptly, looked away. "It ain't none of my business," he said half apologetically, "just forget I said anythin'. Shore, Knight, we like our jobs fine. Let's drop the subject."

Jerry smiled. "I don't talk much and I never did have a habit of repeatin' what I hear."

"I kind of sized you up thataway at first" — Wing smiled sheepishly — "and blurted out a lot of palaver."

"I'm interested and I don't talk," Jerry said. "What did you mean by somethin' funny goin' on?"

"You tell me and I'll tell you." Wing frowned. "You see, this Randall that owns all the land hereabouts . . . or most of it . . . lives in the East . . . Kansas City, I think. He leaves everything to Capron. I just wonder, sometimes, if Capron might not like to run the company in a hole."

"And then what?"

Wing shrugged his broad shoulders. "I ain't thought that far. On the other hand, it sometimes looks like the Randall Company was out to hog the whole country. The company holds notes on all the ranches hereabouts, and said ranches is losin' cattle . . . more cattle than they can afford to lose."

"What other ranches are there?"

"The Rafter K is about fifteen miles due north from Topango Wells. The Coffee Pot's the same distance to the northeast. South of the Circle F is the Two-M . . . Mart Monroe's outfit. Then there's several small outfits scattered about. They seem to change hands pretty regularly."

"Does the Circle F make money on its beef?"

"It sure should. I don't know what prices it got, but there was a mighty big shipment went East last fall."

"Just one shipment?"

Wing shook his head. "There was several."

24

"Any Circle F shortage on stock?"

Wing shrugged his shoulders. "You got me. I don't get into the saddle enough to know just what's what. You'll have to ask Kelt Flecker, or one of his older hands. Hackett and Reed wouldn't know, either. Why you askin'?"

"Put it down to bein' curious." Jerry smiled. "With cattle disappearin' thataway, it's a wonder some of the ranches haven't called on the Cattlemen's Association to investigate."

"Mebbe they did." Wing frowned, then went on. "There was a *hombre* named Wolcott come here about three months back . . ."

"Range detective?"

"I don't know for sure. He roamed around the country till it happened."

"Until what happened?"

Wing took a deep breath. "Nobody rightly knows. Wolcott was found dead . . . shot to death . . . a few miles to the west of here. A cowhand that worked for the Circle F . . . Ridge Conway . . . was found dead, near him. The two had shot it out. Conway was a right mean cuss."

"Does that pin anything on the Circle F?"

"That ain't for me to say. The sheriff in Topango Wells is still investigating. It was known that Conway and Flecker was right close, though Flecker claims that him and Conway had a fallin' out two days before the bodies was found. Also, that Conway had quit his job directly after said fallin' out. And here's somethin' else.

Wolcott had been shot in the back as well as from in front."

Jerry nodded slowly. "Provin' that Ridge Conway had somebody with him and that between them they got Wolcott . . . even if Wolcott did get Conway first."

"Somethin' like that. Sheriff Drake is still lookin' for that third man."

Knight looked musingly off across the range where the San Lucia peaks etched rugged lines against the western sky. The sun was on its downgrade stretch now. Neither man spoke for some time. Finally Knight said quietly: "I thought a heap of Dennis Wolcott."

Wing stiffened, looked puzzled. "You knew him?" He frowned.

Knight nodded. "Knew him well."

"But . . . say, look here . . . you asked me a few minutes back if he was a range detective . . . just like you'd never heard of him."

Jerry smiled thinly. "That was just a feeler. I wanted to see if you knew anything, or what they thought of Wolcott around here."

"Oh," Wing added after a moment. "Well, was he a Cattlemen's Association man?"

"I don't think so."

"Are you?"

"Am I what?"

"Dang it" — Wing grinned — "You know what I mean. Are you working for the Cattlemen's Association?"

Jerry laughed, looked Wing straight in the eyes. "Far from it, Shorty."

26

"Well, what . . . ?" the other commenced, then paused. "Oh, shucks, it ain't my business. Let it go. But, say, in case you need a pard, keep me in mind."

"Thanks, Shorty. I'll remember that."

Steve Hackett and Frank Reed approached the two. The conversation shifted to other subjects. The sun had dropped below the San Lucia range by this time. There came a sudden banging on a dishpan and the cook's loud call to supper. The cowboys rose and sauntered across the ranch yard to the cook shack.

After supper, Kelt Flecker tried to inveigle Jerry into another poker game, but Jerry refused to rise to the bait: "Nothin' doin'." He grinned ruefully. "I'm aimin' to get some shut-eye. I expect you'll be findin' a job for me tomorrow." A short time later the men turned into bunks.

The following morning after breakfast, Jerry cut a horse out of the saddler's corral, saddled, then found Flecker to get instructions regarding the day's work. Herb Jacklin had already saddled and loped out of sight over the nearest swell of range. The other men were scattered about the buildings. His horse waiting nearby, Jerry stood to receive instructions from Flecker.

"You bein' a stranger to this part of the country," Flecker commenced, "I've drawed you a rough map of the range hereabouts so's you won't get lost. Here, take a look at this." Flecker produced a small black leather wallet that he opened, taking out a sheet of white paper on which was crudely drawn, in lead pencil, a rough map of the surrounding country. "Now, you see," Flecker went on, "here's the San Lucia Mountains to

27

the west. Here we are" — pointing to a dot on the map — "right here. This is the Circle F. Now, heading toward the southwest, you'll cross Aliso Creek, which runs a southeast course after headin' in the mountains. The creek is the boundary line between our outfit and Mart Monroe's Two-M spread."

"You aren't going to tell me you're having trouble over boundaries with the Two-M," Jerry put in.

"Hell, no. Nothin' of that kind. We're right friendly with the Monroe outfit."

"That's good. I'd hate to get mixed into any range wars."

"Cripes!" Flecker growled. "Do you think I'd send an innocent stranger into a mess of that kind?" Without waiting for a reply he went on. "Now, here's what you do . . . cross Aliso Creek, then ride for the point where the creek corners into the foothills of the San Lucias. There's always a bunch of Two-M cows hangin' around there. They're prime stock . . . and they never have no riders near 'em. You commencin' to get my point?"

Jerry's eyes narrowed. "Thought you said you were on friendly terms with Monroe."

"Hell's bells! We are." Flecker chuckled. "But if he's fool enough to leave his cattle unguarded, we'd be bigger fools not to take care of 'em for him. All you got to do is cut out about twenty-five or thirty Two-M critters and drive 'em over to our range. Then you head for Camino Cañon . . . see, on this map. It's about eight miles to the northeast of here. Nice wide cañon, lots of grass. You'll find some of the boys there to take the stock offen your hands. That's all you got to do."

28

Knight was seething with anger. "Looks pretty rotten to me," he stated flatly. "Rustlin' a friend's cows . . ."

Flecker burst into sudden laughter that shook his bulky shoulders. "Sho', now, Knight, you didn't think we aimed to steal them cattle, did you? Shucks, boy, that's a right unkind thought. We just aim to take care of 'em for a spell."

"Yeah," Jerry snapped, "till you can run 'em over the state line and sell 'em . . . said state line, accordin' to this map, bein' just beyond the exit from Camino Cañon. And I suppose you got forged bills-of-sale ready, too. Flecker, you're a lousy cow thief!"

Flecker's face clouded up like a thunderstorm, one hand dropped to holstered gun. The next instant he jerked the hand away as though it had touched something hot. Knight's six-shooter had appeared as though by magic and held a steady bead on Flecker's middle.

"Go on, jerk it!" Jerry invited angrily.

Flecker slowly shook his head. "Not me," he refused. "I sort of lost my temper for a minute, but there's other ways of convincin' you that you're wrong. Put that gun away. We got to be friends, Knight."

"I'm not convinced of that, either," Jerry said quietly. He put the gun away, half expecting Flecker to make a sudden grab for his own weapon. But Flecker's hands still hung loosely at his sides.

"You refusin' to do what I tell you?" Flecker half snarled.

"I'm refusin' to turn cattle rustler!"

"Oh, like that, eh?" Flecker sneered. "You forgot you signed an agreement to work for me, take my orders? You breakin' that agreement?"

"I'm willin' to do the work, honest work," Jerry said slowly, "but no honest man would expect me to live up to an agreement as long as you give crooked orders."

"You're a hell of a *hombre* to talk about bein' honest. Mebbe you'd like to go back to the penitentiary, Knight?"

"Huh?" Jerry stiffened. "What you talkin' about?"

Flecker's loose lips widened in a nasty grin. "Don't try to bluff me, Knight. You ain't a good enough poker player for that. I suppose you're goin' to try and tell me you aren't out on parole right now? And that you've already broke that parole by steppin' out of the state that paroled you, that you'd only served three years of a ten-year stretch. I suppose that's news to you, eh?"

Knight was silent. After a moment he swallowed heavily and said: "Right interestin' information, Flecker."

"Dammit! I told you not to try a bluff on me. I remembered hearin' your name when we met you yesterday. There was an article about you in the El Paso *Gazette* when you were paroled six months ago. Last night I looked up that old paper. Want to see it?" Without waiting for a reply, Flecker produced a newspaper clipping and held it before Knight's eyes. He said mockingly: "Knight . . . better known as Jerry. Fast man with a gun, eh? You was too fast once, wa'n't you?"

"There was mitigating circumstances," Jerry said slowly. "It tells about that, right here."

30

"Mitigatin' circumstances don't bring a dead man to life." Flecker chuckled evilly. "You've done your three years. Then, because somebody offered you a job, the state authorities paroled you. But what's happened to that job? Another condition of the parole was that you wa'n't to leave the state. Knight, you're a hell of a long way from Texas and between here and there there's been a stage hold-up fairly recent, by a feller that answered your description. I happen to know that. And you blow into Topango Wells yesterday with talk about havin' wages in your pocket. All right, make up your mind. I'm losin' patience. Do you want to go back to the pen, or are you ready to obey my orders?"

Knight looked glum, downcast. Finally he sighed, started to climb into his saddle. "Reckon I've got no choice in the matter," he spoke heavily. "Guess I'll have to obey orders."

Flecker guffawed triumphantly. "I figured you'd listen to reason, cowpoke. You be a good *hombre* and we'll all make money. Cross me, and you'll find yourself starin' a series of steel bars in the face. And don't figure to drift out of the country when you leave here. One word to the authorities, and I'll have a manhunt on your trail. Oh, yes, Knight, be sure and pick nice, plump cows."

Jerry gulped, started to swing the pony around.

Flecker said: "Here, take this map with you." He replaced the map in the wallet and handed it up to Knight.

"I won't need that leather case, Flecker."

"Go on. Take it. I don't want it. It's been kickin' around for the past year or so. You'll need that map a lot before we get through. It'll keep better if you got a case to carry it in. I don't aim to be drawin' maps for dumb cowpokes all the time. Get goin', Knight. I'll see you at supper."

Jerry yanked his hat brim over his eyes, turned the pony, and started off.

Flecker snickered: "Don't go away mad. Ain't you goin' to say good bye?"

But Jerry kept going without another word.

Flecker laughed, and turned back toward the bunkhouse. Tim Beadle and George Corwin were sitting on a bench just outside the door.

Beadle said: "Did the sucker take the bait?"

Flecker laughed triumphantly. "Cripes! He didn't have no choice in the matter when he seed what we knew about him."

"Bet he was surprised," Corwin commented.

"He was downright flabbergasted," Flecker grunted. "All right, you two, you better get your hawsses and ride for Camino Cañon. You know, just in case he does get there with some cows. It might not happen today, but it will, one of these days, damn' soon. Jerry Knight, eh? Hell's bells! It ain't goin' to be long before he gets lost in a fog . . . a fog made by powder smoke. And he won't ever find himself again, neither . . . not if old Mart Monroe draws a bead with that Thirty-Thirty of his'n. Men, the scheme is airtight!"

CHAPTER
FOUR

Heading toward the southwest, Knight pushed his pony along at a sharp gait till he was well out of sight of the Circle F ranch buildings. Only then did he slow his pace, his course bringing him nearer to the San Lucia range. It was good grazing country hereabouts, rolling land with here and there clumps of sage, of prickly pear. As ten miles drifted to his rear, the terrain commenced to lift toward the San Lucia foothills and now and then he had to turn the horse aside to avoid tall upthrusts of reddish-brown granite.

Half an hour later Jerry neared the line of low cottonwoods dotted with small alder trees that lined either side of Aliso Creek. He pushed on and drew his pony to a splashing stop in the center of the broad, shallow stream of clear water that didn't reach quite to his stirrups. While the pony was drinking long droughts of the cooling creek, Jerry drew out the map Flecker had furnished and studied it intently.

As he was about to replace the folded map back in the black leather case, a tiny gold fleck in the leather caught his eye. Jerry frowned and studied the case carefully. At some time a name, in gold lettering, had been stamped into the leather. Someone had gone to great pains to scratch out the gold in an effort to obliterate the name, but the marks of the letter stamp were still visible under close scrutiny. An **e** showed up quite plainly, as did a **c** and a **t**. Further study brought out a capital **D** and a capital **W**.

He grunted with satisfaction, reined the pony out on the opposite bank, and rolled a Durham cigarette. Inhaling deeply of the tobacco smoke, he checked the pony's tendency to move on, and again gave his undivided attention to the letters on the black case. One by one the letters revealed themselves to his eyes, till they spelled out the name: **Dennis Wolcott**. It was all clear to anyone who cared to devote a little study to the partially obliterated letters.

Jerry's eyes narrowed as he gazed in deep thought across the range. In a fight with Ridge Conway, who Wolcott had killed, a third man had slain Dennis Wolcott by shooting him in the back. According to Shorty Wing, Conway and Kelt Flecker had been friends. It was Flecker who had given Knight the black leather case. Was it Flecker who had shot Wolcott in the back?

"That," Knight muttered grimly, "is somethin' I aim to find out before I leave this range. The way things are shaping up I may be forced to leave a lot sooner than I expect . . . mebbe on the fast end of a lead slug."

He put the map and leather case away, and touched spurs to his pony's ribs, clearing the trees that bordered the creek, but following its winding course deeper into the foot-hills. Here the grass grew luxuriantly, although jumbled heaps of large rocks barred his way from time to time. Then, quite suddenly, Jerry dipped down into a wide grassy hollow across which were grazing about 300 white-faced cattle bearing on the right ribs a 2-M brand. Jerry glanced quickly and cautiously around. Excepting himself, there wasn't a rider of any kind in sight. He moved toward the cattle.

"Flecker said to cut out twenty-five or thirty nice plump cows," Jerry growled resentfully, "but he's one damn' fool if he figures I'm goin' to waste any time choosin'. I'll cut out a bunch from those nearest me and then fan my tail out of this territory just as fast as I can drive cow critters. I don't reckon it would be very healthy to be caught stealing another man's beef in this section."

He uncoiled his rope and, using it to startle the cows into motion, started toward the nearest animals. For ten minutes he worked strenuously cutting out some twenty cattle from the herd. Then quite suddenly it happened.

Jerry was just reining his pony around a tall upthrust of rock in pursuit of an obstreperous cow when a leaden slug flattened itself against the granite with a sort of silvery splash. At the same instant the report of a rifle shot reached his ears. With one quick motion Knight jerked his pony to a halt, whirled in the saddle as he spun the pony around to face the unseen rifleman. There was nobody to be seen. In front of Knight were scattered only boulders and waving grass. He crouched low in the saddle, one fist clenching the butt of his six-shooter, eyes peering rapidly about but seeing no motion anywhere. Jerry raised his voice:

"Show yourself, *hombre*, if you want another chance! That shot was right close, but if you want another, you got to put in an appearance."

This was largely bluff and he knew it was bluff, but he hoped to frighten the hidden assailant into coming into the open. But the bluff didn't work. The answer, when it came, surprised Knight. It consisted of a single scornful laugh from a point much nearer than Jerry had dreamed. He moved his head slightly to view the high, wide granite boulder — it was nearly the size of a small house — from behind which the laugh had come. And now Jerry saw the end of a rifle barrel pointing his way and the rider behind the gun.

The rider spoke contemptuously: "Jerk 'em high, cowpoke. I've got a bead on you. Take your hand away from that gun. Put 'em up! Quick!"

There was nothing else, under the circumstances, for Jerry Knight to do. Slowly he raised his hands high above his head, then lowered them, clasped, across the crown of his sombrero.

"Now will you come into sight?" he challenged coolly. "Or are you afraid to?"

Again that scornful laugh, as the rider pushed into full view, walking her horse slowly toward Jerry, the rifle still at ready and cuddled against her side.

Jerry said: "Thought it was a girl's voice. Nobody but a woman would miss a shot at that short a distance."

"It wouldn't occur to a dumb man that I might have missed on purpose, would it?" the girl snapped angrily. "Cow thief, I could have bored you plumb center."

"I'm wonderin' why you didn't?" he asked mildly.

"Probably because I'm a fool," the girl said bitterly. "It's a good thing for you it wasn't Dad or one of the boys. Nope, I'll just take you prisoner and let them decide what's to be done. Loosen your gun belts, drop 'em to the ground. Hurry up, now, or I'll forget that I'm soft-hearted. Quick!"

Looking into the girl's flashing black eyes, Jerry saw that she meant every word. At the same moment, even while he was dropping his guns to the earth, he couldn't suppress the involuntary exclamation that left his lips. The girl was really pretty with great masses of blue-black hair coiled beneath her old slouch-brimmed sombrero. Her nose was straight, her lips red, and her chin determined. A man's blue denim shirt, rolled to the elbows, exposed well-tanned, rounded arms. She was in man's overalls and on her feet were a well-worn pair of high-heeled riding boots. The horse she sat was a wiry little chestnut.

The girl said again, contemptuously: "Dirty cow thief!"

"Sort of harsh words, ma'am," Jerry said reprovingly.

"Well, aren't you? I've been watching you, saw you cutting out Two-M cattle. I saw you were a stranger and I hesitated to shoot on that account, but we've lost enough cattle the past year. Well, answer me, aren't you a cow thief?"

"It sure looks thataway, ma'am." He grinned.

The girl frowned at the cowboy, failing to understand such levity under the circumstances. "You mean, you aren't? That you have a plausible reason for . . . ?"

"Yes, ma'am." Jerry's grin widened. "You see, I was only following the boss' orders."

"And he told you to steal our cows?"

"Yes'm. Told me just where to find 'em."

"Well, my grief! What sort of . . . say, cowboy, are you crazy?"

"Just a mite batty, I expect," he said humbly. "Maybe it's the view."

"The view?"

Jerry explained. "Uhn-huh. And a sudden idea. You know, the scenery. It *is* beautiful. I don't know where I've seen such a pretty sight. And then I got my idea. I thought, gosh, it'd be great to be married to such scenery. And the whole idea sort of made my head swim . . ."

"Stop it!" The girl's cheeks flushed red. "You *are* insane, I reckon."

"Yes'm, I don't ever expect to be the same again. My name's Knight. My friends call me Jerry, but I reckon we'll have to put down the whole she-bang on the license."

"What are you talking about?"

"The wedding license. You and me. Say, I bet you ten bucks your name is Monroe."

"A cow thief would bet on a sure thing," the girl sneered.

"I'd put my money on you, any time," Jerry said lazily. "The first name is Marie, Violet, Abigail, or I'm a liar."

"You are," the girl said shortly. "It's Alice."

38

"Right pretty name. But I had to find out somehow. Yep, you and me will get along fine, once we come to an understanding."

"You're going to come to your understanding a heap quicker than you expect. Turn that horse, mister, and ride slow in front of me."

Jerry made no move to obey. He said, instead: "I can't Alice. I got to do what my boss told me to do. I don't think he'd like it if I came back without some of your cows."

"Who is your boss?"

"Kelt Flecker."

The girl's lip curled up disdainfully. "That snake!"

"Ain't you sort of hard on the whole snake family, miss?"

The girl's dark eyes narrowed. She hardly knew what to make of her captive. "I reckon I am, at that," she conceded coldly. "But snakes are cunning . . . at least."

"Don't you think that same applies to Flecker?"

Alice Monroe shook her head. "If he had brains, he wouldn't send anybody quite as thick-headed as you to rustle our cows." Jerry flushed as the girl continued. "I can't see how he came to hire you. I'll bet you're just something the cat dragged home."

"No'm," Jerry said humbly, "Flecker won me in a poker game."

"My grief! In a poker game?"

"Uhn-huh. Flecker was demonstratin' something I already know . . . that three of a kind beats two pair." From that point on, Jerry went ahead and told the girl just how he had happened to go to work for the Circle F.

The girl listened to the tale with growing amazement, believing Knight in spite of herself — and finding herself liking the cowboy at the same time. She relented a trifle and some of the acid went out of her voice. "Well, that beats me!"

"It beat me, too." Jerry grinned.

"I've never heard anything like it. And just because you signed that paper to follow orders, you think you have to turn cow thief? Even after you discovered you were playing with marked cards? Cowboy, you are a bigger fool than I thought."

"It sure looks thataway," Jerry admitted whimsically. "Right now, I'm plumb kicking myself for not looking into this neck of the range a long time ago."

"You find it interesting?"

"She sure is."

The girl's cheeks flushed under Jerry's admiring stare. "We'll talk about the business at hand," she reminded, trying to keep her voice chilly, but not succeeding very well. "I've decided to let you go."

"Supposing I like bein' a captive? Supposing I don't want to be let go. Y'know, you really ought to consider my feelin's in the matter." He chuckled.

The girl had already lowered the rifle muzzle. Now she threw up one hand in a hopeless gesture. "It's no use trying to talk sensibly to you," she stated emphatically. "Here I'm trying to get our talk on a common-sense basis, and you . . ."

"All right," Jerry broke in, "I'll behave. Now, what do you want to do?"

"I want you to pick up your guns and ride back to the Circle F as fast as your horse will carry you. What you do then is no concern of mine."

"We won't argue that right now," Jerry said dryly. What are you intending to do?"

"I'm going to get back to the ranch and tell Dad about you, repeat the things you've told me about Flecker sending you here to rustle our cattle, and so on. It's the proof we've been needing. We never have liked Flecker. We've suspected him, but couldn't get proof. And then we'll get Sheriff Buck Drake on the job and . . ."

"I wouldn't, were I you," Jerry advised, shaking his head. "You wouldn't get any place. Flecker would only deny that he had sent me over here. I'm a stranger in the country. It would be Flecker's word against a stranger's . . . and Flecker would win. You'd have tipped your hand, given your plans away. No, we better let it ride and not say anything about you letting me go. And I'll just consider myself lucky."

"You certainly can," the girl stated flatly. "If Dad or one of our Two-M hands had been watching these cows today, you wouldn't have received a warning. They'd have shot on sight."

"I reckon so . . ." — Jerry broke off suddenly to ask: "Does your dad always keep somebody on guard over these cattle?"

The girl nodded. "Every day. For the past three months. We had to do something, the stock was disappearing so fast. But Dad sent out a warning, notifying he'd shoot on sight anybody he found rustling his cows. Everybody in the San Lucia country knows that, and we haven't, so far as we know, lost a cow since."

"Do you reckon Kelt Flecker knows it?"

The girl laughed shortly. "Better than anyone else. Dad told Flecker, directly to his face."

Jerry frowned, then speaking as though to himself: "Dennis Wolcott was killed by an unknown . . ."

"Yes, he was," Alice Monroe took up the thought. "You know about that, eh? I'll tell you something else. It's suspected that Kelt Flecker is the unknown, but Sheriff Drake has never been able to prove it. Flecker claims he broke with Ridge Conway a couple of days before the killing of Conway and Wolcott. Sheriff Drake is still looking for that third man."

Jerry laughed softly. "And if you'd shot and killed me . . . you or somebody else . . . and something of Dennis Wolcott's was found on me that would sure make it look like I was the third man in the case, wouldn't it?"

"It certainly would. Have you anything of Wolcott's?"

Jerry nodded. "Flecker gave me a black leather wallet that once belonged to Wolcott. By looking close you can make out Wolcott's name, stamped in the leather."

"It certainly looks," the girl's dark eyes narrowed, "as though Mister Kelt Flecker was trying to get some evidence shot."

"A nice piece of framing," he agreed.

"That settles it," the girl said decisively, "now we've simply got to go to Topango Wells and tell the sheriff what we know."

"Not yet," Jerry contradicted. "Before we spill any beans, I want to know a few more things about this range."

Alice Monroe eyed Jerry speculatively. "You aren't a range detective, are you?" she said seriously.

Jerry grinned and shook his head. "Not none. Matter of fact, if I told you who I really am, you'd laugh at me. You wouldn't even believe me, mebbe."

The girl was puzzled, but didn't press the question that rose to her lips. Finally she said: "All right, I *think* you've spoken the truth. I won't say anything for a time . . . to the sheriff. But I am going to tell Dad. Now, you better pick up your guns and ride."

"Tell your dad I'm askin' him to keep his lip buttoned for a spell."

Alice Monroe looked dubious. "I'll do what I can, but he'll have to suit himself."

Jerry nodded, and swung down from the saddle to retrieve his six-shooters. At that instant there came a sharp, whining noise as a leaden slug passed dangerously close to his head. From the hillside at the backs of the two came the flat report of a Winchester.

CHAPTER
FIVE

The next instant, Jerry had whirled to the girl's side and had swept her out of the saddle, keeping the horse between the girl and the assailant on the hillside.

"Down, keep down!" Jerry said sharply.

"I'm down." Alice Monroe's voice was cool. "It's you he's trying to hit. Not me. If you hadn't chosen to get your guns at that very instant, he'd have hit you."

"Who is it?"

"If I knew, I'd tell you."

Cautiously peering above the pony's neck, Jerry scanned the hillside that was covered with trees and brush. There wasn't a soul to be seen.

"See him?" the girl asked.

Jerry shook his head. "Not a sign . . ." He broke off suddenly, catching sight of a horse darting through the trees, but the rider was too far away to be recognizable in the leafy shadows.

"I think," Jerry said swiftly, "we've got him cornered. He figured, when he finished me, you'd turn your horse and clear out as soon as possible. He'll have one tough time coming down out of that brush without being seen by us. You stay here."

"What are you going to do?"

"Try and catch me a skunk." The cowboy laughed grimly. "Keep behind rocks. I'll be . . ."

"But Jerry . . ." There was a note of fright in the girl's tone.

"Yes, Alice." Jerry grinned. "Gosh, we're sure gettin' acquainted . . . first names in use already. Wait here for me."

His guns were already buckled on as he vaulted to the saddle and wheeled the pony. Then he started at a direct run toward the hillside. The girl gazed after him with wide, anxious eyes. Jerry was nearing the line of brush and trees that grew halfway up the slope. Then yards farther, a puff of black smoke burst from the brush. The report of the gun reached her ears. But Jerry's pony was still climbing, its speed undiminished. An instant later, he reined the little beast into the shadowed depths.

Ten minutes passed. Fifteen. Silence on the hillside now. The sun beat down warmly on the anxious figure of the girl, waiting for some sign of Jerry or the unknown gunman. Once she examined her rifle. Abruptly a shot sounded through the silence. Five minutes later there came a second shot. Then two more in quick succession. Alice choked back the cry that rose to her lips, her eyes wide on the motionless hillside.

Meanwhile, Jerry had pushed through the trees and was peering sharply about. Cottonwoods and alders and scrub oak barred his path. Jack pine appeared frequently. There wasn't a soul to be seen. Low-hanging cottonwoods forced Jerry to dismount and lead the pony through a veritable jungle of range growth.

Suddenly, from Jerry's left, a shot roared. This time it was a six-shooter. Although the shot flew wide of its mark, Jerry gave a sharp cry and dropped to the earth. Rolling over and over, he quickly screened himself behind a mass of tall brush and waited.

Silence. Overhead, spots of sunlight pierced the thicket. Insects droned unceasingly in the quiet. A minute passed and reached to five. Stealthy footsteps sounded on dry leaves. A branch snapped loudly. Then, peering to right and left, six-shooter in hand, came Herb Jacklin, his mind intent on finding and finishing the job he had commenced. Seeing Jerry's riderless horse, he stopped suddenly, tensed to shoot. He was facing partly away from Jerry's position. Now Jerry rose to his full height.

"You lookin' for somethin', Jacklin?" he said clearly.

Jacklin's gun hand swung up in a swift arc, and, as he whirled to face Jerry's voice, a vile oath left his lips. His gun roared as Jerry jerked sidewise, his own guns snapping into view. Jerry's right hand thumbed one swift shot. Almost on top of the explosion came the sound of the left gun. Jacklin stiffened, started a scornful laugh that turned to a cough. Then his body jack-knifed, and he pitched forward on his face. He was quite dead before Knight reached him, turned him over.

Gunsmoke fog drifted lazily through the sun-spotted shadows. A breeze lifted, swept away the last remnants of the swirling gray haze. Knight straightened himself from the body, looked around. His face was hard and grim.

46

"That's one, Dennis," he half whispered. "It was probably Flecker that got you, but this scut was in on it, all right."

He stood looking down at the motionless form a moment, considering while rolling a cigarette. A match was lifted to his lips with steady fingers. Then he reloaded his guns and strode to his horse. A short distance away he found Jacklin's pony, slapped it on the rump, and started it off through the brush. Then he mounted and loped quickly down the slope where Alice Monroe awaited him.

He forced a smile as he dismounted at the girl's side. She was white-faced, tremulous. Finally her lips parted in a half whisper: "Well?"

Jerry said easily: "Lots of skunks in those hills."

"Skunks don't use guns."

Jerry smiled down into her eyes, giving her confidence, steadying her shaken nerves. "This one did," he said quietly.

"Who was it?" the girl insisted.

Jerry evaded that. "You tell your dad about this," he said. "Better have him come out and look things over. You better get on your pony and drift now. But first I'd like the lay of the land around here. Who's Bristol Capron?"

"Manager of the Randall Land and Cattle Company. A slimier reptile never lived, in my opinion. I don't trust him."

"The company put him in the job."

"He's a fit man for such a company."

"What've you got against the Randall outfit as a whole?"

"They're thieves . . . land hogs, cattle hogs. They're trying to gobble up every bit of wealth in sight. I tell you, Ira Randall wouldn't dare come to this part of the country." Her voice was bitter. "He'd be lynched on sight. This country hates him worse than poison. He's wise to stay in the East."

"Mebbe you're wronging Ira Randall," Jerry suggested.

"If so, you'll have to show me where," the girl flamed. "His company has issued mortgages to poor farmers who couldn't possibly pay them off. It's foreclosed on ranches. I tell you, the Randall Company is nothing but a greedy, merciless bloodsucker. What do you think Flecker was stealing our cattle for?"

"I'm waitin' to hear."

"So Dad would go broke and have to give up the Two-M. Capron has already made several offers, but they're so small, cheap, that Dad refuses."

"The company holds a mortgage on the Two-M?"

"No, thank God for that . . . but it would like to. Capron is trying his best to ruin us, so the company can get the Two-M."

"Any particular reason for the company to be so eager to get your outfit?"

"Plenty," Alice Monroe snapped. "Palo Verde Pass."

Jerry looked puzzled. "You'll have to explain that."

"Palo Verde Pass cuts through the San Lucias about six miles southeast of our ranch house. It's part of our holdings. The T.N. and A.S. Railroad would like the pass in order to extend its line which, as you probably know, terminates at Topango Wells at present."

"Seems to me," Jerry said, "Your dad would be wise to give the railroad the right of way. He could make some money and . . ."

"You don't understand," the girl interrupted. "You see, right at the mouth of the pass there's a nice stretch of tableland that overlooks this whole valley. Before Mother died, she and Dad had always planned to build a house at that point." The girl's eyes grew wistful, slightly moist. "Someday I want to build a house there myself. This is pretty country. It's a pretty pass. I don't want it ruined by coal smoke and cinders and steel rails. We don't want a lot of money . . . only enough to get along comfortably. If the company would only leave us alone . . . I mean, the Randall Company . . ."

Jerry said gently: "I see your point, girl. But people the other side of the San Lucias need a railroad."

"There's Camino Cañon, then," the girl replied. "It's more on a line with the rails already laid. The T.N. and A.S. would sooner have it. By using Camino, it would have a shorter, more direct route."

"Why doesn't the railroad use Camino Cañon, then?" Jerry asked. Remembering the map Flecker had furnished, he continued: "Camino Cañon is just about eight or nine miles due west of the Circle F, isn't it?"

"Nearer eight." The girl nodded. "The railroad can't get it because Camino Cañon is on Circle F holdings and the Randall Company won't sell . . . that is, it will sell, but at a terribly prohibitive price. The railroad refuses to be held up that way. I don't blame it."

"Oh, I see." Jerry was quiet for a spell, then he changed the subject. "You better be getting along now. Tell your dad what's happened. Also, tell him not to count his cows tonight or he'll find himself twenty or thirty head shy."

The girl started to mount. Now she swung up to the saddle and snapped at him: "What?"

He nodded, repeating: "Twenty or thirty head shy."

"Now, look here, cowboy . . ." Alice bridled.

"Shucks, I got to carry out the boss' orders. Now, now, wait a minute, don't you go to flyin' off the handle thataway. I know what I'm doing."

"I wonder if you do." The girl looked puzzled.

"Yeah, you can bet on it. And you may lose a few cows, but you stand to win in the long run. Take my word for that."

"We-ell" — the girl hesitated — "it sounds crazy, but . . . but . . ."

"But you'll let me leave with the cows and not shoot at me any more? Fine! We're gettin' along right well, Alice. But you haven't seen anything yet. I've got plans . . ."

"What kind of plans?"

"Remember what I said about a license?"

The girl's face crimsoned as she touched spurs to her pony and moved rapidly away.

"I've got other plans, too!" Jerry called after her. "Leastwise, I'll have 'em drawn. Plans for a house . . . a house on that pretty tableland you were telling me about."

The girl kept going.

Jerry raised his voice again: "Hey, I'll be back tomorrow after more cows! You'll be here, won't you?"

The girl turned in the saddle. "You couldn't stop me, now, cowboy" — she laughed back — "but I'll have the whole Two-M crew with me. ¡Adiós!"

Her horse broke into a swift lope, and a moment later she had dropped behind a rise of land.

Jerry mounted, again set to work cutting out 2-M cows. In a short time he had gathered twenty-five head and turned them toward Camino Cañon. It was about three in the afternoon when he arrived at the cañon, driving the cows before him. Tim Beadle and George Corwin were awaiting his arrival, although they seemed somewhat surprised at seeing him.

Beadle said: "Got here all right, eh?"

"Sure, didn't you think I would?" Jerry said gravely.

"Didn't have no trouble, or nothin'?" Corwin persisted.

"None at all."

"Wa'n't nobody ridin' herd on the cows?" Beadle appeared puzzled.

"Flecker told me they left the cows unguarded," Jerry stated. "Didn't you know that?"

Beadle and Corwin exchanged glances, but didn't bother to answer Knight. Beadle said to his partner: "I reckon they must have give up watchin' . . ."

"Who?" Jerry cut in.

"Never mind," Corwin replied. "Come on, we'll throw these cows in with the others."

The three men got behind the small bunch of Herefords and drove them into the cañon whose sloping walls were covered with grass and scrub oak. Rounding a bend in the cañon, Jerry saw about fifty more 2-M cows, penned up in a crude corral built of loose rock. The trail through the cañon was little frequented and the rock corral was screened, to a large extent, by tall brush and cottonwoods. So there was little likelihood of the rustled cows being discovered by anyone unless he were led to the spot.

Jerry said: "Huh! More cows, eh? Were you fellers over on Two-M range today?"

Beadle shook his head. "No, these is just strays we've picked up from time to time. We been holdin' 'em here for a spell. In case any of the Two-M hands did discover this beef stock, we could always say they'd strayed over here, and we was just holdin' 'em till we had a chance to turn 'em back."

"Strays, eh?" Jerry said thoughtfully. "I shouldn't think them cows would be likely to stray away from good grazin' and cross Aliso Creek to come over here."

Beadle winked at Corwin. "Knight," he said humorously, "you'd be surprised where Two-M critters stray sometimes."

Corwin laughed and nodded, then said: "You can go back to the ranch now, Knight. Tell Kelt you delivered the cows OK and that we was here waitin'."

"You two comin' in?" Jerry asked.

Beadle shook his head. "Nope, we got some drivin' to do tonight."

Jerry reined his horse around, waved one hand in farewell, and headed for the Circle F.

CHAPTER
SIX

The ranch cook was just beating the dishpan to announce supper when Jerry rode in, turned his horse into the corral, and carried his rig to the bunkhouse. Kelt Flecker and the three Circle F hands were already seated at the table in the cook shack, delving into spuds, bacon, and beans. Flecker looked up in some surprise when Jerry entered and greeted the rest.

"You carry out my orders?" he demanded.

Jerry reached for a platter of bacon as he nodded. "Sure, delivered those Two-M critters to Corwin and Beadle."

"Never mind that," Flecker said hastily. He looked quickly at Wing, Hackett, and Reed who were gazing questioningly at Knight. Flecker went on: "We'll talk it over later, Knight. And you mean Circle F critters . . . not Two-M, don't you?"

"Reckon I do." Jerry nodded.

"Didn't lose that map, did you?" Flecker said after a time.

Jerry shook his head. "It helped a heap."

"Sure," Flecker said heartily. "You hang onto that map and the case you carry it in. It'll come in handy."

Supper was finished in silence. Afterward, Flecker drew Knight outside and asked for details regarding the 2-M cows. Jerry supplied the story, adding: "Corwin and Beadle had another bunch of cows waiting in Camino Cañon. Said they were Two-M strays."

"We've had them a long time," Flecker boasted brazenly, "just waitin' to add a few more before runnin' 'em over the state line. Say, you didn't see nobody over on the Two-M range today, did you?"

"You mean Two-M hands?"

Flecker nodded.

Jerry shook his head. "Nary a hand," he said smoothly.

The two were standing near the corral. Darkness had descended, only the squares of light from the cook shack and bunkhouse punctuating the dense gloom. Overhead only a few stars showed through.

Flecker said after a time: "Herb Jacklin wasn't with George and Tim, was he?"

"I didn't see him in the cañon," Jerry replied truthfully.

"I wonder why in the hell he ain't back?" Flecker sounded irritable.

"Where'd he go?"

"I sent him on a job," Flecker returned vaguely.

A sudden movement several yards away took the attention of the two men. A dark shape moved in the gloom. Flecker reached for his gun, then halted, and went cautiously forward. A moment later he scratched a match, then a violent oath left his lips.

54

Jerry hurried forward. "What's wrong?"

Flecker swore again. "Here's Herb's horse. Now where in hell's Herb?"

Jacklin's horse had finally wandered home. Jerry scratched matches while Flecker removed Jacklin's rifle from the saddle boot and examined it.

"Looks like two shots were fired," Flecker announced after a time. "That's providin' Herb started out with a full magazine, and I reckon he did. But where in hell is Herb? Hope nothin's happened to him."

Jerry said: "Mebbe his horse bucked him off, and he's walking."

Flecker shook his head. "That horse can't be made to buck. I 'member the day Herb took all the buckin' out of him. The horse pitched Herb off . . . just once. Then Herb took to beatin' it over the head with a loaded quirt every time it moved sudden. Nope, that horse was sure broke of buckin' . . . say, Knight, you didn't hear any shootin' today, did you?"

"Come to think of it, I did," Knight admitted.

"Huh! What? Why didn't you say so before?"

"Reckon it slipped my mind."

"When was this? Where?"

"It was just before I pulled out with the Two-M cows," Knight replied truthfully enough. "Up on the hillside, among the trees and brush. There were several shots fired."

Flecker swore violently. "Why didn't you see what was goin' on?"

Knight laughed scornfully. "Listen, boss, would you have stayed, under the circumstances? Here I was on a strange range, picking up another man's cows. Hell's bells! You're lucky I delivered the cows at the cañon!"

"But you might have . . ."

"How did I know that Jacklin was over there? What did you do, send him to spy on me? That's a lousy trick . . ."

"Take it easy now, Knight. I didn't say Jacklin was over there." Flecker's voice was placating. "As a matter of fact, that shootin' didn't mean anythin'. Pro'bly somebody shootin' at targets or out to get a few birds for supper."

"That's probably it," Jerry agreed, grinning in the darkness.

Flecker appeared worried. He and Jerry walked slowly toward the bunkhouse. Finally Flecker announced: "Look here, Knight. You know where that corral is in the cañon now. Tomorrow, you go over to the Two-M range, get some more cows, and bring them to that corral. I'm ridin' tonight."

"Where're you going?"

"I'm worried about what's happened to Herb," Flecker snapped. "Can't tell what's shapin' up, with him not returnin'. I'm goin' to saddle up and join Corwin and Beadle. We got to get them cows out of the cañon, in case there'd be any sort of investigation on the way. You stay here and carry out the job like I've told you. We'll probably be back in three days."

"Take that long to get those cows over the state line?"

Flecker nodded. "Two days to go and find a buyer and so on. Me 'n' George and Tim can return in a day. But, hell, I'm losin' time, foolin' around here."

Muttering to himself, Flecker dashed to get his saddle, returned to the corral, and saddled up. Five minutes later, he was riding, fast, out of the ranch yard. Suddenly he pulled up short in a scattering of sand and gravel, and yelled: "Hey, Knight!"

"Yeah, what you want?"

"You take charge till I return. Carry out the job I give you, but give them other hands enough work around the ranch to keep 'em busy till I get back."

"I'll take care of it!" Jerry called in reply.

Again came the rush of hoofs as Flecker departed rapidly. Jerry chuckled. "Kelt Flecker is sure disturbed. Jacklin's not showing up has got him worried."

He made his way toward the bunkhouse and found Shorty Wing standing in the doorway.

Shorty said: "I heard Kelt givin' you orders. So you're roddin' the outfit till he returns, eh?"

"Looks thataway." Jerry smiled.

From inside the bunkhouse, Steve Hackett asked: "What job you got picked for us tomorrow?"

Jerry stepped into the bunkhouse, nodded to Frank Reed who was also there, then said: "You *hombres* are due for some riding early tomorrow. Kelt has about seventy-five Two-M cows that he figures to sell over the state line. We four are going to cut out a hundred Circle F critters and take 'em over to the Monroe outfit. We've got to keep the account balanced, pay a debt with interest, if you want to put it that way."

"What!" The three cowboys spoke as one.

"You heard me." Jerry chuckled. "Game to do it?"

"Cripes, yes!" Again a blending of three voices. Shorty Wing added: "Say, what sort of game you pullin'?"

Jerry said: "Kelt's worrying because Jacklin hasn't showed up."

"But where is he?" Reed asked.

"I killed him," Knight said tersely. "Flecker sent me rustling Two-M cows in hopes I'd get shot while doing it. He sent Jacklin to spy on me. I met a girl there . . ."

"Alice Monroe?" Hackett said.

Jerry nodded. "We got acquainted. I reckon Jacklin, watching me, figured I might tell what I knew, so he took a shot at me. I climbed the hillside after him. We shot it out."

"Well, may I be damned!" Wing said in amazement.

"Mebbe we'll all get shot," Jerry speculated, "when Kelt learns I'm bucking him."

"Ain't that the truth!" Reed exclaimed fervently. "There'll be plenty lead thrown. Looks to me like the air was due to get fogged up with gunsmoke."

"Say, Jerry," Wing queried, "why should Kelt send you over there to get you killed?"

"He'd like it to look like I was the third man in the Dennis Wolcott killing."

Wing interrupted to say: "I told Steve and Frank about you knowin' Wolcott. They both think you're a range detective."

"I'm far from it." Jerry smiled a bit grimly. He added details about the map and the leather case with the obliterated name.

The four cowboys talked for another hour before turning in for the night. The following morning they were in the saddle by sunup, paying no attention to the questions of the inquisitive ranch cook who was curious to know where they were going.

It was about an hour past mid-morning when Jerry, accompanied by Wing, Hackett, and Reed, pushed about a hundred head of Circle F cattle across Aliso Creek and onto 2-M range. Clearing the trees that bordered the course of the stream, Knight saw Alice Monroe and a spare elderly man, seated on horses, watching the approaching cattle with puzzled eyes. Jerry rode forward to meet the girl. Alice put her pony into motion as did the man beside her.

"Hi, you, Alice," he greeted cheerfully. "I'll bet this is your dad."

"You guess right." The girl smiled. "I've already told him you were crazy, but, after seeing these cattle, I guess he knows it."

Jerry reined his pony around, put out his right hand. Mart Monroe accepted it rather dubiously. He looked suspiciously at Jerry, and then toward the approaching cows and cowpunchers.

"Look here, young man," he said crisply, "I don't understand this at all."

"I bet you don't, either." Jerry grinned and changed the subject. "Find any skunks up on that hill yesterday?"

Mart Monroe said grimly: "One . . . name of Jacklin. We buried him, right there." His piercing blue eyes drilled into Knight's. "That's one thing that leads me to trust you, but . . . but I don't understand these Circle F cows. Why did you bring them here?"

Jerry explained: "There's about seventy-five Two-M Herefords on their way into the next state right now. I'm just paying you back, Mister Monroe. I'd hate to see you lose any stock."

Monroe gasped. "But . . . but . . . look here, I can't take these cows. We'll have to do this legally. Do you think I want Flecker accusing me of rustling?"

"We're doing it legally." Jerry grinned. He drew a sheet of paper from his pocket, handed it to Monroe. "Here's a bill of sale for one hundred head."

Monroe accepted the paper, read it. He looked about ready to explode. "Now, look here," he stammered, "we can't do this. Your name is signed on this paper. You haven't any right to sell Circle F cows . . ."

"That paper clears you, see?" Jerry said earnestly. "If trouble comes from this, it descends on my head. You're in the clear. Now, don't ask questions. I know what I'm doing."

"Are you a . . . ?"

"No, I'm no range detective working for the Cattlemen's Association," Jerry said calmly.

Monroe's eyes opened widely. "How did you know I was going to ask you that?"

"Nearly everybody else has." He grinned. "Nope, Mister Monroe, you'd be surprised if you knew what I am."

"Well, what are you?"

Jerry didn't reply to that. By this time the cows and cowpunchers were much nearer and he turned his pony to rejoin them. He shouted to Shorty Wing: "Keep 'em moving, Shorty!"

Again he wheeled his pony and drew to a stop near Alice Monroe and her father.

"I don't know as I like this," Monroe was saying, shaking his head. "This might make trouble."

"Sure, I expect that," Jerry said calmly, "but trouble for Kelt Flecker. You know you've lost cows . . . far more than this hundred head."

Monroe started to swear, glanced at Alice, checked himself, and nodded vigorously. "A heap more. By the great shorn spoon!"

"You'll get back every head," Jerry promised, "or at least the same number of head, if you'll leave things to me. Of course, I'll have to steal a few of your cows now and then to make Flecker believe I'm on the job. If you'll just warn your hands not to throw any lead my way, I'll be much obliged. I might get hurt if that continued."

Alice smiled, said: "You almost did, cowboy."

Monroe was still protesting. "But why can't we just tell the sheriff what we know? That will settle Flecker's hash."

"Sure, but will it return property that folks around here have lost?" Jerry asked.

"Well," Monroe conceded, "mebbe not. You figure to right the wrongs the Randall Company is guilty of?"

"I'd sure like to try."

"You're carvin' out a big job for yourself, son." Monroe's blue eyes held a sympathetic light. "And you're running big risks."

"Mister Monroe," Jerry asked, "can you get me a list of the folks that have lost money through the Randall Company? You should be pretty well acquainted in Topango Wells."

Monroe shook his head dubiously. "I can get you the names that are still in this part of the country, but a good many families, discouraged, have left for other parts."

Knight nodded. "Do what you can, anyway. I reckon I'll have to get most of the information from Bristol Capron."

Monroe laughed scornfully. "Capron wouldn't tell you a thing."

"Mebbe I could persuade him," Jerry said grimly. He looked up, saw the Circle F cowboys approaching, and said: "Well, we'll run off some more of your cows and get going. Better separate those Circle F animals, so you can keep count."

Monroe still looked puzzled, but he nodded consent. "I'll head back now, and send out a couple of men."

"I'll see you tomorrow," Jerry said.

Monroe turned his pony and dashed away. Alice waited a few minutes. Jerry said: "Does the clerk in this county issue a pretty engraved license, or is it just one of those plain ones?"

Alice crimsoned. "Jerry . . ."

"And about that house we're going to build on that tableland," he interrupted, grinning, "how many rooms do you plan to have? Mebbe you ought to draw up some sketches."

"They're all drawn . . . ," the girl started, then stopped.

"I'll be over some night to look at 'em," Jerry stated.

"Cowboy, stop this foolishness."

"Who says it's foolish? Do you?"

"We-ell, no, of course . . . that is . . ."

"Certainly, you don't." He chuckled. "Just as soon as we can get Flecker taken care of, we'll . . ."

"Jerry, you will be careful, won't you?"

"What do you mean . . . careful?"

"Not to get shot or . . . or . . ."

"Doesn't make a bit of difference, does it?" Jerry asked airily. "I'm only a crazy cowpuncher. You said so yourself."

"Well, I didn't mean it that way."

Before anything more could be said, the three Circle F men rode up and awaited further instructions from Knight. Jerry lifted his hat to the girl and, with a — "See you tomorrow." — led his men off in the direction of the grazing 2-M herd. By the time they had finished cutting out an even twenty-five head, Alice Monroe had disappeared in pursuit of her father.

That afternoon, the cowboys delivered the 2-M cows to the corral in Camino Cañon, then returned to the ranch. The following morning they drove a second hundred Circle F beef animals to the 2-M and turned them over to a pair of 2-M hands who had accompanied Mart Monroe and his daughter. This time, Jerry had a longer opportunity to converse with

Alice, but what words were exchanged between the two have no place in this tale.

Again, a bunch of 2-M cows were cut out and driven to the corral in the cañon, but by this time, when Knight and his men returned to the ranch, they were met by a frowning George Corwin who braced them in the bunkhouse, after they had taken care of their weary horses.

CHAPTER
SEVEN

"Where in hell you fellers been?" Corwin demanded angrily. He frowned down on the four from the doorway of the bunkhouse as Jerry and his friends trudged up from the corral, lugging saddles.

Jerry said, surprised: "You fellers back already?"

"I am," Corwin snapped. "Kelt got to thinkin' one of us should be here, to see there wa'n't no loafin' goin' on. Kelt and Tim will be back tomorrow. I didn't go all the way with them ... but say, what you fellers been doin'?"

Jerry grinned insolently. "Oh, just riding around. You know how cowboys like to ride."

"Cut it!" Corwin snapped savagely. "I'm askin' a serious question. I want an answer."

Jerry said coolly: "Just how badly do you want it, Corwin?"

Corwin started to swear and suddenly cooled down before the hostile eyes of Jerry and his friends. He glanced from man to man, noting six-shooters in holsters. Quite suddenly he turned back into the bunkhouse, muttering over one shoulder: "Cocky, eh? All right. We'll see what Kelt has to say when he comes back. I only asked a civil question. No need you flyin' offen the handle."

"And I answered you," Knight said crisply. "I said we'd been riding. Don't worry, I've been taking care of the Randall Company rights."

"T'hell with the Randall Company!" Corwin suddenly whirled to face the others who had now entered the bunkhouse. "All right, wait till Kelt hears about this. If he don't make it tough for you . . ."

Jerry said: "To hell with Kelt and you, too, Corwin!"

Corwin's eyes bulged. One hand jerked toward a holstered gun.

Jerry said calmly: "Go on, jerk it. I asked you a spell back how badly you wanted it."

Corwin's face flamed, then the color died out to be replaced by an ashen paleness. He turned away, shaking his head. "I'll leave this to Kelt," he muttered. "I can see you *hombres* have come to some sort of an understandin'. You ain't goin' to gang up on me. I'll let Kelt handle things."

Knight laughed sarcastically. The other men didn't say anything. Saddles were put down and men trooped to the cook shack to eat supper. The meal was consumed in silence, Corwin now and then casting uneasy glances in Knight's direction. Suddenly, unable to bear it any longer, Corwin muttered an oath and rose from the table. Without a word he passed out of the building and headed toward the bunkhouse. Jerry rose and, watching from the cook shack doorway, saw Corwin emerge from the bunkhouse, bearing his saddle.

Jerry stepped outside.

Shorty Wing said quietly: "He's heap bad medicine with a six-gun, Jerry."

Jerry snapped: "I never did like taking medicine."

"We better go along," Steve Hackett proposed.

"You three stay here," Jerry jerked back.

The three cowpunchers watched Jerry from the doorway, saw him overtake Corwin halfway to the corral.

Jerry said quietly: "Where you heading, Corwin?"

Corwin stopped, set down his saddle, and faced Jerry. "It ain't none of your business, Knight, but I'm headin' to find Kelt to tell him how you're actin'. I don't like it. I'm goin' . . ."

"You're going to stay right here," the other declared flatly. "I'm rodding this outfit."

"Hell's bells!" Corwin snarled. "Kelt didn't put *me* in your charge. He meant them other three."

"I don't care what Kelt said," Jerry repeated. "I'm rodding this outfit."

"T'hell with you."

"That works two ways," Jerry said calmly. "First thing you know, Corwin, you'll be hitting the trail Herb Jacklin took."

Corwin backed a few paces, eyes narrowing. "What do you know about Jacklin?"

Jerry laughed coldly. "I know he won't ever be back. We shot it out, Corwin. That plain? Mebbe you want some of the same."

Corwin stiffened. "You can't give it to me!"

A third time Jerry said carelessly: "How badly do you want it, Corwin?"

Still Corwin hesitated, torn between the desire to reach Kelt with this story and at the same time to put Knight out of business.

Jerry continued tauntingly: "Here's something else, Corwin. I know who the third man in the Wolcott killing was."

Corwin's eyes bulged, the tip of his tongue licking at lips suddenly gone dry. His arm commenced slowly to bend at the elbow. "Oh, is that so," he sneered. "I suppose you've told the sheriff some wild tale . . ."

"Haven't mentioned a word to the sheriff," Jerry admitted, "but I'm intending to. You big enough to stop me?"

Corwin swore an oath. His right arm stabbed down. His gun snapped up in a crashing roar that was drowned in the double explosion of Jerry's twin six-guns. Powder smoke swirled between the two men. Corwin staggered back, then sat down abruptly on the ground. His mouth was sagging; his eyes looked about to burst from their sockets. Slowly he sank back, threshed about a minute, and lay still. A dark crimson stain spread slowly on his left breast.

Running steps at his rear caused Jerry to look around. Wing, Reed, and Hackett were arriving at a run. Shorty Wing gasped: "Gawd, that was fast. You hit, Jerry?"

Knight said grimly: "Never touched me."

"He reached first," Steve Hackett put in.

68

"Thought sure Corwin had you!" Reed exclaimed. "Is he dead?"

Jerry said: "We got a job of buryin' to do, *hombres*."

"What started it?" Wing wanted to know.

Jerry gave the necessary details.

"There'll be hell to pay when Flecker gets back," Hackett said seriously.

Knight laughed shortly. "I reckon I'll have enough to foot the bill."

The following morning Jerry and his men delivered another hundred Circle F cows at the 2-M together with the necessary bill of sale, but this time, after Jerry had had some conversation with Alice and Mart Monroe, the men returned to the Circle F without driving any 2-M steers to Camino Cañon. Jerry expected Flecker to return about noon and wanted to be there when he arrived.

It was about three in the afternoon before Flecker showed up. He found Jerry, Wing, Reed, and Hackett seated in the bunkhouse. At once he commenced asking questions, but Jerry forestalled him with: "Where's Tim Beadle?"

"Tim rode over near Two-M range to check up on you," Flecker growled. "We noticed when we rode through Camino Cañon that there wa'n't as many Two-M cows there as there should have been. I bet you been loafin' all day." He halted suddenly at the slip in front of Reed, Hackett and Wing, and added: "I mean Circle F cows. I don't know what's got into me, gettin' mixed that way."

"And where did you say Tim had gone?" Jerry asked smoothly. "He wasn't worried about me, was he?"

"Why in hell should he be?"

"I was wondering." Jerry smiled.

Flecker broke in: "Say, where's George Corwin?"

Jerry said calmly: "Last I saw him, he was six foot down. We buried him deep."

Flecker gave vent to a sudden howl of amazement. "What did you say?"

"Look here," Jerry asked, "you left me to rod the outfit when you were gone, didn't you?"

"Certain. What's that got to do . . . ?"

"Corwin didn't like the idea. We had some words."

"You crazy fool! Them orders didn't cover Corwin. What happened?"

"We had some words," Jerry said calmly. "He went for his gun. I didn't have any choice in the matter."

"And you killed him?" Flecker gasped. "You mean to sit there and tell me *you* beat George to the draw? And you say he went for his gun first? Knight, don't lie to me. I want the straight of this mess."

"I'm not lying. Ask these other *hombres*. They saw Corwin reach first. Ask cookie. He saw the whole thing from his cook shanty."

"By Gawd, I will!"

Flecker heard Reed, Wing, and Hackett verify Knight's story, then he whirled to go in search of the ranch cook. Ten minutes later he returned, muttering angrily.

"Well, what did cookie say?" Jerry asked calmly.

"He backed you up," Flecker snarled. "But there's somethin' damn' funny about this whole business. I don't understand it. Knight, don't you throw a leg over a horse till this business is settled to my satisfaction. I aim to keep you here till I can decide what's to be done. I'll talk things over with Tim Beadle."

"Mebbe," Jerry proposed innocently, "we'd better go to Topango Wells and tell the whole story to the sheriff. I'll tell what I know and you can tell your side."

Flecker's eyes slanted viciously at Knight. "No, we don't tell nothin' to the sheriff," he snapped. "Seems to me you're gettin' plumb cocky all of a sudden, Knight."

Jerry said quietly: "It isn't as sudden as you think, Kelt."

Flecker appeared nervous. He glanced at Reed, Wing, and Hackett. "And you fellers keep your mouths shut, too. I'll tell you what to tell and what not to tell. And don't stir offen this ranch, you hear me?"

The three cowboys commenced a protest but a glance from Jerry silenced them. Thinking he held the men under his domination, Kelt Flecker swaggered out of the building.

Shorty Wing remarked worriedly: "Jerry, there's goin' to be hell to pay when Beadle gets back."

"I'm not worrying." Jerry laughed.

"I would be, in your boots," Reed said seriously.

Jerry laughed again. A moment later he said: "Shorty, will you do me a favor?"

"Certain sure. What is it?"

"Sneak down to the corral and take my saddle. Put it on a good horse, then hide the horse in that brush back

71

of the corral. I'll try and keep Flecker busy so he won't see you."

Steve Hackett asked: "You figurin' to light out?"

"Tonight, if I get a chance. I've got business in town. Don't worry, I'm not aiming to leave you *hombres* in the lurch. I'll be back."

Wing nodded. "Don't worry about us. I'll take care of saddlin' up for you as soon as possible."

Time drifted past. Jerry found Flecker in conversation with the cook, trying to find a flaw in the story the cook maintained was the truth.

"S'help me Gawd," the old cook was saying, "I saw George reach for his gun before Knight even made a move."

"What were they talkin' about before that happened?" Flecker asked for probably the twentieth time.

And for probably the twentieth time the cook had replied crustily: "You think I got ears that can hear what's said down near the corral?"

"Dang it," Jerry drawled, "I told you what happened, Kelt. Can't you take my word for it?"

"No, I can't," Flecker said flatly. "There's somethin' funny goin' on and I aim to get at the bottom of it." And so they argued the afternoon away.

Meanwhile, Shorty Wing had succeeded in slipping down to the corral and saddling a horse for Jerry. However, not without being discovered. Flecker had happened to glance out of the cook shack window just in time to see Wing leading the saddled horse into the tall brush back of the corral. Flecker started to speak, then checked himself, and remained silent.

Shortly before supper Flecker spotted Beadle riding hard into the ranch yard. He hurried out to meet the rider, with Knight following close behind. Beadle was bursting with conversation as he pulled his foam-flecked horse to a savage halt.

"Do you know what, Kelt?" he exclaimed excitedly. "This range is overrun with crooks."

"I sort of suspected that," Jerry said dryly.

"What you talkin' about, Tim?" Flecker demanded.

Beadle stepped down from his pony, face crimson with indignant rage. He looked quickly about and lowered his voice a trifle: "I rode over on Two-M range, like you said, thinkin' I might see Knight."

"Knight didn't go over there today," Flecker cut in. "He ain't explained why yet. There's somethin' else that . . ."

"And so you know what, Kelt?" Beadle interrupted angrily. "I was spyin' around, not showin' myself. Do you know what? Them dirty Two-M waddies has been rustlin' us blind."

"Talk sense, Tim," Flecker said irritably.

"I'm talkin' sense," Beadle snapped. "They got about three hundred Circle F cows and men ridin' herd on 'em. Now can you beat that?"

"The dirty cow thieves!" Flecker bellowed. He whirled suddenly on Knight: "What do you know about this?"

Jerry said innocently: "Surprising, isn't it? Can you imagine, cow thieves on the range? I never heard of such a condition."

"Don't get funny," Flecker snarled. "I'm askin' you."

"Why should I know anything about it?" Jerry evaded. "Mebbe Monroe is just getting even with you. The best course is to go to town and lay this all before the sheriff and tell what we know."

"T'hell you say," Flecker sneered. His eyes narrowed, considering past events. "Seems to me, you're mighty anxious to get in to see the sheriff. What you got up your sleeve?"

"Nothing but my elbow," Jerry replied.

"It's li'able to have to do some fast bendin'," Flecker said ominously. "We'll look into this cattle rustlin' later." He turned back to Beadle: "Tim, George is dead."

"Dead? Dead!" Beadle looked blank. "What do you mean he's dead?"

"Dammit! Ain't I tellin' you?" Flecker snapped impatiently.

"But . . . but what happened?"

"Him and Knight had a scrap."

Beadle's face went ugly. He whirled on Jerry. "Damn you, Knight, I'll . . ."

"You'll what?" Jerry queried coldly. One gun was coming out, covering both Flecker and Beadle as he retreated two steps.

Beadle went pale but kept his nerve. "Put that gun away, give me an even break."

"Cut it, Tim!" Flecker said harshly. "George had an even break, but he . . ."

"I don't believe it," Beadle rasped.

"Cut it, I tell you!" Flecker insisted. "There was four witnesses, Tim. Knight claims it was self-defense. I reckon it was. Now, cool down. Knight, put that gun away."

"I will when Beadle gets through going on the prod," Jerry jerked out.

A quick glance was exchanged between Beadle and Flecker. Beadle relaxed, said sullenly: "I'm sorry, Knight. I thought a heap of George Corwin, but if Kelt says it was on the square, that's all right with me. How'd it happen?"

Jerry started to explain, but Flecker interrupted with: "Knight, I got private talk to make with Tim. I'll tell him about your blow-up with George. By the time I get through, you'll see Tim won't hold any grudge."

Jerry nodded shortly, turned, and strode away. Beadle glared after his nonchalant, square-shouldered bearing. "I'll kill that smart, young . . ."

"Later, Tim, later," Flecker said soothingly. "We got to give him his head till he can run into the open."

"When'll that be? There's somethin' funny about this. I don't suppose Herb Jacklin has showed up?"

Flecker shook his head.

Beadle's face darkened. "There's something funny in the wind," he declared. "First Jacklin, then Corwin. Now them cows of ours over on Two-M property. How do you explain it, Kelt?"

"I don't yet," Flecker said heavily. "It's got me worried. Knight is plumb cocky all of a sudden. If our cows is on Two-M range and being guarded by Two-M hands, there's something bad in the wind. We got to learn what it is. I got a hunch Knight has made some sort of friendly contact with Monroe."

"Why don't you turn him over to the authorities? He's broke his parole."

"And him knowin' what he knows now?" Flecker said sarcastically. "Don't be a fool, Tim. He knows too much about us. We wouldn't dare chance it. If I'd known things was goin' to turn out like this, I'd never have brought Knight out here."

"What about him and Corwin shootin' it out?"

"Here's the story as Knight told it to me. The others say George went for his gun first. I guess he did, but what led up to that I don't know. We've only got Knight's word." Flecker added other details pertaining to the fight, and ended: "One thing's certain, Knight has got to go!"

"What you figurin' on?"

"A little spell back," Flecker explained, "I saw Wing saddle a horse and hide it in the brush, back of the corral. Now, there ain't no reason for Wing doin' that unless he's saddlin' a horse for Knight. I got a hunch Knight figures to go some place tonight."

"Where?"

"I don't know, and I won't feel right till I do know. It's for you to find out. You get your supper, and then take a fresh horse and leave. I'll tell the others I've sent you over to see Monroe. I think Reed and them other dumb cowhands know what we've been doin'. I sort of spilled the beans myself a while back. But we'll take care of them later."

"Knight comes first," Beadle said.

Flecker nodded. "You just ride away from the ranch far enough so you can see where Knight heads when he leaves here. Once you got that part straight in your mind . . . well, Tim, you got a gun and you know how to use it. Don't forget that Corwin was a friend of yours."

"I get you, Kelt. Knight meets his finish tonight."

CHAPTER
EIGHT

All through supper Flecker sat glowering at his plate, speaking very little. Now and then he glanced up, glared at Knight and the other three cowboys. The air was tense — especially when Jerry met Flecker's glares with insolent grins. Reed, Wing, and Hackett felt apprehensive. They knew just enough to realize trouble was in the wind, but exactly what part Knight was playing in the swiftly shaping events was something beyond their comprehension.

Flecker was worried, no doubt about that. His hand trembled a trifle when he lifted his coffee cup. Jerry snickered. Flecker slammed down the cup, splashing the hot contents over his trousers. Jerry laughed louder.

Flecker swore and scowled at him. "You damn' redhead! What's ticklin' you?"

Knight said: "I was thinking about a mistake you made, Flecker."

"Me? A mistake? What you mean?"

"In bringing me here under false circumstances or understanding or whatever you want to call it."

"Cripes! Talk sense!"

Knight's grin widened. "Mebbe you've forgotten about that stage hold-up bandit you mentioned."

"What about him?" Flecker snarled.

"Remember, you said I answered his description and that the law was on his trail?"

Flecker's eyes widened. "Well, you dang' fool! You got a nerve to spill that."

Jerry shook his head. "You're mistaken, Flecker. It wasn't me, after all. If you'd read the papers, you'd have seen where they caught that *hombre* two days after the hold-up. Yeah, he confessed. Sure, he did look like me . . . red-headed, tall, and so on. But it wasn't me."

Flecker choked; his face grew apoplectic. The other cowboys looked interested. Nobody spoke for a moment. Flecker was fumbling in a vest pocket and finally produced a newspaper clipping which Jerry recognized as the article having to do with the paroling of Jerry Knight. Flecker read swiftly through the article. Then he bent his beetling brows on Jerry.

"Your name's Knight, ain't it?" he demanded. "Known as Jerry?"

"You've got that part, all right," Jerry admitted.

Flecker smiled thinly, relaxed somewhat. "That's all I want to know," he stated confidently. He went on eating.

A few minutes later, however, the worried frown returned to Flecker's forehead. Abruptly he rose from the table, knocking his knife and fork to the floor with a loud clatter.

Jerry said: "Where you going?"

Flecker whirled around. "I don't know as it's any of your business."

"It might be," Jerry said calmly.

"Well, it ain't," Flecker sneered, "but I don't mind tellin' you I'm aimin' to ride to the Two-M and ask Mart Monroe to explain how he happens to be holdin' a herd of Circle F animals on his range. He's goin' to square that or I'll know the reason why."

Knight nodded carelessly. "Thought that's where Tim Beadle went when he rode away just before supper." He had been wondering for the past hour where Beadle was headed.

Flecker was caught off guard. Before stopping to think, he commenced: "No, I sent Tim on some other business." He stopped suddenly, then continued. "That is, I told Tim to go see Monroe. But I just got a hunch I ought to be there, too. I wouldn't want no trouble to come off about those cattle. I just want an explanation, that's all."

He hurried from the cook shack and a few minutes later the cowboys heard him riding away. There was silence for a few minutes, then Shorty Wing said: "Jerry, you reckon Kelt and Tim will do any iron-pullin' over to Monroe's?"

Jerry shook his head. "Not with Monroe's crew on hand. No, Flecker will be peaceable, but those cows have got him worried. He doesn't understand and he can't wait to learn what it's all about."

Shorty Wing said: "Me 'n' Flecker got somethin' in common."

Jerry smiled. He didn't say anything.

Steve Hackett commented: "Flecker might get tough at that. Tim Beadle's hot-tempered, and with Tim there . . ."

"Beadle isn't there," Jerry said. "Flecker was just bluffing. I don't know where he is. I wish I did know."

Shorty Wing said shrewdly: "Jerry, do you suppose Flecker could have spotted me hidin' that horse for you this afternoon? In that case, he might have sent Beadle to keep an eye on where you went ridin' when you left."

Knight laughed suddenly, brow clearing. "Thanks, Shorty. I've been wondering. I'll bet that's exactly what Flecker did. Now, I'll keep a weather eye open for trouble."

"You goin' into town?" Hackett asked.

Jerry nodded. "I figured I'd have to wait till after Flecker had gone to bed, but, with him riding to the Two-M, I can pull out any time."

"What you aimin' to do?" Frank Reed asked.

Jerry shrugged lean shoulders. "I'm not sure yet," he replied cryptically. "Haven't got it figured out."

Supper was finished a short time later. The ranch cook cleared away the dishes and the cowpunchers returned to the bunkhouse. Jerry sat by himself, thinking in silence. Reed, Wing, and Hackett sat looking at old magazines and newspapers, the light from the oil lamps throwing into bold relief faces that appeared but little interested in reading. Knight finally rose and sauntered to the doorway, looked out. A soft breath of sage was lifted to his nostrils on the night breeze. Stars gleamed overhead. There wasn't any moon yet. The other three cowboys watched him intently, breathed a sigh of relief when he turned back inside.

Shorty Wing cleared his throat and said awkwardly: "Any of us . . . or all three . . . will be glad to ride to Topango Wells with you, Jerry."

Jerry smiled and said thanks, but didn't accept the offer. He didn't want to hurt their feeling; at the same time, when he left, he wanted to be alone. He returned to his chair and sat down, his mind following, foot by foot, the trail between the Circle F and Topango Wells. Having only been over the trail once, this took time, but finally he had constructed mentally every foot of the way. Mostly the road ran across rolling grazing lands, with no points of ambush on either side — except one. About four miles from the ranch a huge pile of boulders bordered the side of the road with a sloping hillside behind the rock. Here, if any, was the place where Tim Beadle might wait to dry-gulch him.

It was all clear in Jerry's mind now. He nodded with satisfaction, rose, said abruptly — "I'll see you later." — and stepped outside without waiting for a reply. Two minutes later he had reached the waiting horse in the brush in back of the corral and climbed into the saddle. Turning the pony's head toward Topango Wells, he set out at a fast lope.

Twenty minutes later, he drew to a halt and tethered his pony to a scrubby bit of brush not far from the road. Then, leaving the road, he circled widely to the south. The stars didn't afford a great deal of light and Jerry slipped along with the silence of a Sioux Indian. Gradually his steps carried him up a slow rise of land. For another five minutes he ascended, then again turned slightly back toward the road he had left. Sage and cactus grew sparsely here and there. Jerry dropped down to hands and knees and crawled through the grass, taking advantage of every bit of growth possible to hide his movements.

Finally he rose cautiously and peered down the slope. A hundred feet below him was the pile of boulders, well beyond the roadway, the suspected point for an ambush. Jerry didn't move a muscle. Five minutes passed. Suddenly a man coughed, clearing his throat. From the darkness surrounding the boulders came an impatient curse. A minute later a match flared, showing Tim Beadle's face. Beadle was lighting a cigarette. The match went out. A pinpoint of crimson gleamed through the darkness, went out, brightened again.

Beadle was seated on a rock, rifle across his knees, ready to blast the unsuspecting Knight when he came along. Jerry's face grew grim. Drawing one six-shooter, he crawled noiselessly forward. It took him fully five minutes to close the distance between himself and Tim Beadle, so carefully did he move every inch of the way, but, when again he stopped, Beadle wasn't five paces away.

Jerry said quietly: "Drop the rifle, Beadle. You're covered."

Beadle gasped, said: "My God!" His rifle clattered to the rocks. Then, in shaky tones: "That sounded like you, Knight."

"Correct!"

"But . . . but what's the idea?"

"Want me to tell you?"

"I'd sure like to know," Beadle said nervously.

Jerry laughed. "You've been waiting for me to leave. You knew I had that horse ready. You waited not far from the ranch house, to see which way I'd head . . . town or the Two-M. Once you heard my horse, you knew. You set out for here."

Beadle commenced a cursing protest. The cigarette clung to his lips.

"Keep your mouth shut!" Jerry said sternly. "Don't lie. I heard your horse. You were moving fast. So was I. Mebbe I could have beaten you to this point, but I figured to let you get here first. I pulled off the road, circled behind you."

"But, my God, Knight. What's the idea. Why should I do that?"

"You figured to dry-gulch me."

The two men were facing each other in the darkness. It was too dark to see their faces. Beadle had dropped his cigarette. He was still sitting on the rock. Jerry was in a crouching position a few feet away, covering Beadle with a six-shooter.

"Why in hell should I try to dry-gulch you?" Beadle was saying. His voice wasn't steady.

"Flecker's orders. I know too much."

"You're wrong, I swear it!"

Jerry laughed softly in the silence. "Nope, I *do* know too much . . . for instance the name of the third man in the Wolcott killing."

Beadle swore, abruptly slid from his rock seat, and dropped behind a huge block of granite. The movement had come so fast that it caught Jerry unprepared. Jerry

84

heard the rasp of metal on leather holster and threw himself flat. Beadle's gun roared, the bullet passing over his head. Jerry lifted himself on one hand, gun ready in the other.

Silence from Beadle's direction. Jerry didn't make a move; his eyes strained unsuccessfully to pierce the darkness. A full minute passed, seeming like an hour to the two men. Jerry's supporting arm was growing cramped, but he didn't dare move now.

Beadle finally muttered: "By God, I believe I got him."

He raised cautiously above the rock, but couldn't see Jerry's form in the darkness. In his hurry to get behind the rock his sense of direction had slightly gone awry. Now he lifted his gun for a chance shot. The gun crashed out of the silence, the bullet passing within scant inches of Jerry's body. But the momentary flash from Beadle's gun was what Jerry had waited for. His gun roared in reply. A groan of pain was torn from Beadle's throat. Then silence again.

Jerry waited five minutes, then he rose cautiously and moved toward the rock. Reaching down his hand, he encountered a face already growing cold and stiff to the touch. Jerry wiped his hand on a wisp of grass at his feet, struck a match. Then he straightened up, reloaded his gun, and made his way to the road below where Tim Beadle's horse was waiting. Hoisting himself to the saddle, Jerry continued on his way to Topango Wells.

CHAPTER
NINE

A tall man in city clothing stood at the far end of the Topango Bar talking to Sheriff Buck Drake. Drake was a stockily built individual with a bulldog jaw and iron-gray hair that showed a tendency to curl at his shirt collar. He was in corduroys and wore his star of office pinned to an open vest. The evening was still young — as saloon evenings go. A few customers, ranged along the bar, sent cigarette and cigar smoke curling upward to the oil lamps suspended in brackets above the bar. There were lots of talk and some laughter. Tiny drops of perspiration shone brightly on Hippodrome Casey's round, good-natured features.

Casey glanced toward the door, saw Jerry coming in, and violently gestured for him to leave at once. Jerry frowned and came up to the nearest end of the bar. Hippodrome looked worried. He kept making futile gestures toward the sheriff and his companion at the inner end of the barroom. The two hadn't noticed Knight's arrival, so engrossed were they.

Hippodrome grunted and leaned across the bar. "That's the sheriff," he whispered. "The feller with him is named Naughton. Naughton come here and asked for a feller named Jerry Knight. I swore I'd never heard of you."

"You old liar." Jerry grinned easily.

"All right, laugh, you dang' fool." Casey was still whispering. "I heard Naughton tell Buck Drake that he was on the parole board of the Texas State Penitentiary. They been talkin' mighty serious, but I couldn't make out what they said. Now, if this doesn't mean anythin' to you, forget I said anythin'."

Jerry huddled close to the bar, the other customers hiding him from Naughton and the sheriff. He said: "If you mean, do I want to see Mister Naughton now . . . I don't. I'd just as soon he didn't see me. We had a sort of argument" — Jerry grinned — "last time I talked to him. I'll be slipping out in a minute, Hippo. I just called to see if Bristol Capron was in here."

"No, he ain't here. You been down to his place . . . I mean that buildin' where the Randall Company is? He lives upstairs, y'know."

"It was all dark so . . ."

"He's probably gone to bed. Capron turns in early."

"That explains it. I'll go back."

"Move fast, cowpoke. Naughton might see you. Lucky for you, you didn't run into the sheriff the day you hit town or . . ." He looked at Knight significantly.

But Jerry was already taking his departure, without waiting to reply or hear more. Hippodrome looked relieved, and turned to catch Naughton and the sheriff looking after Jerry's retreating back.

Naughton said: "Say, barkeep, that looked like Knight." He started toward the door in pursuit of Jerry.

"No, sir, Mister Naughton" — Hippodrome gulped for the proper words with which to detain Naughton — "that's . . . that was . . ."

"Well, Hippo," Sheriff Drake said sharply, "just who in hell was he?"

"Friend . . . friend of mine," Hippodrome stuttered.

Naughton looked dubious, but he came back to the bar.

"What's his name?" Drake snapped. "He's a stranger to me."

"Name's Pete . . ."

"Pete what?"

Hippodrome wasn't a fast thinker. To cover his confusion and stall for time, he started to clear a couple of empty beer bottles from the bar.

"What's his last name?" the sheriff demanded again.

Hippodrome happened to glance at the label on one of the beer bottles and had an inspiration. "Name's Schlitz . . . Pete Schlitz," he stated defiantly.

"Schlitz, eh?" The sheriff looked curiously at the barkeep. "Damn' funny I ain't seen him in town before."

Hippodrome had another inspiration. "It ain't so surprisin' at that. Pete Schlitz never stays in one town very long. He hops around a lot."

Naughton looked a trifle dazed. "Schlitz . . . hops?" he muttered, and gazed queerly at the bartender.

The sheriff walked past and out to the street. By this time Jerry was out of sight. In a few minutes, the sheriff returned. "You tell your Pete Schlitz friend I want to see him, Hippo, next time he comes around here.

Sometimes I think you try to be funny. It don't set well on a fat man."

"Maybe you're right," Hippo agreed. He was sweating profusely by this time. He wiped up the bar with a damp cloth and announced that the house would buy a drink. To his relief, Naughton and Sheriff Drake accepted the invitation.

Meanwhile, Jerry had mounted and rode down the street till he came abreast of the two-story brick building that housed the office of the Randall Land & Cattle Company and the living quarters of its resident manager, Bristol Capron. Dismounting, he looked in both directions along the street. A few lights shone from buildings, but there were no pedestrians in sight. Two blocks away a brightly lighted window proclaimed the location of the Topango Wells Hotel where the man known as Naughton was probably staying the night.

Yes, sir, I'll bet Mister Art Naughton would like to see me. Jerry grinned in the gloom. *He's probably getting worried about my whereabouts by this time. Ten to one he's told the sheriff all about me, and I wouldn't be surprised if they started for the Circle F first thing in the morning. Oh, well, mebbe I can learn something from Bristol Capron before then.*

Approaching the door of the Randall Company's office, he lifted one hand and pounded loudly. There was a few minutes' silence, then a window on the upper floor rasped open. Capron's irritable voice reached Jerry's ears: "Who's there?"

"It's me . . . Knight."

"What do you want?"

"I've got to see you, Capron."

"What about?"

"Expect me to yell it right out in the street."

"Any reason why you shouldn't?" Capron demanded. "I haven't anything to hide."

Jerry laughed scornfully. "Your story and Flecker's don't agree, then."

There was a moment's silence. Then Capron lowered his voice: "Did Flecker send you in to see me?"

Jerry said impatiently: "My gosh! Aren't I trying to tell you that?"

"I'll be right down," Capron said. His voice sounded uneasy as the window slammed shut.

Jerry waited. In a short time he heard steps descending from the upper floor. They approached the door. A bolt slid back; a key turned in the lock. The door opened a few inches. Jerry started inside, only to feel the door refuse to give. Through the opening the barrel of a revolver was shoved toward his head.

"You stay right there, Knight," Capron snapped. "Give me Flecker's message."

"Aw, I'm not going to stand here talking. I'm coming inside."

More of the gun barrel was shoved through. "You'll get a bullet if you try to come in here, Knight."

Jerry laughed softly, stepped to one side, and grasped the gun barrel in his right hand, pointing it skyward. "Now, you damn' scoundrel, shoot and be damned. And the sheriff is only a coupla blocks down the street if you want to bring him on the run."

90

Capron was cursing viciously, trying to wrest the gun from Jerry's hand and at the same time endeavoring to hold the door against Jerry's pushing weight. "Let go my gun, Knight," he panted. "What do you want? I demand to be told just what . . ."

His voice broke in a hopeless grunt as Jerry wrested the gun from his grip and shoved open the door. Once inside, Jerry thrust the gun into the waistband of his overalls and slammed the door at his back. "All right, Capron," he snapped. "No more funny stuff. Get a light."

"I won't do it," Capron whined. "I won't have you breaking in here and acting like this." The man's nerve was going fast. "Wait till I tell Kelt about this."

"Get a light," Jerry growled menacingly, "or I'll blast you from hell to breakfast and there won't be enough for Kelt to recognize."

"But, look here, Knight . . ."

Jerry drew one of his own guns, pulled back the hammer. "Hear that?" he asked coldly. "I won't waste time on you much longer, Capron. I'm going to count three, and, if a lamp ain't lighted by the time I get through, I'll pull the trigger. One! Two! Thr . . ."

"Hold it, hold it!" Capron half shrieked. "I'll light up. Give me time."

His bare feet scurried over the plank floor, searching feverishly for a lamp and matches. Jerry grinned in the darkness, but tried to keep his voice stern as he urged: "Hurry it up. This ain't my night to be gentle."

A match scratched loudly and a moment later a lamp shed a soft glow over the big office. Capron was white as a sheet, his thin hair tousled over his pasty forehead. He had drawn on trousers over his nightshirt and his suspenders dangled at his sides. Jerry looked quickly about the room, then moved toward the front wall to draw down the shades that covered windows and door glass.

Capron watched in trembling silence. "Look here" — he had finally found his voice — "you don't need to go to all this trouble. Just tell me what Flecker said and . . ."

"Shut your trap!" Jerry snarled menacingly. He didn't particularly care for the rôle he was playing, but to further the ends in view it was necessary that he thoroughly intimidate Bristol Capron. "Now, come over here and open this safe."

Leading the way to the safe, placed against the wall not far from Capron's desk, Jerry repeated the order.

"I won't do it!" Capron said defiantly.

Jerry laughed and the cold chills ran down Capron's backbone at the sound. Still, he tried to hold his nerve. "I won't do it," he said again. "You better get out of here, Knight. I know all about you being paroled. Flecker told me about you. You were in prison . . ."

"For what crime?"

"For killing a man," Capron declared.

"All right." Again Jerry laughed. "Just keep that in mind, if you get stubborn with me."

Capron turned a sickly yellow and started for the safe.

Jerry continued: "And I suppose Flecker told you just why he wanted me on the Circle F."

"He didn't say."

"Don't lie, Capron! He wanted to frame me as the third man in the Wolcott killing. You know that damn' well."

Capron choked and looked fearfully at the cowpoke's cold face. "How . . . how . . . ?" he stammered.

"Never mind that. Get this safe opened."

Capron knelt before the safe, his fingers trembling with the combination dial. A moment later the heavy door swung outward. He rose to his full height. "I . . . I don't like this. I want to see Flecker or one of the others."

"Sit down in that chair over there," Jerry ordered. His gun barrel indicated a seat near the desk. "One move out of you and you'll get just what the others got."

"Oh, my God," Capron whispered hoarsely. "You've killed Flecker and . . . and . . . ?"

"Shut up!"

The lighted lamp on the desk revealed the safe's contents. Jerry reached to a cash drawer, removed a stack of bills that, with a wide grin, he stuffed into his pockets.

"Is . . . is this a hold-up?" Capron choked.

"What do you think?"

Capron fell silent, his uneasy glance following the cowboy as he lifted out of the safe a couple of heavy ledgers and a packet of papers. These he spread out on the desk before seating himself. Then he opened the books.

An hour drifted past, lengthening to an hour and a half, while Jerry examined books and documents. Finally, recovering his courage somewhat, Capron ventured: "I don't see what you're going through those records for. You wouldn't know anything about the Randall Company's business."

Jerry sneered: "I know more than you think. For instance, you were ordered to quote the T.N. and A.S. Rail-road a decent price for a right of way through Camino Cañon. You lied to the railroad people when you asked . . . *demanded* . . . four times that price."

"Oh, my God!" Capron shrank back in his chair. "Did . . . did Flecker tell you that, too?"

Jerry was quick to grasp that advantage. "You'd be surprised some of the things Kelt has told me."

Capron groaned. "I'm ruined if that gets out. Listen, Knight, I'll give you some money and you get out of the country. There won't be a thing said about you breaking parole. I'll fix that with Kelt."

"Shut up, you worm!"

"Is Kelt dead or isn't he?"

Jerry laughed. "What do you think?"

Capron groaned and commenced to sob.

Jerry eyed the man with disgust, decided to try a bluff. "You not only deceived the railroad company, but you've tried to force Mart Monroe to sell out so you could offer the railroad the right to go through Palo Verde Pass. Flecker has rustled Monroe blind in an attempt to ruin him."

94

"Listen, Knight, I'll do anything you say. I didn't think Kelt would ever tell that. He claimed to be my friend."

"*Will* you cut out that sniveling?"

Fifteen minutes more passed while Jerry continued to pour over the books. To only a small extent had he found what he searched for. It was time for another bluff. Abruptly he picked up his six-shooter, turned it toward Capron.

"I'm through fooling with you, Capron," Jerry stated harshly. "I want the other book."

"What other book?" — but Capron's eyes had shifted nervously, and Jerry knew his guess had been correct.

"The one Flecker told me about," Jerry said reluctantly. "You know, showing your private transactions."

"But there isn't any such book."

"Oh, cripes!" Jerry lifted the gun a trifle. "I reckon I might as well let you have it now and get this business over with. I never could stand a sneakin' liar."

"Don't shoot, don't shoot!" Capron half shrieked. He threw himself half across the desk, begging and sobbing. "I'll get it."

Jerry drew back, grinning inwardly. This was easier than he had anticipated. "Go ahead. Hurry it up!" he growled.

Capron scurried around to a point near one end of the desk and commenced clawing feverishly at boards in the floor. A board came loose, then a second one. Reaching down, Capron produced from under the floor a large ledger bound in gray buckram. Staggering to his feet, he dropped the book on the desk and wilted back to his chair.

Fifteen minutes later, Jerry lifted his head from the book and asked a few sharp questions. Capron, shaken to the very core of his thieving heart, answered promptly and fully. Jerry continued to peruse the pages, asking questions from time to time.

Finally he closed the book and looked disgustedly at Capron. "You're pretty low," he said coldly. "You were put here to look after the Randall Company's interests and you've cheated the company from the start. You've sold twice the number of cattle you've reported annually and pocketed the difference. You've foreclosed mortgages on ranches and small farms you had no right to foreclose, and then sold them again and pocketed the money, forging records to suit your dirty means. You've cheated poor wretches out of their money by selling land to farmers . . . land that was never meant for farming, is no good for farming purpose. You've foreclosed on them again and again, always reselling in your own name and pocketing the money. You've . . ."

"What . . . what are you going to do to me?" Capron groaned.

"I know one thing," Jerry said sternly. "Your bankbooks are here, showing that you've become pretty wealthy at the expense of the Randall Company. Restitution will be made so far as is possible. You've made the name of Ira Randall a thing to be hated and feared in this country. That's an injustice if there ever was one. That will have to be straightened out. You've murdered when it suited your convenience."

"I never killed a man, so help me, I never . . ."

"You were in it with Flecker and his crew of snakes."

"Flecker made me . . ."

"Don't lie. I don't doubt Flecker had the nerve for it, but it's your cowardly mind that planned it all . . . oh, hell, Capron! I'm sick of talking to anyone as dirty as you. C'mon, we'll go see the sheriff."

"I'll tell him you're paroled."

"Tell and be damned, skunk! C'mon, I say."

"No, no!" Eyes staring, lips slobbering, Capron staggered up from his chair as Jerry rounded the desk. He threw himself on Jerry, clutching at his arms, fighting to get his guns. Jerry struggled to throw the man off, but the wretch was fighting like a cornered rat with a strength that was almost maniacal.

Then the door opened quite suddenly, closed as quickly. Kelt Flecker's voice sounded harshly through the scraping of feet: "Stick 'em up, Knight. You're covered!"

In desperate eagerness, Capron released his hold on Jerry and staggered back: "Thank God you're here. Kelt!" he half sobbed, then his voice rose and he screamed savagely: "Kill him, Kelt. Kill the nosy bustard! He knows everything. Don't let him go. Kill him!"

CHAPTER
TEN

Knight swung slowly around to see the triumphant look on Flecker's face. Flecker's fingers were trembling on triggers. "Gawd! What luck," he said ominously. "I expected to find Tim Beadle here when I saw his horse outside. Wondered what Tim was up to. Then I heard Capron screamin' like a maniac. I come in and . . . say, where *is* Beadle?"

Jerry laughed quietly. "I'm not sure, but I bet you a plugged *peso* he's down in hell explaining to Jacklin and Corwin just how it happened."

"Damn you!" Flecker scowled. "I'll square that, too."

"Kill him, Kelt, kill him!" Capron snarled. "We don't dare let him loose. Use your gun! Quick!"

"Shut up, you fool!" Flecker said roughly. "Think we want a shot to bring the sheriff on the run. Bristol, you get his guns. Then we'll tie him up tight while I talk to him. Mebbe we won't have to do any killing. Mebbe we can make a bargain with Knight. He can pro'bly use money. Hurry, get his guns."

Cautiously Capron approached Jerry from the rear, lifted from holster first the right, and then the left gun. But in his excitement he overlooked his own gun that Jerry had captured and thrust into the waistband of his overalls. During the struggle with Capron, the weapon had slipped down considerably. He was between Flecker and the light and Flecker couldn't see the gun.

"Hurry, now," Flecker was urging. "Get a rope."

Capron was depositing Jerry's guns on the desk at the rear. Jerry knew there'd be no bargaining once he was tied up. Probably Flecker would employ a knife and then dispose of Jerry's body. Abruptly he jumped to one side, reaching for the gun in his waistband. Too late to prevent the movement, Flecker realized what Jerry was doing. Flecker's right hand tilted up in a savage arc as he cursed Capron's stupidity. The gun crashed loudly even as Jerry leaped halfway across the room. Then he had Capron's gun free of his waistband.

The gun in Flecker's left spat smoke and orange flame. Something red-hot drilled into Jerry's right side, staggering him. He lifted Capron's gun — pulled trigger — once — twice! The weapon was of smaller caliber than a Forty-Five and of cheap construction. The first shot missed; the second bored in, high in Flecker's left shoulder. With a howl of pain the big man staggered back.

A yell of rage behind him caused Jerry to turn. Capron was lifting one of Jerry's guns. Jerry laughed grimly through the fog of powder smoke, raised Capron's gun, and hurled it fully at the face of its owner. Blood spurted from Capron's nose, and he sat down violently on the floor. Jerry leaped to the desk, secured his own guns, just as Flecker prepared to make another attempt.

"Drop that gun, Flecker!" Jerry yelled. "I'll let daylight through you, sure as hell, if you don't!"

With a curse of rage, Flecker dropped the gun and leaned back against the wall, his left arm dangling weakly at his side. Capron was climbing to his feet now, sobbing with rage and fear.

"You, Capron," Jerry spoke tersely, "get over there against the wall with Flecker, and on your way, just kick his gun down here."

Reluctantly Capron obeyed and stood shivering at the side of his partner in crime. Now that he had the situation well in hand, Jerry felt rather weak and relaxed. Seating himself on top of the desk, he laughed grimly. "Your game is up, scuts."

Flecker swore a vile oath and took one step toward the desk, but the lifted guns in Jerry's fists destroyed any idea he may have had concerning further resistance. Again he slumped back against the wall and contented himself with staring contemptuously at the whining Capron.

And thus the three were when Sheriff Buck Drake, followed by the man named Naughton and a crowd of the town's citizens, poured in through the doorway a few moments later.

"Well, what's the shootin' about?" Drake roared. He took in the situation at a glance, added humorously: "The shootin's over, 'pears like." With that he shooed the crowd of curious citizens outside and again closed the door.

The man named Naughton was eyeing Jerry curiously. He said: "So it's your doings, eh, Jerry?"

100

Jerry grinned and said: "Correct, Mister Naughton."

"You ready to go back to Texas with me?"

"Well, I'm not sure if I'm ready, but I'll go back if you insist . . . for a spell, anyway, till things get straightened out."

Naughton said bitterly: "I thought you'd get into trouble. Looks like you almost got yourself killed. How would I feel if I had to go back to Texas without you?"

Sheriff Drake cut in with: "So this is Jerry Knight, eh? Naughton's been telling me about you, Knight."

"I can imagine what he said." Jerry laughed.

The door opened suddenly and Mart Monroe, followed by Alice, stepped into the room. Monroe gave a sigh of relief on seeing Knight.

Alice cried: "Oh, Jerry, we were afraid . . ." She didn't finish but came across the room to stand at his side.

Jerry took her hand. Neither said anything for a few minutes. Mart Monroe concluded: "Alice was afraid you would have trouble over those bills-of-sale you gave me, Jerry. You see, when Flecker came to ask about me having Circle F cows on the Two-M, I showed him the bills you'd given me. He was right mad, said he was coming to town to turn you over to the sheriff. After he left, Alice got worried and . . . well, she dragged me in to see about it. But what's happened . . . ?"

"He's a crook, that's what he is!" Capron had suddenly found his voice. "He's a paroled prisoner! He's broke his parole."

"Hush up that noise," Sheriff Drake growled.

"Just the same," said Kelt Flecker, "Capron speaks the truth. Just as soon as I can get my wound fixed, I aim to swear out a warrant, chargin' him with theft of cows delivered to Mart Monroe."

"And he took money out of that safe, too!" Capron cried.

Naughton and the sheriff exchanged grins that matched the one on Jerry's face. Naughton said: "Let me see those bills-of-sale, Monroe."

Monroe produced the papers, passed them to Naughton. Naughton examined them, passed them back, saying: "They're all in order. You see, folks, Knight had a right to sign those . . ."

"What, sign for the Randall Company?" Flecker yelled.

"You dang' fool," the sheriff snapped, "*he* is the Randall Company. Owns it lock, stock, and bar'l!"

"All right," Jerry said lightly, "you would spill it. I see Mister Naughton's been talking to you."

"Well, I . . ." Alice gasped. "Jerry, you never . . ."

Flecker and Capron looked on in dumb amazement, mouths hanging open. "But he has broken his parole!" Capron objected.

"Wolcott broke the parole . . . ," Naughton commenced.

"Aw, forget that," Jerry cut in. "Look, I've got all the dope on Capron we need. I know the third man in the Wolcott killing."

Kelt swore and went white. Knight talked swiftly, giving details, and ended up: "That's all. Let's get out of here. I want to get to a . . ."

"Just a minute," Naughton cut in. "I guess Mart Monroe and his daughter would like to know a little more about you, Jerry."

Jerry said: "Aw, I don't see . . ." He suddenly fell silent. Alice pushed herself up on the desk beside him and Jerry's head dropped to her shoulder. Alice looked startled, but she didn't say anything.

Naughton was talking: "You see, Ira Randall is Jerry's uncle. Jerry could have had a good job with the Randall Company, but he refused, wanted to make his own career. He took his mother to Texas and managed to build up a cow outfit of his own. His independence made Ira Randall angry. He thought Jerry was foolish. Later, Ira was taken ill. He's had a bad heart for years. He turned the management of the company over to the man he thought was his friend . . . Bristol Capron. Well, you've heard what Capron did. We won't think any more about him or Flecker. They'll both get their just deserts."

Capron moaned. Flecker didn't say anything. Mart Monroe had managed to tie up Flecker's shoulder while Naughton was talking.

"Meanwhile," Naughton went on, "a friend of Jerry's named Dennis Wolcott got into trouble in a small town in Texas. I guess it was self-defense, but the man who was killed had friends, and Dennis Wolcott was sent to prison under the name of Jerry Knight . . ."

"But I don't see," Alice commenced, "how he happened . . . ?"

"I'll explain, Miss Monroe," Naughton interposed. "You see, Wolcott was a stranger in the town where the killing took place. He was Knight's closest friend. When they arrested Wolcott, he gave the name of Knight. Wolcott had relatives in the East who would have been broken-hearted if they'd known Dennis had killed a man. As soon as possible, Dennis got in touch with Jerry and told him what he'd done, and Jerry agreed that, if anybody would be saved any pain, Wolcott had done the best thing. So, Wolcott went to prison under the name of Knight and was paroled under the same name, of course."

"Well, I'll be danged," Mart Monroe muttered.

Naughton went on: "Ira Randall was finally compelled to go to Texas for his health. He and his nephew patched up their differences and Ira grew to love the boy like a father. Randall appointed me his lawyer . . . he'd met me through Jerry and we became friendly and he asked me to manage the Randall Company. You see, we'd talked over the affairs of the company and Ira was commencing to distrust Capron, but was too ill to investigate for himself. About this time, Jerry was working to get Dennis Wolcott paroled. I happen to hold a position on the Texas Penitentiary Parole Board. I arranged matters. Jerry gave Dennis a job on his own ranch, then later Ira Randall, who also liked Dennis, sent him here to secretly look into the affairs at the Circle F. Randall caught a man named Ridge Conway rustling cattle and wrote Jerry about it. Somehow, Flecker and his crew must have heard or suspected something about Wolcott. Maybe he caught the gang red-handed. Perhaps Flecker will tell us about that."

Flecker growled through the pain of his wound: "Try to get me to tell."

"You'll tell in good time, all right," Naughton said coldly. "Anyway, the next thing we heard was that Wolcott had been found dead and Sheriff Drake was unable to find the man who had done the killing. About the same time, Ira Randall had a bad heart attack and signed all his holdings over to Jerry and his mother. Ira hasn't much longer to live, but he'll finish his days in comfort down on Jerry's ranch. After Wolcott's death, Jerry insisted on coming here to investigate. I thought it too dangerous. In fact, Jerry and I had a quarrel about it, but he insisted on coming anyway. Well, I guess all of you folks know there's no stopping him, once he gets started. To cut a long story short, he's accomplished his mission, but I still wonder he wasn't killed. For which I am very glad. And I guess I'll let him tell the rest of his story, supply details and so on, if you don't already know them. I've been wondering how he got in with the Flecker gang . . . ?"

A startled exclamation from Alice interrupted the words. "He . . . he's . . . *something is wrong*," Alice said excitedly. "His head was on my shoulder. I thought he was just resting. My grief! His side is all wet. He's been wounded! Jerry, oh, Jerry, why didn't you tell us?"

There was a rush of feet toward the desk, but Jerry didn't answer. His head rolled loosely and he nearly fell to the floor.

★　★　★

It was late afternoon the next day when Jerry awoke. He looked about, discovered himself in bed. His side felt stiff and sore. His exploring hand found bandages. There was a sudden movement at the side of the bed. Alice stood looking down at him. Jerry said: "Hello! Where am I?"

"At the doctor's house. Wait, you're not badly hurt. Just weak from loss of blood."

"Huh, that's funny. I don't remember much. Is everything all right?"

"Of course. Capron and Flecker are both in jail. They've both confessed ever so many things. Oh, my dear, you shouldn't have run such risks."

"It's funny," Jerry repeated. "Last I remember I was sitting on that desk at your side, waiting for Naughton to get through talking so I could get to a doctor."

"You fainted . . . from loss of blood."

"Fainted?" he said scornfully. "Can you imagine that for a fool thing. Fainted! Just like a weak old woman. Gosh, what a fool I am."

"Cowboy, dear! I said you were a fool the first time I saw you, a fool or crazy."

Her eyes were moist.

"And now you believe it, eh?" Jerry grinned. He was feeling stronger. One arm went around Alice's neck as he drew her face down to his. "Sure I'm crazy . . . about you."

"Jerry! Stop! Father or Mister Naughton may come in. They're just outside. And your cowboy friends at the Circle F are due to arrive . . ."

106

"Let 'em arrive." Jerry smiled happily. "The sooner the whole town knows it, the better."

"Knows what?"

"About the house we're aiming to build on that pretty tableland near Palo Verde Pass. Lady! Don't you realize I got plans for you and me?"

Alice bent down to complete the first plan.

The Red Raider

CHAPTER
ONE

The man with the red serape and the high-peaked sombrero moved silently into the shadow of a building fronting on the narrow street of the little Mexican town of Conejo Lures. The street was deserted save for a drunken Mexican who reeled noisily along the beaten path that led to one of the town's three saloons. Once he fell sprawling over the mandolin that he carried, but was soon up and in a few minutes disappeared into the doorway, leaving the street to the watcher in the red serape. Occasionally a dog barked somewhere out of space, but aside from that all was silent. It was almost four o'clock in the morning, and, except for the patrons of the bars, the town was asleep. Overhead the stars began to wink out, one by one, and the moon had long since made her luminous way across the purple night.

The man with the red serape slunk deeper into the shadow, as a couple emerged from a doorway several rods away. The man was dressed in the ordinary cowpuncher rig, and the girl wore the black-lace *mantilla* familiar to Mexican women. Their murmuring voices reached the man in the darkness, as the cowpuncher embraced her hungrily. For a time he held her close, then the girl moved around, swinging her lover into the light, with his back to the watcher. The time had arrived for action! The skulking figure slowly drew a gun from its holster at his side and took careful aim.

Crack! Cr-r-rack! Crack! Three times he fired, and the flashes cut the cool night air. The man with the girl turned stumblingly and endeavored to draw his guns, but, as they left the holsters, his strength departed and he slumped to the ground, inarticulate words mingling with the death rattle in his throat.

At the sound of the shots lights appeared along the way, and in a few minutes partly dressed forms began to pour into the street. They were too late, however, for the girl, as soon as the man fell, stooped swiftly to his side, took something from inside his shirt, and handed it to the man with the red serape who came running up, wreathed in the smoke of his shots. The killer spoke a few low words after the girl as she flitted away into the shadow of the building and then, turning swiftly, ran to where his horse was tethered and, leaping quickly into the saddle, wheeled away in the direction of the border with New Mexico.

A few vagrant shots flew after the galloping rider from those who had the presence of mind to try to stop him, but none of them found their aim, and he escaped unscathed. His victim lay with unseeing eyes staring at the dawn-streaked sky, his shirt a sodden mass of red.

CHAPTER
TWO

Old Dad Flint, owner of the Circle X outfit, stood in the doorway of the ranch house and shielded his eyes from the level rays of the late afternoon sun to gaze at a rapidly approaching cloud of dust.

Wonder who that can be? he mused. *The boys wouldn't be back this soon, an' besides they'd have the cattle with them. Waal, they'll be a-comin' on in another twenty minutes now, an' then I'll know.* He swung his burly form around and went to a rocking chair that stood in the shadow of the verandah, where he seated himself.

Dad Flint had been in a quandary a short time before. He had just succeeded in disposing of all his saleable cattle, when he received a wire from one of the packers in Chicago requesting, if possible, an immediate shipment of Hereford beef steers. The packer's request was one that called for several hundred head. Not having the cattle, and yet disliking to refuse the packer with whom he had dealt for many years, Dad had immediately wired an answer to the effect that the shipment would be made inside of a month. Then he had called on his neighboring ranchers to get the steers required, only to learn that at the price quoted they were disinclined to let such cattle as they had go, or that they had already disposed of whatever stock was for sale.

This meant that Dad Flint had to do some tall scurrying around the country for cattle or break his word to the packers. It was Dad's boast that he had never broken his word to any man, and as he put it: "I don't reckon I cares to begin breakin' my word now, and, God willin', I'll keep my word if I have to mortgage my ranch to get money to buy what cattle they need." At this time Dad was in no condition to enter a deal where he stood to lose money. Ranch improvements and other expenses had eaten to no small extent into his bank account. However, he figured that he would buy at a loss, if need be, just so the shipment of cattle would be made at the promised time.

Riding from ranch to ranch he had had no success in getting cattle. As he worked south, though, he had been able to contract at small ranches for something like a hundred head of steers. With several hundred still to be procured, he had crossed the border into Mexico. Stopping at the small town of Conejo Lures, he learned that Valesquez Pancho, a wealthy Mexican rancher in that vicinity, had just about what he wanted. The next day Dad offered Pancho a check for the steers, which Pancho refused, saying he wanted cash. He accepted the hundred and some odd dollars that Dad had on him as deposit, and Dad hurried back to the ranch and thence to the neighboring town of La Roda, where he drew from his bank the sum of $12,000.

114

This amount he entrusted to his son Jimmie, a youth of about twenty years, and who, the next morning, accompanied by all but two of the cowpunchers of the Circle X, started for Conejo Lures to turn the money over to Pancho and drive the steers back to the ranch, where they would be fattened up for a week and then shipped to Chicago.

Reason dictated that the money be entrusted to Buck Thomas, the ranch foreman, as Jimmie was a bit unsettled in his ways and prone to flights of foolishness at times. However, since Jimmie's mother had died, Dad had taken his wayward son in hand and tried to make a man of him. Family pride, too, would not let Dad turn the reins over to any but one of his own blood, so the boys left with the full understanding that Jimmie, who it was one day expected would be the head of the ranch, was boss. At the last moment before they left, Dad had pangs of misgiving and, taking Buck Thomas to one side, had asked him to watch over Jimmie and see that he behaved, in putting the deal through, as a Flint would behave. Now he was waiting for the boys to return with the cattle. His old heart swelled with pride as he thought of Jimmie at last arriving at manhood and concluding a big deal in cattle like any of the old-timers. He glanced up at the cavalcade of riders that emerged from the approaching cloud of dust. They were riding furiously, and, as they approached, the old man had a sense of impending evil. *Something must be wrong*, he thought, as he tugged at his gray mustache. His eyes tried to discern Jimmie among the riders, but Buck Thomas was riding at their head, and Jimmie was not to be seen.

As the foam-flecked horses and riders drew near, they slowed down, but did not stop as they wheeled in the direction of the corral. Only Buck Thomas, a lean man of about thirty, with bronzed, clear-cut features, drew rein and pulled up at the door of the ranch house, stopping so suddenly that his horse reared back on its haunches. Leaping from the saddle, he drew off the handkerchief that had fended the alkali dust from his mouth and nose, and brushed the coating of gray powder from his chaps.

"Hello, Dad," he said shortly, not meeting Flint's eyes and engrossed in the brushing process.

"Buck, where's Jimmie?" the grizzled old man asked.

"We left him behind a ways. Come on in the house. I've got something to tell you, and I don't reckon it'll be very good news."

Dad stepped inside, followed by Buck's lean figure. When they were seated, he asked: "What's all this here idea in Jimmie comin' behind? Is he hurt . . . or . . . or . . . anything?"

Buck stared uneasily at the floor for several moments before he replied. "Truth is, Dad, Jimmie's following in a buckboard. I said I had bad news for you, and I guess I have. Jimmie won't ride a horse any more. Fact is, Jimmie won't do anything any more."

"Why? . . . why?" stammered the old man, as the terrible truth began to dawn upon his consciousness, "Is Jimmie . . . is he . . . ?"

116

"You've guessed it, Dad," Buck returned slowly, not meeting the old man's questioning gaze. "Jimmie's dead."

Dad Flint looked at him unbelievingly for a time, as he slumped into a chair. Finally, his will asserting itself, he straightened up and his blue eyes steeled as he asked: "Tell me about it, Buck. I rather reckoned I'd more or less placed my boy in your care, but I guess I must've mistaken my man," he finished bitterly.

"I know how you feel, Dad," Buck answered, unoffended, "an' I done my best, but it seems like my best wasn't enough. Mebbe after I've explained, you'll see how it was."

"Waal, get to it, get to it," the old man said impatiently.

"You'll remember," the lean cowpuncher began, "that when we left here you placed Jimmie, although he didn't know it, more or less in my care. Well, we reached Conejo Lures without any mishaps of any kind, but that's where the trouble began. We got in town toward evening, an' the boys being somewhat dry after the long ride wanted to stop and get a few drinks. I was all for riding directly out to Pancho's but Jimmie said the boys were in need of a little relaxation, an' he reckoned *he* wanted a few hours' rest, too. Inasmuch as he was heading the outfit an' was boss, I let him have his way. Besides, he had the money an' I knew he wouldn't give it to me. After all, I thought, what harm can it do to wait till morning? So I cautioned the boys to go easy on their drinks an' keep an eye on Jimmie. Myself, I didn't drink at all that night." Buck stopped

117

to light a cigarette he had been rolling, and Dad nodded impatiently for him to go on.

"Everything went all right," Buck continued, "till we went in that new dance hall that opened up in Conejo Lures a few weeks ago. I didn't want to go in, but Jimmie was all for seeing all the sights the town had, so I trailed along with him and the other boys. They had a few drinks and then one of those *señoritas* they have there begins to roll her black eyes at Jimmie. He goes over an' has a dance with her, and then they sat down at a table an' talked in low tones. I didn't like the looks of things, an' besides it's after two in the mornin', so I went over and suggested to Jimmie that we rustle up a bed an' get some sleep. He answers me kinda short-like, but in a few minutes he broke away from her and came over to the bar with the rest of the boys. Still he was kinda reluctant to leave."

"Jimmie allus was strong for the women," Dad said wearily. "Go on."

"Well, the *señorita* disappeared after a time, and Jimmie said he was ready to pull out just as soon as he had another drink. I waited while he ordered his drink, which he lingered over considerable. Suddenly, while we're waitin', the lights go out. I didn't suspect nothin', because the proprietor calls out . . . 'Just a minute, gents, the gasoline tank must be empty again. We'll have lights in just a minute.' They got one of those gasoline-tank lighting rigs that comes from Chicago," Buck explained, and then went on: "Well, I didn't think nothin' about it, an' in about five minutes the lights lit up again. Then I turned to speak to Jimmie an' he was

118

gone. I saw it then clear as a flash. He'd fixed it up with the *señorita* to empty the gasoline tank, and then, when the lights went out, he got away from us, figurin' he could have a few drinks with her out of my parental reach, and then join our party again. Poor Jimmie, he probably figured he was as much of a man as the rest of us and could take care of himself."

There was a pitiful look in the old man's eyes and his lips quivered as he motioned Buck to go on.

"Well," Buck explained, "I felt kinda uneasy about him, but I thought he'd turn up safe and sound anyway. Nevertheless, we started out to see if we could find him. We scattered into groups, and, while we couldn't get into all the houses, we did get into several, but no trace of Jimmie. While I was looking for him at one end of the town, I heard three shots. Seems like I knew then just what had happened, because it all seemed to dawn kinda clear on me that there was more to Jimmie's affair with the *señorita* than just a little spoonin' affair. Well, when I got there, Jimmie was lying dead on his back. I felt for the money, an' that was gone, too."

Dad Flint brushed a tear from his cheek, but didn't speak.

"As I figure it out," Buck went on, "Pancho must 'a' told someone that we was comin' after his cattle with cash money. The news probably got around, and somebody thought they needed the money more than Pancho, so they waited for us, framed poor Jimmie, and got away clean."

119

"Damn' rattlesnakes!" the old man ejaculated. "I'll get even if it takes me to my dying day and . . ." He broke off suddenly. "Any idea who done it?"

"We got the girl," Buck said. "Leastwise, we got the girl Jimmie was with in the dance hall. She's in the Conejo Lures jail now. Of course, she denied havin' anything to do with the affair, but we found out she'd been hanging out the last few days with a pair of galoots by the name o' Lannon . . . Black Bart and Wolf are their first names. This Black Bart Lannon's a bad sort, known as a killer in Conejo Lures. Seems like he had quite a followin' down there, too. He dresses like a greaser . . . big red serape, high-crowned sombrero, and that sort of truck . . . but he's not all greaser. He's a mixture of Mex, Indian, and white, and Lord knows what else. Anyway, from eyewitnesses who saw him get away, I judge it was Black Bart Lannon. We found a red serape near the body, too. By the time we got our horses, he was clean out of sight. We followed his tracks the next morning to where he crossed a creek over on the American side, but after that we lost him. There was nothing to do then but come back for Jimmie and bring him home, and then get further orders from you. Mebbe I've failed you, Dad, but I did the best I know how. I guess mebbe I'm sorta dumb sometimes, an' I'm goin' to miss Jimmie . . ."

"No, you done all you could, Buck," the old man said slowly. "I reckon I spoke kinda hasty. I was all upset-like . . ." His voice broke, and Buck crossed the room and patted his shoulder with the awkward air that marked any show of sentiment among these simple

120

men. At that moment a team was heard outside. "That'll be Jimmie, I guess," the old man said, as he rose and went to the door.

In a few moments the lifeless form of Jimmie, wrapped in blankets, was brought in and laid on a bed in an inner room. Buck left Dad with his dead and slowly made his way out to the bunkhouse.

When he arrived there, most of the boys were sitting disconsolately. Three of them were half-heartedly engaged in a game of draw, but the rest were talking in low tones of the tragedy.

"How'd Dad take it?" Slim Rollins called out to Buck as he entered the door.

"Pretty hard, Slim, I guess, but you'd never guess it to look at him. The old man's got a poker face and hangs onto his feelings pretty good."

"What's he gonna do?" Cash Jordon asked.

Buck shook his head. "I don't know yet. I know what *I'd* like to do, though. I'd like to git the snake who did the shootin' and string him to the nearest tree."

"Me, too," chimed in the others.

CHAPTER
THREE

It was late that night when Dad Flint sent the Chinese cook down to the bunkhouse with word that he wanted to see Buck. Not knowing just what was wanted, Buck strapped on his guns and then drifted up to the ranch house, where Dad Flint sat dejectedly in his chair.

"Sit down, Buck," the old man said. "I been figgering this whole thing out and I guess there's nothin' I can do but go after Jimmie's murderer. I didn't say so this afternoon, but I know this Black Bart Lannon . . . have known him for the past ten years. He's a mean *hombre*. He worked for me once, but I caught him runnin' off a bunch of cattle and turned him over to the sheriff. He swore the day he was convicted he'd even up with me someday, but after they put him behind bars I kinda let him drift out of mind. Seems like he got even, all right," Dad finished grimly, "but I ain't through yet with him by no manner o' means."

"What d'you aim to do?" Buck queried.

"I'm goin' to ride over to La Roda first thing in the mornin' and see if the bank won't let me have enough money to buy them cattle from Pancho. Then you go down and get the cattle and send them on to Chicago . . ."

"Why not forget the cattle . . . ?" Buck broke in, but the old man interrupted him.

"I wired I'd ship them cattle, and, by God, I'll do it," Dad said stubbornly. "Anyway, you're left in full charge to carry that deal through."

"What're you goin' to do?" Buck asked.

"I'm goin' after Black Bart Lannon, and I'll stay after him till I get him, or he gets me."

"But, Dad, why don't you take care of the cattle deal and let me go after him?"

Dad Flint shook his head. "Nope, you didn't sign up here to chase murderers. You're a ranch foreman, and a damned good one, but I ain't goin' to have you riskin' your life on my behalf. Besides, I know what Lannon looks like and you don't."

"But, Dad," Buck objected, "I'm a younger man than you are . . ."

"That's just it, Buck, you've got all your life ahead o' you. Now that Jimmie's gone, I've neither kith nor kin. I happen to know that you're right smart interested in that little schoolmarm down at La Roda and I don't reckon it's up to me to risk your life none."

Buck's blush showed through his tan. "It's your affair, Dad, but I'd sure enjoy taking a hand in puttin' that measly snake out of the way."

"I appreciate that, Buck, but I been settin' pretty easy the last few years, and I guess it's about time I got into harness again. I'll either get Lannon or Lannon'll get me." He hesitated, then went on. "If I don't come back, Buck, the ranch is yours. No, wait" — he held up an admonishing hand to stop Buck's words of surprise

— "you've been with me three years now, Buck, and you've been just like a son to me. Fact is, next to Jimmie, there wa'n't anyone I liked better, so I been drawin' up a will leavin' the ranch to you in the event anything happens. I'll take it down to La Roda with me in the mornin' and get it drawn up in regular fashion before Lawyer Higgins. Just so nothin'll happen between now and then, though, I'm going to sign it now and have Slim Rollins and Big Ike witness it. Hey, Tom," he called to the Chinese cook, "fetch Slim and Big Ike in here."

In a few minutes the two cowpunchers came in, and, despite Buck's protestations, the will was signed and witnessed, after which they departed. Buck tried to get him to change his mind, but Dad Flint was very obdurate, so Buck finally gave up trying to persuade him.

A sudden feeling of uneasiness caused Buck to look up at the window. There, peering through the pane just above a leveled gun, he saw an evil face gazing at Dad Flint.

"Look out, Dad!" he shouted, but the warning came too late. The roar of a .45 rang through the shattered glass. Buck saw Dad stagger back and fall to the floor as he leaped through the doorway.

As he emerged from the door, Buck saw two shadowy forms a short distance away leap on their horses' backs. From the level of his hips both of Buck's hands spat jets of flame through mushrooms of blue smoke as lead flew after the retreating forms. One of the horses crashed down into the dust, and, as Buck

124

ran past, he saw its rider pinned down under the kicking horse, trying to draw his gun. Buck fired once at him as he passed and ran after the other rider, shooting as he went. None of his other shots took effect, however, and, as his hammers were by this time falling on empty cartridges, the rider was soon lost in the darkness.

By the time he returned, the bunkhouse had been aroused and he could see the tall figure of Cash Jordon running through the darkness.

"That you, Buck?" Cash called.

"Yeah . . . look out for that *hombre* in the road there. I don't know whether I got him or not." As he spoke, he heard a smothered exclamation from Cash as he stumbled over the fallen horse and rider.

"Damn it," Cash said as he rose. "I didn't know he was so near. I guess he must be dead. He didn't move when I fell on him."

"Well, stay there and make sure. I'm going back to the ranch house. Dad's been hit . . . I don't know how bad. I'll send Slim and Big Ike after that other galoot," Buck said as he hurried in the direction of the ranch house.

When he entered the ranch house, Dad was sitting up on a bench, and Tom and Slim were ministering to him.

"Get him?" Dad asked as Buck came in.

"Got one of them," Buck answered. "Hurt bad?"

"Nope," Dad answered. "His bullet just creased me a mite. A fraction of an inch nearer the temple, though, an' it'd've finished me. I sent Big Ike and Hawkins and

Ramsey down to the corral for their horses." As he spoke, the staccato pounding of hoofs on the dirt and the creak of straining leather sounded outside the window. "There they go now. I told them to follow up whoever it was and bring 'em back, if possible. I don't suppose it'll do much good, no-how, because he's got too big a start."

"I'll go out and look at that other galoot and see if there's any life left in him," Buck said as he started for the door.

With Cash's help, he managed to extricate the man from beneath the fallen horse, and they carried him into the house and laid him on the floor. He was still breathing faintly, and now and then a froth of blood bubbled through his white lips.

"Looks like you got him through the lungs," Cash said as he rolled the man on his face. "Yep, that's what. Here's another shot through his shoulder. You must have got him when he was going away from you."

"Let's see if we can make him talk," Buck said, pressing a flask to his lips and passing an arm under his shoulders.

In a few minutes the man stirred, and then coughed, sending flecks of blood down the front of his shirt. His eyelids fluttered, and then opened. He gazed a minute at the circle of faces around him and gasped: "I guess . . . I'm a . . . goner . . . this time . . . boys." He tried to smile, but it ended in a cough.

"Where's Black Bart Lannon gone?" Dad said, guessing at the identity of the other midnight rider.

126

"You might just as well speak the truth now. It may help you when you go up above to your Judge."

"You . . . you Flint?" the man gasped.

Dad nodded.

"Well, you better . . . watch . . . out. Lannon's . . . goin' to get you . . . first . . . chance."

"Where is he?" Buck demanded.

The man's eyes were already growing glassy as he gasped: "He's . . . Indian reservation . . ." The words died away in his throat as a shudder passed through his frame and his head fell back.

"He's gone," Buck said, letting him down on the floor.

"Too bad he couldn't 'a' talked longer," Dad said. "Anyways, I know where to look for Lannon now. Indian reservation, he says. But which one?"

"Probably the Mescalero," Buck answered. "It's the nearest."

Dad nodded. "I 'spect so. Well, roll this galoot in a blanket an' put him with Jimmie. He don't deserve no such respectable treatment, but, after all, I'm not his judge. I'll send the undertaker down when I get to La Roda in the mornin'."

"Goin' to carry through with your plans as you said before?" Buck asked.

"We carry on just as I outlined," the old frontiersman said grimly.

"But your head . . . ," Buck started to object.

"My head's all right. Leastways, it will be by morning," Dad said.

★   ★   ★

During the night Big Ike and Hawkins and Ramsey returned and reported that the trail had been lost when the fleeing horseman crossed an outcropping of hardpan.

"What way did you go?" Buck asked.

"We kept on the south trail for Mexico," Big Ike said.

"Wrong direction," Dad said briefly. "He's circled east. Of course, you couldn't be expected to know that. Well, we better all get a few winks of sleep now, 'cause we're goin' to be plenty busy for the next few days."

But Dad didn't get away after Lannon the next day. He made the trip to La Roda, and, while there, met Steve Van Stone, owner of the Lazy D. Steve listened intently while Dad related what had happened, and then offered to take the cattle deal off Dad's hands. This left Dad more freedom, but by the time he returned to the ranch his wound was bothering him considerably, so he decided to wait a day. The following day Jimmie was buried, and that night Dad cleaned his six-guns and rifle, the lines on his weather-roughened face setting deeply, and a flame behind his old eyes. Life held little for Dad now. Jimmie must be avenged. There was nothing else. Buck tried once more to persuade Dad to let him go after Lannon, but — "Nope . . . Lannon's mine." — was Dad's reply. Dad was a veteran of the old order of things. He left his bed before dawn and was in the saddle and away before sunup.

CHAPTER
FOUR

On the western rim of the Bolson Plains the Organ range lay like a great exclamation point northward from Pyramid Peak till it sank in the alkali flats and salt marshes of the lost Lake Otero. It was a region of isolated but sometimes lofty and massive mountain peaks that rose abruptly from the level plains like volcanic islands from the sea. Eastward to where the peaks of the Sacramento and Guadalupe ranges showed dimly on the horizon stretched an arid waste of barren tableland — a land of greasewood and cactus and alkali beds, thin encrustations of snowy whiteness on dead lake bottoms.

In a deep gully at the edge of this lonesome land a sputtering campfire of greasewood burned briskly in the quickly chilling desert night air. It reflected dully from the dust-laden leaves of the scrub oaks on the sparsely timbered slope of the low foothills, and picked out sharp highlights on the greasy cheek bones of Black Bart Lannon, a tall man with a red serape draped across one shoulder. On the opposite side of the fire slouched a young man, Wolf, brother of Black Bart. The leaping flames shone on his flat face, and his beady eyes, barely glinting through narrow slits, showed little of good and much of mixed bloods. The lithe grace of his movements as he shook tobacco from a muslin sack into a wisp of paper resembled those of a puma. Beside Wolf, erect and motionless, sat a young buck Apache, while behind him, lumped under their blankets, a dozen other Indians slept on the ground. Wolf picked a crackling twig from among the burning brands, lighted his cigarette, and snarled at the older man across the fire.

"Mebbe you're a helluva brother, you are! Mebbe you don't make me sick" — and the youth tossed the twig back to the flames.

"You're so wise, what's eatin' you?" The sneering speech accented the evil leer of the hard face that differed from the younger brother's only in degree of hardness. Both were killers — the older merely a more mature killer. Both men were hated and feared as rattlers are feared, and they hated each other.

"We're in a swell mess now, ain't we?" Wolf answered the sneer. "Owin' to your wise play, and 'speshally that damn' red blankit o' yourn, the soldiers headed us off, an' if it hadn't've bin for Kicking Horse here, even this dinky bunch wouldn't o' got through."

"Aw, quit yer damn' preachin'." Black Bart Lannon glowered at the fire. "We got enuf men as it is for what we wanna do."

"Yeah . . . hell!" The young man's weasel-like eyes contracted to the merest slits as he contemptuously sneered up at the taller man. He knew his brother too well to fear him. "I suppose you called it enuf this mornin'. Lotta good raidin' that mangy bunch o' shacks at Escalona done. All we done was scare a lotta ol' wimmin."

To this there was no reply.

"An' where in the flamin' hell," Wolf continued, "was the sense of takin' that fool trip to the Circle X an' gettin' Strang shot an' that ol' he-grizzly of a Dad Flint trailin' us all over like that feller in La Roda was tellin' me the day they buried that cocky young Flint? Served him damn' good an' right." He bared his yellow teeth in a twisted grin at the recollection.

"Aw, shut up, will you?" snapped his brother. The thought of the cold-blooded murder bothered him not at all, but the idea of the grim, relentless old man taking his trail chilled Black Bart Lannon's heart to its cowardly core. Besides, he did not care to discuss the division of the proceeds of that murder just then. Later would be time enough for that.

The Indian, who till now had been staring stonily into the fire, turned his piercing eyes on Black Bart Lannon. "Yeah . . . Black Bart Lannon talk much," Kicking Horse grunted disgustedly. "Black Bart Lannon heap talk, no do. Black Bart Lannon good for scare women. Much talk 'bout heap whiskey, plenty fun, steal plenty guns . . . bah! Heap talk, all wind! Kicking Horse plenty sick. Kicking Horse t'ink he take him braves and go home." The tall Apache relapsed into a moody silence once more.

"Kicking Horse hits the nail right plumb on the head," Wolf Lannon said. "When he pulls out, I pull out, too. Mebbe you was good oncet, Bart, but it 'pears to me that you've slipped a mighty heap. I kin go back to Conejo Lures an' get more cash than I rustle packin' along with you."

Black Bart Lannon rolled a cigarette and lit it before he spoke again. He wasn't ready to have his gang broken up, just as they were getting nicely into action. He had the $12,000, or nearly all of it, that he had taken off Jimmie Flint's body, and reason dictated that he pull out of the country in a hurry and enjoy the proceeds of his murder. On the other hand, Wolf was to come in for a share, also Wolf's woman, who had played the part of the lure that tragic night in Conejo Lures. By the time the division was made Black Bart Lannon stood to get about $5,000 of the money. Another thing: thousand-dollar bills weren't any too numerous in that part of the country, and they were hard to get changed into smaller bills without attracting notice. He was sure by this time that the country for miles around would be aroused and on the look-out for him. Besides, Black Bart Lannon had another axe to grind. His hate for Dad Flint was one of the things that brought him back across the borderline of New Mexico, and his strongest obsession was to wipe Dad out. If things worked out right, the $12,000 would only be a drop in the bucket compared to what he would get later.

"Well, you lost your tongue, or ain't you got nothin' to say?" Wolf's jeering tones broke in upon Black Bart Lannon's abstractions.

"Yeah! You he-whelps of pukin' buzzards make me plumb disgusted," Lannon said. "You want to remember that this here Rome the books tell about wa'n't built in a day."

132

"Yeah, but it burned all to hell in a night," Wolf answered. "I know. I read them same books. An' that's jest what'll happen to us. We'll get our tails burned all to hell some night, trailin' around with you."

"What I mean is," Lannon said sullenly, "you got to have some patience. I was plannin' a reg'lar raid on the Circle X an' mebbe on La Roda, jest as soon as we git enuf men together. Now, we won't have to go to the Circle X, ef what you tell me is true, that Dad Flint's takin' my trail."

"It's true, all right," Wolf said. "What you so God Almighty keen on knockin' off old Flint fer?"

Black Bart Lannon glowered darkly. "That's my business," he said vindictively.

" 'Nuther thing," Wolf said, "when you goin' to split that money? Don't forget Mariposa comes in for her share, either!"

"To tell you the truth," Lannon lied, "I ain't got the money with me. I got it cached in a safe place." He knew Wolf wouldn't leave him till he had received his share of the money.

"That's a lie, Bart," Wolf cried, "an' you know it's a lie! I'd bet a thousand coyote pelts the bills are inside your shirt this minnit. I got a good notion to see fer myself." He started in Black Bart Lannon's direction, but his brother made a quick movement of his hand and the firelight shone on the blue steel of a Colt.

"Don't start no ruckus now, Wolf," Lannon warned in nervous tones. "I got you covered, an', while I don't aim to shoot you up, bein' as I have need fer you, still I don't take no chances."

Wolf's hand relaxed as he slipped his gun back in the holster. He knew that he could shoot as quickly as his brother, but if one of them were killed, he'd never get his share. Besides he couldn't be sure that Black Bart Lannon hadn't cached the money some place.

"All right, have it your way," he gave in sullenly.

"That's right, take it cool-like, Wolf," Lannon pacified. "You leave it to me, an' we make a big clean-up in a few days. You never went wrong on one o' my plans yet, did you?"

"Oh, you can plan, you can," Wolf said.

While the two brothers had been talking, Kicking Horse was watching them silently. Now he spoke: "Mebbe Wolf like. Kicking Horse no like. Kicking Horse go home when moon goes."

"You're a blamed fool, ef you do," Lannon growled. "Few days now, we have plenty money, plenty whiskey, plenty guns ..." He reached to his hip pocket and produced a flask of whiskey, which he handed to Kicking Horse. "Sluice down your guts with that, old-timer," he said in an attempt to be jocular.

The Indian tilted the flask up and up, and then handed it back to Lannon — empty. "Heap good," he said. "Sometimes Black Bart talk straight. Kicking Horse want more." The Indian's eyes had taken on a strange glitter as he talked.

"You'll get more. Listen, Kicking Horse, we get guns, plenty bacon, plenty whiskey. Then quick Kicking Horse and his brothers make camp in mountains. Pretty soon come young squaws to Kicking Horse and his brothers. Make big camp. Papoose come. Kicking

Horse have big camp, Kicking Horse be big chief. Plenty guns, all white men afraid o' Kicking Horse. No bother Kicking Horse. Be big chief, squaws do work. Kicking Horse smoke pipe all day. Drink plenty whiskey . . ."

Kicking Horse lurched over to where Black Bart stood. Stretching out a dirty hand, he said: "Give Kicking Horse whiskey now, then Kicking Horse do heap fight." The Indian began to boast in maudlin tones, as the potent liquor he had swallowed began to take effect. "Kicking Horse be big chief, take plenty scalps, have two . . . t'ree . . . four squaws. Many ponies, many blankets. Much kill white man. Kicking Horse like kill white man, see much blood, red blood." He drew a wicked knife and staggered in Wolf's direction.

Wolf drew both guns and leveled them at the drunken Indian. "Put that knife away, quick, you drunken fool!" he shouted.

Kicking Horse reluctantly slipped the knife back in its sheath. "Me want more whiskey," he said.

"You see what you've started, Bart," Wolf said. "Now we've got to keep an eye peeled on these here redskins all night long, or they're liable to jump us."

"I can keep 'em quiet," Black Bart said. "Last time I made camp here I cached a couple o' jugs o' whiskey. I'll get 'em." He moved back in the shadow of the underbrush and, after digging among the rocks, produced two large jugs of rot-gut, which he brought out and handed to the Indian. Kicking Horse drew the cork with his teeth and lifted the jug to his lips. He gurgled noisily for a few moments, the whiskey slobbering down off his chin.

The other Apaches awoke and came up for their share. Far into the night the drunken band stumbled and sprawled around the fire, till the whiskey was gone, while Black Bart and Wolf watched them warily. Gradually one by one the Indians dropped off to sleep. In the morning they awoke, mean as rattlers, saddled, and rode into the white sand of the desert.

CHAPTER
FIVE

Dad Flint was already ten miles away from the Circle X before the sun rose above the purple hills. By ten o'clock he had reached the Rio Grande and, after some trouble, found a fording place where he crossed over into Latham. Here he drew rein for the first time, at the Harvey Eating House for coffee and beans. The man in charge eyed him a few moments before he began to talk.

"Not headin' east, be you, stranger?" he said genially.

"Mebbe," Dad answered laconically, "why?"

"It's none o' my business, o' course," the man said, "but the country's liable to be right unhealthy t'other side o' Pyramid Peak. The 'Paches is out."

"Indian uprising?" Dad asked in surprise.

"Well, it ain't what you'd call a general uprisin'. Just about a dozen young braves feelin' their oats, I reckon. The government got wind of it in time to stop a general uprisin', but a small bunch o' 'Paches, headed by a galoot of the name o' Black Bart Lannon, raided Escalona, about forty miles northeast o' here, yesterday afternoon. They didn't do no damage to talk of . . . shot up a few stores an' got some money, from the station agent . . . because the El Paso and Northeastern

Limited pulled in an' scared 'em off. The sheriff of Otero County was in Escalona at the time and recognized this Lannon *hombre*, but when he tried to spoil the getaway, Lannon threw so much lead in his direction that the sheriff figured this idea was plumb unpopular and hid behind a row of milk cans till they got away. I'm kinda afeared that sheriff lacks guts, but then we're all human."

"Where'd they go then?" Dad asked.

"Who? Lannon and the 'Paches? They was headed off northwest. Better keep your eyes peeled for 'em if you're headin' thataway."

"Oh, I'll watch for 'em all right," Dad answered meaningfully as he drained his coffee and rose to go. In a few minutes, he had filled his canteen, watered the horse, and was back in the saddle as he headed northeast, in the direction of the desert.

The sun was directly overhead by now, and, as Dad passed through the foothills around Pyramid Peak, he could feel the sting of the alkali dust as it found its way into his eyes and through his clothes. Gradually, as the short brush and mesquite were replaced with white sand and gypsum dust, horse and man became covered with a coating of fine gray particles.

"Thank God, this desert ain't as big as some I've seen," Dad commented to himself, "but it's plenty bad enough. I ain't so young as I usta be." Once his horse shied at a rattler lying in the dust, but it must have been fed recently, for it acted torpid and made no effort to strike. "A few more hours o' this, Circle," Dad said to the horse, "an' we ought to see the foothills of the

Sacramentos." In a short time he crossed the tracks of the El Paso and Northeastern Railroad and saw the huddled buildings of Escalona far to the right and south of him. Soon that, too, was lost to view.

The sun began to shift around to the west, and Dad, bent on conserving every available drop of energy, glanced searchingly around the horizon and thereafter withdrew his attention from non-essentials. The Sacramento Mountains were dimly visible in a blue haze ahead of him. Some time later, warned by an inner sense, Dad roused himself and glanced around again. The mountains had moved perceptibly nearer. He glanced over his shoulder.

There, to his left and back of him, a file of horsemen was loping through the white haze of heat. They were too far away to be recognized, but he was sure they were Apaches. He could see the sun glinting on their bronzed bodies. Dad spurred Circle and headed for a group of rocks about a mile away. In a few minutes faint yells sounding behind told him that he had been seen. Circle was tired after the all-day trail, and Dad had been pushing him to the utmost. Consequently the Apaches began to gain, and in a few short minutes Dad heard the report of a carbine and felt the breeze of a bullet as it zipped by his ear. No more shots followed, however, and Dad judged the Apaches must be conserving ammunition in the hope of capturing him alive.

Dad and Circle had just reached the rocks toward which he was headed, when another report sounded, and Circle crashed to the ground, shot through the head. More shots followed, and the death-dealing lead spattered against the rocks all around, but Dad was uninjured as he scrambled to safety behind the huge boulders.

CHAPTER
SIX

While the Apaches were approaching, Dad was calmly and coolly looking over his guns to see that everything was in working order. He glanced up and around at his fortress. It couldn't have been a better place to stand off his attackers if he had planned it himself. Behind him was a high, overhanging bluff, which made it exceedingly difficult for anyone to approach him from the rear. In front and on both sides were huge boulders of various sizes.

As the Apaches approached, they spread out fan-fashion, yelling and shooting as they neared him. "Probably drunk as hoot owls," Dad muttered to himself as they advanced. He raised his rifle to his shoulder, took careful aim, and fired. The shot found its way to the heart of a huge buck, who topped from his horse, kicked convulsively a few times, and then lay still as the horse of the following Apache swung aside to avoid stepping on the body.

"That's one accounted for," Dad muttered, as they circled away. "There's . . . let's see . . . two, six . . . and four is ten . . . thirteen 'Paches and two whites. That big, dark *hombre* with the red serape will be Black Bart Lannon. Wonder who that other rattlesnake is. The two whites don't seem so anxious to come within reach of my lead. Cowardly coyotes." He spat. "Let the 'Paches do all the dirty work. Just like the mean skunks." As the Indians circled near him a second time, Dad raised the Winchester to his shoulder and fired rapidly six times before they passed out of firing range. Another Apache slipped from the saddle and two horses fell, tumbling to the ground, sprawling their riders in the dust. One lay silently where he fell, but the other at once rose to his feet and started to run out of gun range. Dad's rifle spat death again, and the Apache slumped to the ground. "Three more," Dad commented calmly, as he reloaded and awaited the next onslaught. He pulled his pipe out of a shirt pocket and, filling it, drew the blue smoke into his lungs. At each attack the bullets had been flattening against the rock all around him, but, so far, he was unhurt. Ordinarily Dad Flint would have continued to fire, even when the chances were small of his bullets finding their mark, but now the opportunities for missing were too great to risk wasting ammunition, so each time they attacked he had waited till they were well within reach before pulling the trigger.

Something had happened. The Apaches had drawn well out of gunshot range and appeared to be holding a consultation with Lannon and the other white man. "Guess they're gittin' sorta sick o' my brand of medicine." Dad chuckled grimly. He crawled to where Circle lay, already stiffening in death, and, groping for his water canteen, drank deeply of its contents.

Truth was, Black Bart Lannon and the Apaches *were* getting sick of the brand of medicine old Dad was handing out. Lannon was urging the braves on to greater efforts, but the loss of four of their number had somewhat taken the savagery out of them. They wanted revenge, but the cool way in which Dad had met their attacks was disconcerting. The liquor had worn off and the Apaches were taking a more sober view of the situation.

"What in hell's the matter with you redskins?" Lannon was growling. "Getting 'fraid of a little lead?"

"No, us not 'fraid," Kicking Horse responded. "Us do all the fighting, Black Bart Lannon stay back. Black Bart Lannon 'fraid. Prett' quick come soldiers. Put Indian in jail. No get out for many, many moons. Kicking Horse think Lannon and his brother better fight own fight. Indians go back. Be good Indians."

"Ye're damn cowards!" Wolf Lannon snarled.

Kicking Horse drew himself up proudly and his eyes gleamed as he said: "Four of my brothers lie in sand . . . dead. Does Wolf think they were cowards?" He quickly translated the conversation for the benefit of the other Apaches, and cries of disapproval and anger arose.

"Better not get 'em mad, Wolf," Black Bart admonished in low tones. "They might turn on us. Let me talk to Kicking Horse." He turned to the waiting Indian and said: "Look here, Kicking Horse, I know you're ain't afraid. You don't go after Flint right, that's all. You stay too far away. Rush up on him and he can't shoot you all at once. Then you got him, see?"

Kicking Horse nodded gravely. "Will Black Bart Lannon and Wolf come with Kicking Horse?" he asked.

Black Bart disregarded the question. "Then pretty soon after old Flint is dead," Lannon said, "we go find little town, lots of women, lots of whiskey, many rifles. All yours, Kicking Horse."

"Why kill Flint?" Kicking Horse asked. "Flint no hurt Indian."

"You're sure wrong there, Kicking Horse," Lannon lied. "Flint keeps poor Indians on reservation. Steals all poor Indians' land. Make plenty cheat with poor Indians."

The tall Apache eyed him doubtfully for many moments before he asked: "You no speak with forked tongue, Black Bart Lannon?"

Lannon with an effort looked into Kicking Horse's eyes with an unwavering glance as he again lied: "No, Kicking Horse, I do not speak with a crooked tongue. I have heard Flint say all Indians should die."

Kicking Horse, when the words had reached his comprehension, quickly translated for the other Apaches, who raised howls of vengeance. Then he turned to the two white men. "We fight," he said briefly, and then, as Black Bart's face lighted in triumph, he added persistently: "We fight if Wolf and Black Bart Lannon come with Kicking Horse and other Indians."

Black Bart started to remonstrate, but Wolf said: "Why in hell shouldn't we fight? It's our battle. Come on. Are you afeared?"

144

At the taunt that he was afraid, Black Bart straightened up, looked his guns over, and leaped into the saddle. The others followed suit. As they started off, Black Bart swung his red serape off his shoulder and let it drop to the ground. "Guess I won't take that," he said to Wolf. "It's too bright, and I don't want to make no bright marks to shoot at."

"Jesus! You *are* afraid," Wolf sneered. "I'll show you." He laughed. Wolf swung his horse around and went after the serape. Leaning from the saddle as he galloped by, he swept the serape from the ground and swung it back gaily over his shoulder as he rode ahead to overtake the others.

"Better not wear it," Lannon advised.

Wolf laughed. "Hell, I ain't afraid. It's damn' warm to wear out in the desert, though. You allus did have funny ideas, such as the wearing o' these here red blankets. It seems every time you lose one, you get another. Got an idea the wimmen like 'em on you?" Black Bart didn't answer. The Indians were spurring their horses as they approached Dad Flint's fortress.

Dad had been watching them as they held their consultation. Wolf and Black Bart Lannon were directly behind the Apaches when the serape changed hands, and the distance was too great to note any dissimilarity in the two men. As they approached, Dad knocked the ashes out of his pipe and picked up the Winchester. "They seem to be comin' right in this time," he said to himself. "It looks like a last stand, so I'll have to see if I can't give a good account of myself." The fact that he would be probably face to face with death in the next few minutes never seemed to enter the old man's mind, so coolly he went about the business of getting ready.

The Indians began firing before they were near enough to take careful aim, and the bullets were chipping off fragments of rock all around him, but Dad held his fire till they were close enough to make his shots tell. He took careful aim, and a stream of fire darted out of the rifle. Straight at Wolf Lannon the vicious lead flew, and the wearer of the red serape slipped out of the saddle.

"Ha!" Dad exulted. "That's Black Bart Lannon. Jimmie's avenged. I knew my aim was right that time. Now I can put some heart into this here battle. Come on, you measly coyote. I'll show ye how we used to clean up on dung beetles sech as you in the old days." A wild, eerie yell burst from his tightly drawn lips, and his teeth showed in a wolfish snarl. All the time he was busy, coolly drawing a careful bead before firing. Finally the hammer fell with a *click*. Dad stopped and reloaded, but the attacking party was coming too close and fast for him to take aim. He fired as fast as his finger could manipulate the trigger into the thick of them as they approached. The gun barrel was almost red-hot, and Dad could feel it burning into his fingers. The Indians — there were only six left — had leaped from the saddle and were approaching Dad on the run, as he threw down the empty gun and drew from their holsters his long .45s. No one had noticed that Black Bart Lannon had stayed behind when the fighting reached close quarters. Three of the Apaches leaped around the corner of the boulders, and Dad threw

146

down on them with both guns spitting flame and lead. He didn't know how long he had been pulling the hammer on empty cartridges when the Indians closed in. Dad felt something like a red-hot knife pass between his ribs, and something else hit his shoulder with a staggering smash as he closed his powerful arms around the nearest Apache.

It seemed there were Apaches all over him now. Twice he went down and twice he staggered to his feet, carrying a tumbled heap of forms with him. Over and over again ran through his brain the thought that Jimmie was avenged, and he began to take a sort of fierce joy in the combat. Shots sounded dully in his ears, and again and again he felt hot stabs reach all parts of his body. A knife slashed across his forehead, and the warm, wet blood trickled down into his eyes, blinding him. Still he fought on, in the dark now, but the grunts of his opponents attested to the fact that he was making his blows tell. Gradually, however, he grew weaker. His whole body was bathed in spurts of warm lifeblood that soaked into his dusty clothing. Suddenly his grasp relaxed and Dad Flint fell to the ground.

CHAPTER
SEVEN

As the Apaches staggered back from the now prostrate body of old Dad, Black Bart Lannon cautiously approached from behind the rock where he had been hiding.

"Is he finished?" he asked, drawing near the body. Assured of that fact, he commenced to curse in savage tones and, drawing his Colt from the holster, discharged its contents into the lifeless body.

"You brave man," Kicking Horse said contemptuously as he reached suddenly for Lannon's rifle and examined it. He peered into the barrel and placed it to his nose, then said: "Black Bart Lannon not fire one shot. Wolf Lannon no 'fraid. Black Bart Lannon heap coward." He spat violently on the ground as he finished the words.

"That'll do, Kicking Horse," Lannon snarled. His right hand flew to his holster, but he remembered in time that he was outnumbered, and brought his hand back empty. At that moment he glanced off to the southwest and saw a cloud of dust that announced the approach of a number of galloping horsemen.

"Quick, Kicking Horse," he said to the Apache, motioning in the direction of the cloud of dust, "we've got to get away." He leaped into the saddle of his horse that stood near and, after riding to where Wolf lay on the ground, took one look at him and then rode furiously in the direction of the Sacramentos, leaving his brother for dead. Kicking Horse quickly gathered together the Apaches who were unwounded and they ran for their horses. There were just four of the Indians without a bullet wound of some kind, although they showed the mark of old Dad's fists on their bronzed faces. Three more, when helped into the saddle, were able to ride. The others were stone dead. In a few minutes they were under way, riding rapidly after the fleeing form of Black Bart Lannon. In a short time the band was lost to view in the tangled mass of trees that grew among the foothills.

When Buck Thomas arrived on the scene at the head of a party of twenty cowpunchers that he had gathered at neighboring ranches as soon as he learned that the Indians were out on the warpath, there wasn't a living soul in sight. The dead Indians lying about and the body of Wolf Lannon soon showed what had happened. The cowpunchers made their way to the rocks where Dad's body lay. The torn and trampled ground and empty cartridge shells and the blood-soaked clothes of the still figure told plainly the story of the brave defense.

"Poor old Dad," Buck said, "he sure put up a fight while he lasted. There must be twenty-five cuts on him. Got some bullets in 'im, too. And to think that he disposed of seven Apaches and Black Bart Lannon all by himself." The men removed their wide-brimmed sombreros in awe as they stood back.

"That ain't Black Bart Lannon," said Steel Hansen, a cowpuncher from the Bar-30 Ranch, who had been looking at Wolf's body. "It's his brother Wolf. I've seed 'em both before, an' I know."

"Well, where's the red serape come from then," Slim Rollins demanded. "I thought Black Bart Lannon allus wore it."

"I don't know about that," Steel answered, "only I know it ain't Black Bart Lannon."

Buck had been examining the body of old Dad. "He's still warm, boys, so the snakes what did this can't have much of a start on us. We'll cover Dad up with stones so the coyotes an' buzzards can't get at him, in case we don't get back right away, an' then we'll get on after the scuts. Those other bodies can lay where they fell for all I care."

In a few minutes the boys had erected a sort of tomb around Dad's body, and, once more regaining their saddles, they rode away over the trail Black Bart Lannon and the Apaches had taken. But Wolf Lannon wasn't dead. Neither Black Bart Lannon, Steel Hansen, nor any one else had examined the body very closely or they would have discovered he still lived. He had been hit twice. Dad's first shot had creased his temple and stunned him for the time being, while the second shot, deflecting from the silver dollar in his shirt pocket, had passed upward through his shoulder. Although bleeding freely and weak from loss of blood, the cool air of evening revived and stimulated him. Staggering to his feet, he made his way past the stiff bodies of the dead Apaches to the pile of rocks under which Dad lay. He realized then that Black Bart and the Apaches had been driven off, but that help had arrived too late to save the life of the old cattleman. Glancing quickly over the ground, he found the imprints of several booted feet, mingled with the moccasin treads of the Apaches.

A sudden fit of fear overcame Wolf. He must get away or they might return and find him. That would mean death, sure. He looked about, but his horse was nowhere in sight. The horses of the dead Indians had run away, also. He stuffed some scrap tobacco into his mouth and, chewing it into a cud, wadded it into the hole in his shoulder to stop the bleeding. He staggered on his way again, but in a few minutes lost consciousness and dropped to the ground in a faint.

Dawn was streaking the sky when Wolf regained consciousness again. He was on his feet, stumbling along, before he was fully awake, with only one thought in mind, and that one thought intent on making an escape before the cowpunchers returned. He thought he was headed straight for the foothills of the Sacramentos, but the loss of blood had made him delirious, and, losing his sense of direction, he was headed straight into the desert. The sun rose above the horizon and climbed higher and higher, but still Wolf stumbled on, a vacant glaze in his eyes.

The cool blue of the sky with the rays of the sun sending down waves of furnace-like heat seemed to change to a sheet of blue flame. For some reason Wolf clung to the red serape, hardly knowing he had it with

151

him. It dragged down at his feet and tripped him more than once, but he always rose and staggered on. All around was stillness and heat and scorching sand. It was so still the very silence seemed to crackle in the white, quivering air. Twice Wolf stopped and, tilting his head far back, drank long from the canteen of water he carried at his waist. The third time he raised the canteen to his parched lips no water trickled down his throat. The canteen was empty, and with a curse forcing its way through his swollen lips Wolf let the canteen fall from his weakened grasp to the ground.

He had wandered for years, it seemed, always doggedly dragging one foot after the other. Growing more delirious, a crazy, cracking laugh at odd intervals careened from his blackened lips. He tried to talk, but the words wouldn't come. Bloodshot eyes endeavored to pierce the swaying heat waves in search of trees and hillsides, but all he could see was sand, sand, and more sand.

Once Wolf thought he saw a train of cars pass a mile or so away, but in a moment of lucidity he realized it was only a desert mirage. As he stumbled on, the scorching sands sending wave after blasting wave into his tortured face, the mirages became more frequent. Once he was sure he saw a stream a short way ahead. Breaking into a stumbling, staggering run, he threw himself down on the very banks only to have it disappear as the other mirages had, and to find his face pressed into the burning sand.

His throat became choked with alkali dust and his face was caked and dry. It became more difficult to breathe. Overhead two huge buzzards stirred the sultry air with sluggish wings, waiting for their prey to drop for the last time. Wolf raised his tortured sight to gaze up at them. "Ye won't get me, damn you, you won't get me," he tried to cry out, but his tongue was swollen and distended between his lips and made only horrible sounds. Suddenly, as he looked up, he saw mountains just above him. He eyed greedily a silver stream, finding its source high up among the rugged purple crags and wending its gleaming way through the pine trees, till it spread into a lake, which, in his delirium, he thought stretched to his very feet. Had Wolf known it, he was standing on the very edge of a huge crack in the earth, but his thirst-crazed mind had no warning to offer him at this time. All he could see was a large blue lake sending slow waves to the shore. A lizard strayed into his shadow and watched this queer being with unblinking eyes.

Wolf's demented mind told him to do but one thing. It suggested treacherously that he leap into the water. He poised, but as he was about to leap, the mirage cleared away and he saw below him the huge crack in the earth with a nest of rattlesnakes at the bottom, hissing their venom at the intruder. One moment Wolf swayed and tried to save himself, but he lost his balance and plunged down into the hell of darting red tongues and beady eyes. Once he struggled to rise, but when he fell, his head had crashed against a rock, and in a few moments even the angry hiss of enraged rattlers and the stench of the nest passed into oblivion.

CHAPTER
EIGHT

Buck Thomas and his cowpunchers reached the foothills of the Sacramentos that evening and quickly picked up the trail. They rode all night without making camp and in the morning, just rounding a bend of the mountain trail, they saw the Apaches riding like mad. As they gained on the fleeing horses, the cowpunchers set up a yelling and whooping, which, mingled with the short *crack-crack* of their six-guns, brought the Indians to a stop.

Kicking Horse threw his gun to the ground and the others followed suit as the cowpunchers surrounded them. In a few minutes the Indians were dismounted and their hands tied behind them. Black Bart Lannon wasn't to be seen.

"Who's chief here?" Buck demanded.

For an instant none of the Indians replied, then Kicking Horse stepped forward. "Me, chief," he answered sullenly.

"Where's Black Bart Lannon?" was Buck's next question.

Kicking Horse shook his head. "No und'stand," he said.

154

"You can't get anything out o' these redskins when they don't want to talk, Buck," Slim Rollins put in.

"Frisk him," Buck said. "Frisk all of them."

The cowpunchers quickly got to work, and, as the Apaches wore little but breechclouts, although two of them had shirts and Kicking Horse boasted, in addition, a civilian vest, they soon completed the search. None of them had anything to show but knives, a little tobacco, and some cartridges. That is, none of them with the exception of Kicking Horse. From inside his shirt Cash Jordon brought forth a black leather wallet, which he handed to Buck. The Indians stood silent, making no physical objections to the search, but their eyes glittered with hate and the cowpunchers kept them well covered while the frisking was in progress.

The wallet was Black Bart Lannon's. As Buck opened it, he found it to be filled with bills. "Holy Jehosophat! This must be the money Lannon got off Jimmie. Let's see, till I count it. There's five . . . seven . . . nine . . . eleven . . . eleven thousand and . . . wait a minute . . ." Presently he concluded the count and made the announcement: "Eleven thousand in thousand-dollar bills and eight hundred and sixty dollars in yellow backs. Yep, that's about the right amount. I suspect he had trouble getting them grand notes cashed." Further search of the wallet disclosed nothing more than an empty envelope addressed to **B. Lannon, Conejo Lures, Mexico**, a few cards from gambling houses, and a flattened bullet that had doubtless been removed from his body at some time or other. Buck swung around on Kicking Horse.

"Look here, Indian, I know where this came from. Where's Black Bart Lannon?" His voice rang out crisply. "Come on, speak up, or I'll have your dirty hide. The more you tell now, the better treatment you'll get when you get back on the reservation. Either you talk plenty or I'll know the reason why. You savvy?" His gray eyes steeled to fine points.

"Me savvy," Kicking Horse grunted. "Me talk. What you want?"

"First off," Buck said, "where'd you get this?" He shook the wallet under the Apache's nose.

"Me take 'um," the Indian answered stolidly.

"Sure you did," Buck said, exasperated, "but who did you take it from?"

"Lannon," came a single, sullen grunt. More silence.

"By God, you'll talk, or I'll put you in jail for the rest of your life!" Buck cried. At the word "jail", the Indian pricked up his ears and nodded his head.

"Me take him from Lannon last night," Kicking Horse said. "Lannon heap coward, and I take 'um money. Heap money, heap whiskey, Indian have good time."

"The hell you will," Cash Jordon put in. "Not with that cash."

"Where's Black Bart Lannon now?" Buck demanded.

The Indian shook his head. "We tie him up last night. This morning he gone. Guns gone. Kicking Horse not know where Lannon gone. Kicking Horse good Indian. All my brothers good Indians. Black Bart Lannon tell us come with him. Plenty whiskey, plenty good time. Me good Indian. Black Bart Lannon make good Indian go bad. Me good Indian. Black Bart Lannon tell Kicking Horse plenty . . ."

"Oh, for heaven's sake, shut up," Buck cut him short. "I know the whole rigmarole by now . . . 'Me good Indian, plenty whiskey, me good Indian, plenty good time . . .'" He broke off in disgust and turned to the others. "I guess we can't get any more out of him, boys. He and Black Bart Lannon had some kind of a fuss and this Kicking Horse takes his money and ties him up. Sometime during the night, Lannon slipped his ropes and got away and the Apaches went on till we caught up with them. I guess that's all we can do. Slim, you and Cash and Big Ike and Ramsay, come with me. We'll see if we can find Lannon's trail. The rest of you boys take these Indians back to the reservation and see that you escort them with care. If we shoot 'em up, the government'll be on our necks."

A short camp was made and coffee, bacon, and beans served all around, before the two parties started on their respective ways. The Indians, now wholly subdued, rode silently, surrounded by the other cowpunchers headed by Steel Hansen. As they rode down the trail, Slim remarked to Buck: "All the pep seems gone outta them redskins. I don't think they'll give no trouble no more."

"No, they'll be pretty good Indians from now on," Buck answered. "They know they're in bad, an' they'll do everything they can to get light sentences."

For three days the four men scoured the adjacent country for signs of Black Bart Lannon, but not a trace could they find. Each morning they split into parties of two, but it seemed that the object of their search had vanished from the face of the earth. On the fourth day, as they rose from their blankets, Buck was already up and preparing the coffee and bacon.

"Early breakfast, Buck." Big Ike yawned, stretching lazily.

"Yeah, we might just as well get back. Black Bart Lannon is probably miles away from this section of the country by now."

By noon, the four men were back at the scene of old Dad's last stand. Reverently they removed the stones that covered the still form encased in blankets. Then, with flat pieces of stone, they dug a shallow grave at the spot where Dad Flint had waged his brave but losing fight. It was slow work and the sun was on the downward grade when they finished, but into the digging went the labor of love. Finally the blanket-wrapped body was laid in the hole and the sand scraped back till it was well covered.

"Knowin' Dad as I do, I think he'd sooner be buried here where he made such a good showin', than in any town cemetery," Buck said, brushing the tears from his eyes. The others, too, showed their feelings in various ways. Big Ike swore roundly while they piled stones high over Dad's grave. Cash Jordon tried to talk in the usual tone of voice, but a lump came up in his throat and choked him. By the time they had finished, Slim was blubbering outright like a big overgrown kid and there was a set expression on Ramsay's face that betokened ill to Black Bart Lannon if the two ever met. Buck didn't say much, but he knew that the others were

158

thinking, as he was, of the many kindnesses that Dad had shown them in the past. They all uncovered and knelt by the mound of stones while Buck said a prayer. It wasn't the prayer that an ordained minister would have said, but the fervent — "Amen." — at the end attested the fact that it served its purpose fully. As they donned their hats and got into their saddles, none of the four said a word and it wasn't till they crossed near the crack in the earth that served as a rattler's nest and into which Wolf Lannon had fallen that the pall of despondency into which the conversation had dropped was thrown off.

It was Slim who first noticed the buzzards floating in the air over the hole in the earth. Curiosity impelled them to ride over and see what attracted the birds. One look was enough. There, lying with one end of the filthy red serape twisted between his legs, lay Wolf Lannon — or what was left of him. His features were bitten almost beyond recognition, and in some places bits of flesh had been torn out by the buzzards. At first, the four men didn't notice the snakes, but as their shadows fell across the nest, the familiar whispering rattles commenced and the body seemed to be lying on a wave of sinuously moving shapes. A huge rattler, disturbed from its torpid sleep, drew a scaly length across what once had been a face, and the four men started back from the hole with a sickness at the pit of their stomachs. They were back in the saddles before anyone spoke.

"Well, that's sure the end of Wolf Lannon, anyway," Cash said.

"Yeah, and what a way to die!" Slim added, shuddering.

"I was wonderin' where that body with the red serape had gone to," Big Ike said. "I missed it when we first came back, but judged mebbe a puma had come down at night and took it."

"Wherever that red serape goes, it seems like death follows," Buck said slowly. "I'm sorry it ain't Black Bart Lannon, instead. He's the one I'm after from now on. He'll heave into sight someday and then I'll get him, an' I'll get him good." His eyes grew cold at the thought.

"How do you reckon Wolf got in a fix like that?" Slim asked.

"He was probably still alive when we were here before," Buck answered, "only we were too dumb to examine him. When he came to, he was likely woozy in the head an' got lost in the desert."

CHAPTER
NINE

The morning sun was well above the hilltops when Buck Thomas loped his horse along the trail that crossed the wagon tracks leading to the Circle X ranch house. In a few minutes he pulled up before the door and alighted from the saddle. Going into the house, which he found empty except for the presence of Tom, the Chinese cook, he asked for Cash Jordon.

"Him allee same gone blunkhouse," Tom informed him.

"Bunkhouse, eh," Buck said. "I'll trail down an' find him."

Three months had passed since Buck and the rest of the cowpunchers had returned to the ranch after old Dad Flint had been killed and Black Bart Lannon had made his escape from the Apaches. Buck had returned and assumed the ownership of the ranch and made Cash Jordon foreman, or rather the decision had been left to the other cowpunchers. Big Ike and Slim Rollins had been working for Dad as long as Cash had, so Buck put the question squarely up to them, and they elected Cash their boss. Cash Jordon was a rather quiet sort, steady, and like lightning on the trigger. All in all, he made Buck a good foreman.

A month after they had returned, a party of leading citizens of La Roda and cattlemen had called on Buck and offered him the sheriff's office. The present incumbent of the sheriff's office was unsatisfactory to the residents of Dona Aña County. He was a weak, unscrupulous man, some said in the pay of certain cattle rustlers and badmen with which the county was infested. From the first, Tutt Arnold had proved an unsatisfactory sheriff and all the promises he had made before the election had been forgotten as soon as that event was over. Consequently there had reigned in Dona Aña County a siege of lawlessness not often equaled, even in the wildest days of the pioneer West.

Buck had at first refused the office, saying that even were he elected, he had no time to devote to the administration of the law, but his petitioners were obdurate, and despite his plea of ranch business they insisted that he run for office. Finally he gave in, but only on the condition that he was to do very little campaigning. Two of the country's largest ranchers assured him that there'd be very little campaigning to do. The people were sick and tired of Tutt Arnold and were ready to elect any honest man put up for their vote. Through long association with Dad Flint, whose honesty had been unimpeachable, the people were pretty well acquainted with Buck Thomas and he with them.

Buck had put Cash Jordon in full charge of the ranch, and such small campaigning as he had done was mixed with an unceasing search for Black Bart Lannon. Every town within a radius of 150 miles had been scoured mercilessly, but not a trace of the object of his vengeance could Buck uncover. Buck thought this was strange, and that he must be in hiding some place, for with his predilection for red serapes he would have been sure to attract notice in any towns through which he might pass. A few days before, Buck had received word from a passing cowpuncher that Black Bart had been seen in Conejo Lures. He had at once saddled up and rode down to the little Mexican town but could find no one who could, or would, admit they had ever seen Black Bart.

While in Conejo Lures, Buck had gone to see the girl, Mariposa, who was being held in jail pending the trial of Black Bart for Jimmie's murder, if, or when, Lannon could be found. She denied knowing anything of the affair at all, till Buck told her how Wolf Lannon had died. Then she broke down and, while still maintaining her innocence and the innocence of Black Bart and Wolf regarding the murder, admitted to Buck that Black Bart Lannon had left for eastern Texas some weeks back. Even then, Buck felt she was lying to him, so he hit the trail for the Circle X, resting secure in the belief that Black Bart would someday again put in an appearance.

As Buck entered the bunkhouse door, Cash Jordon was seated on a bunk, mending a piece of harness. He looked up as Buck's shadow fell across the doorway.

"Hello, there, old wasp!" he called out, an affectionate grin crinkling the leathery skin around his eyes. "I didn't know you were back."

"Hello, Cash," Buck returned. "H'are you? Yeah, I just got in. Where's everybody?"

"They weren't much to do, so I sent the boys out to mend fence. Slim an' Big Ike are paintin' sheds. What'd you find out. Anything?"

"I saw that Mariposa girl and she tells me Lannon headed Texasward a few weeks back. I don't believe her, though. I can't dope it out, no-how, Cash, but I got a hunch that Black Bart is still hanging around this here neck o' the woods. Anyway, there wasn't any trace of the dirty skunk in Conejo Lures."

"He'll show up one of these here days," Cash answered. "An' then we'll get him, an' get him right."

"How'd the election come out," Buck asked next.

"There, I'd plumb forgot to tell you. You're elected. The delegation was down here yesterday to present you with your star of office, but you weren't here. They want you to come down to La Roda as soon as you get back. They tell me it was a pretty close vote, too. You only beat Tutt Arnold out by a couple hundred votes. Buck, there's a right bad element in Dona Aña County right now."

"You're a shootin'-tootin' there is," Buck answered, "an' my first job will be to see what I can do toward cleanin' out some of these badmen."

"Well, don't forget to swear me in as one of your deputies," Cash said. "I'd sure admire to sit in on any kind of game you're shootin' in." He looked enviously at Buck.

"Well, I'll swear you in if I need you," Buck said, "but I guess mostly, Cash, that you'll have your hands full running this ranch. My headquarters will be in La Roda an' I'll have to leave all of the ranch business to you for a time, till I get settled around."

"Where you goin' to start in?" Cash asked.

"That's just what I can't figure out," Buck answered. "We both know there's a bad crowd hanging around La Roda. But there doesn't seem to be any leader, leastwise one you can lay a finger on. Anyway, I figure most of the troublemakers center in La Roda, and, if I can clean up there, the big work is done. I only wish I knew who to start on."

"Tutt Arnold," Cash suggested.

Buck shook his head slowly. "I don't think so," he said. "Tutt Arnold's probably got something to do with it, but Tutt's no leader. There're bigger brains than Tutt's back of some of these hold-ups that're being pulled so right smart every once in a while."

"Mebbe Black Bart Lannon's," Cash suggested.

"I don't know. It wouldn't surprise me none, and yet . . ." Buck broke off and shook his head in a puzzled way. "I don't know what to think, Cash. The only thing I can do is keep an eye peeled till something turns up."

The two men talked a while longer, and then Buck went out to speak to Slim and Big Ike. When he returned to the ranch house, Cash Jordon was talking to a dapper little man in city clothes who Cash waved toward Buck: "This here gentleman is Mister Buck Thomas."

The dapper man came forward, holding out his hand to Buck, who shook it perfunctorily. "What can I do for you?" Buck asked.

"My name's Wilkens, Homer H. Wilkens, of Albuquerque," the little man said suavely. "I've been traveling through your country, looking over various ranches, and have just about decided to buy the Circle X if you'll name your figure."

"The Circle X isn't for sale," Buck said briefly.

"Oh, I realize that you probably haven't planned to sell out," the little man said, unperturbed. "However, the firm I'm acting for is prepared to offer you an attractive figure . . . a *very* attractive figure, one that you cannot afford to refuse."

"The Circle X isn't for sale," Buck repeated emphatically.

"My dear young man, won't you consider our offer? We are prepared to pay at least twenty-five percent more for your property than the regular market price. You simply can't afford to let such an offer slip by. No doubt, you have many dreams you'd like to have brought to a consummation. With the money we offer, you could travel any place you cared to . . ."

"For the last time," Buck cut in sharply, "let me tell you that the Circle X *isn't* for sale. As for traveling . . . this is God's own country an' it suits me right down to the ground."

"But . . ."

"Furthermore," Buck continued, not heeding the interruption, "if your company is so danged anxious to pick up ranch land, there's plenty to be had around here, just as good as the Circle X, and a danged sight cheaper."

"I hear as how Trent's place, the Flying L ranch, is fer sale," Cash Jordon said. "Missus Trent ain't well, an' Trent's got to move to another climate. You should get the Flying L at your own price."

"I shall make a note of that," Wilkens said. He turned to Buck again. "And now, Mister Thomas, won't you consider our offer? We'll be glad to make any concessions that you may . . ."

"No!" Buck said sharply. "The Circle X suits me, an' the country suits me, an' I'm plumb satisfied. That's all there is to it." His voice changed. "Mister Wilkens, I'm sorry, but I'm a right busy man these days, and I can't give you any more of my time. I've got to be in La Roda by nightfall."

"In that case, can't I offer the service of the wagon that brought me here?" Wilkens said. "I'm going back to La Roda now."

"Nope. Thanks just the same. I prefer to ride my horse down. Good bye." With these words, Buck turned and walked from the room, leaving Cash Jordon to get rid of Wilkens. In a few minutes the creak of wheels was heard, and, looking out of a side window, Buck saw Wilkens being driven rapidly in the direction of La Roda. He returned to the room and found Cash staring at the floor.

"Persistent cuss, eh, Cash?" Buck broke in upon his foreman's abstractions.

"Persistent ain't no name for it," Cash returned. "That *hombre's* powerful anxious to get hold o' the Circle X for some reason or t'other."

"I wonder why," Buck mused. "I don't like his looks nohow. Reminds me of a weasel with his little quick motions an' those shifty eyes."

"He doesn't want any ranch but the Circle X," Cash said. "He didn't even make a note, when I told him about Trent's place. 'Nother thing. I know that *hombre* ain't been travelin' around the country like he says. I was talkin' to the geezer what brung him out an' he says Wilkens just landed in La Roda this mornin'. An' all that talk about you goin' travelin' . . . ? Looks to me like somebody wanted you out of the way, Buck."

"Kinda appears that way, doesn't it? Well, I got to get movin', so tell Tom to rustle some grub for me, will you?"

CHAPTER
TEN

The children were leaving the door of the little schoolhouse that nestled in the hills, surrounded by short scrub trees and tall grass, as the afternoon sun began to touch the hilltops. Parents were loading the children into their buckboards when Buck first glimpsed the sign — **Rural School No. 4, Dona Aña County** — that, affixed to the peak of the roof, Buck could see plainly through the tops of the trees. He drew rein, dismounted, and seated himself at the side of the road to roll a cigarette till the people were out of sight. Buck's interest in Helen Fanning, the pretty, blonde schoolteacher, was well known and he had no desire to undergo the merciless kidding that he knew awaited him if he rode up to the schoolhouse before parents and children had left.

Wonder why they didn't build that school nearer to town, Buck mused, exhaling a cloud of gray smoke. *It makes a right smart haul in those buckboards every afternoon to bring the children home.* Finally the last buckboard had passed out of sight around a bend in the road and Buck thought it safe to go in. He swung into the saddle and in a few moments had alighted at the schoolhouse door.

As his tall figure darkened the doorway, Helen Fanning, who was seated at her desk at the end of the room, looked up. When she saw who it was, the blushes mounted to the very tips of her corn-silk hair. Buck thought he had never seen a prettier sight as she turned to speak to two small children who lingered near, then raised her head and welcomed him in.

"Good afternoon, Mister Buck Thomas, I see you haven't forgotten that you were to ride home with me this afternoon."

"I don't forget anything like that, Miss Fanning," Buck said as he crossed the floor to a chair near her side. The two children looked at him in wide-eyed wonder. One, the boy, was a sturdy youngster of about ten years. The girl was a flaxen-haired little fairy two years younger.

"Won't you shake hands with Mister Thomas, children?" Helen Fanning said in her soft tones. She turned to Buck. "They're Seth Houghton's children. You know Seth Houghton who runs the general store, don't you? He's late coming after them today."

Buck nodded as he took the boy's small hand in his own grasp, after shaking hands with the little girl.

"You're Buck Thomas, ain't you?" the boy said.

"Don't say 'ain't', Tad," Miss Fanning reproved Buck answered: "Yes, sir, Buck Thomas is my name."

"The new sheriff, eh?" the little fellow continued.

"Seems to me, I heard some news to that effect," Buck answered.

"Well, are you, or ain't you?" the boy persisted.

"I guess I am."

170

"Well, my paw says the county couldn't have elected a better man. He says you're going to have a regular clean-up when you take office."

"I'm goin' to try, anyhow." Buck laughed.

"Well, I don't want no more clean-ups," the boy said.

"Why, Tad?"

"Well, my maw makes me spend too much time now washing my neck and ears," he answered. "Pretty soon, I s'pose, we'll be taking a bath all over every day, if you have . . ."

"That will do, Tad," Miss Fanning said, a slow smile on her lips. She turned to the chuckling Buck. "Allow me to congratulate our new sheriff," she said.

"Mebbe you'd better withhold congratulations till the new sheriff shows what he can do." He laughed. "That's one thing I wanted to talk to you about, Miss Fanning. Can I talk to you *alone?*" Buck finished meaningfully.

The girl nodded and turned to the children. "Run outdoors and play now, children. Your father will be here soon."

Child-like, they preferred to stay and listen to the older folks talk, till Buck suddenly turned fiercely on them, and, drawing his guns from the holsters, said in savage tones: "You two big, tough galoots better be getting along now, before I fill you full of lead." The children burst into screams of laughter and ran shrieking through the door.

Buck hardly knew how to commence. He made two or three efforts, but a lump rose in his throat.

Helen Fanning knew what he wanted to say and helped him out. "You were about to say something about your being sheriff, Buck," she prompted softly.

A grateful look shone in his eyes as he answered: "Yes, you see, Helen . . . Miss Fanning, now that I'm elected, I won't have much time on my hands for a while. I've got a big job ahead, living up to the things folks expect of me, so I'll be right busy for a spell. I just wanted you to know that, even if I don't see you, I'm thinking of you all the time." He hesitated and gulped for more words.

"Yes, Buck, I'll understand," she answered, the tones just reaching his ears.

He rose and went to the window where he gazed out for a few moments before coming back to her side.

"And I was wondering," he went on, a look of determination on his face, "if, after all this ruckus is cleaned up, if you and I couldn't . . . couldn't get married. I've got a ranch that'll pay pretty well, and . . . and we can fix the house up right comfy . . ."

"Oh, Buck," she said as she threw her arms around his neck, "oh, Buck, I don't care anything about the ranch. It's you I care for. And Buck, you must be terribly careful and come back safely to me."

He held her close for a few minutes, when suddenly from outside the door they heard the little girl scream. In one bound, Buck reached the door, followed by the schoolteacher.

There, transfixed with fear, stood the little girl. In front of her stood Tad, bravely facing a giant puma that stood, violently switching its long tail from side to side, at the edge of the clearing. Its tawny body stood out in bold relief against the gray-green of the background and its red mouth was opened in a snarl that exposed wicked, yellow fangs. The puma was just about to leap when Buck emerged from the door. The movement distracted the beast's attention, and, as it turned its head, a veritable hail of lead and fire rained from both of Buck's guns.

Crack! Crack! Cr-r-r-r-rack! Crack! In a second the puma was a squirming, spitting, dirty-yellow mass tumbling about the ground and snapping at the red holes in its body. Suddenly before the blue gunsmoke had drifted away, a convulsive twitching set in, and then the puma stretched out and lay still.

"Oh, Buck, is it dead?" the schoolteacher cried as she followed Buck down the steps and over to where the puma lay in a pool of blood.

"I reckon he is," Buck answered, reloading and slipping his guns back in the holsters as he touched the body with the toe of his riding boot. "I emptied about twelve pieces of lead at him and I'll bet a mess of hop toads every one went home. I *couldn't* miss at that distance."

The little girl was crying, but Tad looked disgustedly at Buck. "Why didn'tcha leave him alone? I could 'a' licked him all right," he boasted.

At that moment a buckboard drew up and Seth Houghton leaped from the seat. "Drat it all," he said, "I was held up at the store again." Then, catching sight of the dead puma and the drying tears on the little girl's face: "What's happened?"

His face paled as Buck explained in a few words, and then he wrung Buck's hand in gratitude.

"I don't know how I'd ever have explained to Maw, if anything had happened to them two kids of mine," he said. "Well, Sheriff, you seem to be takin' hold in the right fashion, an' I'm in your debt already." The two men talked a few minutes longer, then Houghton loaded his two children into the wagon and headed back for La Roda. He offered to take Helen and Buck back with him, but they said they had their horses, and he drove on.

Although the schoolhouse was only about five miles distant from town, the moon was high in the heavens before Buck helped Helen dismount at the little gray house in La Roda where she lived with her mother. Under certain conditions, a journey can be unusually prolonged.

CHAPTER
ELEVEN

The morning sun was shining brightly along the main street of La Roda when Buck Thomas stepped from the doorway of the rude wooden building that served as City Hall. He glanced down, half proudly, half self-consciously, at the shiny silver star pinned to his vest. Buck straightened himself proudly. The star was symbolical of the trust that the good citizens of Dona Aña County accorded him.

As he sauntered along the rough boardwalk into the shadow of the La Roda House, the town's one hostelry, a voice hailed him. He turned and beheld Homer H. Wilkens, hurrying down the steps. Buck waited till he had come up.

"Ah, good morning, Mister Thomas . . . pardon me, I should say, Sheriff Thomas, shouldn't I?"

" 'Mornin', Mister Wilkens," Buck responded to his greeting in a curt tone. "What can I do for you?"

"This little matter of the Circle X, Sheriff. Have you reconsidered my offer?"

"No . . . and I'm not intendin' to." Buck turned his back and started away, but the little man caught hold of his sleeve.

"But wait . . . we are prepared to offer you . . ." Wilkens drew an envelope from his pocket and made some rapid calculations on the back of it with his fountain pen. "We are prepared to offer you . . . just that figure." He held the envelope up for Buck's inspection.

The amount written on the envelope staggered Buck for a minute. "That's a heap of money, Mister Wilkens," he said slowly. "You could buy two Circle Xs for that amount."

"Yes, but there's just one Circle X we want," Wilkens said blandly. "What do you say? Do we make the deal?"

Buck eyed him quizzically for a moment before answering. At last he said quietly, speaking slowly that his hearer might get the full import of his words: "Mister Wilkens, I don't know what the rule is in the country where you come from, but out here men don't sell presents that have been given to 'em. The Circle X was willed to me, and the man that I got that ranch from holds a right soft spot in my heart. I'm not selling."

"Well, have you a clear title to your outfit?" Wilkens asked.

"The Circle X is mine, all right," Buck answered. "Lawyer Higgins has the will he drew up for old Dad Flint a few days before he was . . . before he died. I just haven't had time to get the papers transferred over to my name yet, but the Circle X belongs to me, and I have the last word when it comes to selling or not . . . and I'm not selling. That's final!" Buck turned his back and walked away, leaving Wilkens staring after his retreating form. Wilkens left town that night and Buck never saw him again.

As Buck walked about La Roda that morning, he was greeted on every side with congratulations on his election and everyone with whom he talked seemed to have so much confidence in him that it was with a feeling of trepidation that he began to wonder if he could live up to their expectations. Toward noon, he sauntered into the Silver Dollar Saloon, ostensibly to get a drink, but in reality to look over the crowd. The Silver Dollar was the worst saloon in the town and catered to the lowest element. As Buck entered, there was a motley array of cowpunchers and half-breeds lined up at the bar, drinking the poisonous stuff that was sold as liquor. At the far end, Tutt Arnold, the ex-sheriff, lounged his burly form against the bar. His shifty eyes, inflamed with drink, noted Buck the instant he came through the door, but he turned his back and poured a drink from the bottle that stood before him.

"Here's the new sheriff!" someone called, and the crowd at the bar swung around to look at Buck.

"The drinks are on the house, boys," the bartender announced. "Step up and drink to the new sheriff." There was a rush to the bar and for a minute nothing was heard but the gurgling of noisy drinkers. Buck just touched his glass to his lips, and then set it down.

"Speech!" someone cried, and the rest of the crowd took up the cry: "Speech! Speech from Sheriff Buck Thomas!"

"I won't try to make a speech, boys, but I'll treat the house," Buck said, throwing a bill on the bar. The idea was met with instant acclaim, but when they had finished drinking, Tutt Arnold, who had not swallowed his whiskey, dashed his glass to the pine floor.

"I reckon I'm kinda pertickler who I drink with," he growled, glowering at Buck.

Buck had no desire to become embroiled in an argument if it could be avoided, so he disregarded the speech as the ravings of an angry, disgruntled man. However, the next words of the drunken Arnold weren't to be disregarded.

"When any see-saw son-of-a-bitch worms his way into an honest man's job, I ain't aimin' to drink with the measly scut," the ex-sheriff said meanly as his hand dropped to his holster.

Four times Buck's guns spat fire. He had begun to shoot as soon as the muzzles of his .45s left the holsters. The first two shots tore into the plank flooring; the impact of the third sent Tutt Arnold's gun spinning from his grasp, and the fourth bored a neat hole through the crown of Arnold's sombrero.

"That last shot was just to show you what I could do if you reckoned on getting unpleasant with your other gun," Buck drawled coolly through the blue, wavering smoke, to the bewildered Arnold as he backed against the bar and fanned his guns over the startled crowd. "Now, if any of you other *hombres* figure on carryin' this ruckus through to a finish, you better start *pronto*. Otherwise, you can put the guns away and we'll go on peaceable-like." No one replied, but several half-drawn guns were returned to holsters, as Buck continued: "You, Tutt Arnold, you'll apologize for the dirty words you uttered a few minutes back, if you're a man and not a rattlesnake."

Tutt Arnold paled. "Bein' as you got the drop on me, I 'spects I'll have to 'pologize, but I dare you to meet me, man to man, without your guns," he sneered.

Buck looked at him a minute, then laid his still smoking guns on the bar. He knew it was a foolish move to make in such a place, surrounded by Arnold's friends, but Buck figured he could carry the move through on sheer bravado.

At the sheriff's action, Arnold's face lit up and he slipped his remaining gun from the holster and laid it on the bar with Buck's. He realized now that he was no match for Buck when it came to a quick draw, but he felt supreme in the thought that he was more than a match for his smaller opponent in a rough-and-tumble battle. Arnold was about two inches taller and outweighed Buck by at least thirty pounds. Rolling up his sleeves, he stepped to the center of the floor and the others quickly formed a ring about him, with the bar at one side.

Buck looked over his bulky opponent and asked: "You reckon on abiding by any particular rules in this affair, or will it be scratch-as-scratch-can?"

"Rules, hell!" Tutt Arnold spat out at him. "Everythin' goes, as you'll soon be learned. An' now come on, an' le's see if you're man enough to wear a sheriff's badge."

Spat! Buck's right fist crashed against Tutt Arnold's cheek bone as he dashed into action. The big man staggered back from the impact of the blow, but recovered in an instant and made a rush at Buck that would have carried Buck off his feet if he hadn't shifted like lightning. It was like the rush of a wounded bull elephant attacking a tiger. As he rushed by, Buck stuck out his foot and Tutt Arnold sprawled on all fours, his shoulder crashing into the brass rail that ran along the floor near the bottom of the bar.

"Everything goes, you said, Tutt," Buck jeered at his fallen enemy. Somebody laughed and Tutt Arnold's face was like fire as he rose to his feet. This time he knew better than to rush at Buck. The two men sparred warily for an instant, till Buck suddenly saw an opening. His left tore into Arnold's body just above the belt, causing the big man to bend nearly double. As his head snapped forward, Buck put every ounce of his one-hundred-eighty pounds into a right swing that landed just under Tutt Arnold's left ear and sent him flying backward into the mass of onlookers that parted as he approached. He was going so fast that, as he brought up with a crash against a table at the farther wall, the table splintered like matchwood under his huge bulk.

"Think I make a good enough sheriff?" Buck taunted as Tutt Arnold extricated himself from the wrecked table. Buck knew that he was entitled, by all the rules of the game, to rush in and kick his opponent in the face while he was down on the floor, helpless, but a sense of fairness prevented his doing so. He stood blowing on his battered knuckles, waiting for Tutt Arnold to return to the fight.

180

"Damn you," Tutt Arnold roared as he advanced toward Buck, a wicked right fist swinging menacingly, "so far you been lucky, but I ain't foolin' no more! This fight don't stop nowhere short of a killin', an' Dona Aña County's goin' to have a new sheriff." As the last words were out of his mouth, he started a vicious swing for Buck's head. Had it landed, the fight would have been finished then and there. But Buck saw it coming. He blocked it with his left and countered like lightning with a snapping right over the heart. Before he could follow up, Tutt Arnold had closed with him. The circle of men was yelling like mad.

For a moment the two fighters swayed in a clinch, then Buck broke loose and beat a veritable tattoo of fists into Arnold's body. *Thud! thud! thud! thud! thud! thud! thud!* With both hands working like pistons, Buck was causing the big man's breath to come in short, agonized gasps. A moment too long Buck concentrated on the body. That was what Arnold was waiting for. He jumped back and his huge fist swung in an arc to Buck's jaw. Buck's knees sagged and he slipped to the floor as Arnold stepped back, painfully trying to get breath to follow up his advantage.

Buck didn't feel himself go down. There was a crashing of drums in his ears. His mind grew blurred — lights flashed — a dull booming deafened his senses. Then, a life of clean living asserted itself. His brain cleared and he realized he was sprawled on the floor. Buck came out of the daze just in time to see Tutt Arnold's heavy boot raised for a murderous kick at his face. As he squirmed his body around, Buck raised his

181

arm to fend off the blow that was intended to finish him. The foot descended, but, as it did, Buck threw his arm around Arnold's leg, and he came down with a crash, Buck underneath. With a mighty heave, Buck threw the heavy body to one side and scrambled on top. Over and over the two men rolled, scratching, cursing, kicking, and clawing, each straining every muscle to get the upper hand. Finally they came up short against the doorjamb, the force of their combined weight shaking the building. Through sheer bull strength, Tutt Arnold struggled to his knees, Buck on his back. For a second he made no attempt to throw Buck off as his right hand fumbled inside his shirt. The meaning of the move flashed upon Buck in an instant. Arnold was reaching for an under-arm holster!

Buck exerted all his strength and forced Arnold to the floor, but he was too late to prevent his drawing the gun. As they crashed down, Buck seized the hand holding the gun and tried to prevent Arnold's rolling over. For a second neither moved, each straining every muscle to the utmost. Then, slowly but surely, as Buck shifted his grip to the wrist, the hand was pulled back along the floor, the sight on the short, wicked barrel tearing a long, jagged shaving from the pine boards as it moved. Beads of perspiration stood out on Buck's forehead and the painful gasping of the two men could be heard above the wild cries of the audience. Slowly, slowly, the fist holding the gun was forced up and back. Once, as Arnold made a final effort, his arm became like iron and Buck couldn't budge it. It was too much of an effort to last, however, and again the gun commenced the slow, upward motion. The muzzle was pointing almost directly toward the ceiling by now. Suddenly Arnold twitched his trigger finger and a bullet roared by Buck's ear, the burning powder scorching his face. An instant later it was too late to fire. Anyway, Arnold had no strength left to pull the trigger. His arm was in a queer, awkward position, the gun barrel pointed obliquely up and over his left shoulder. He groaned with pain. Tutt Arnold screamed and his face went gray. There was a snapping report that sounded like a pistol shot. His straining body relaxed and he slumped forward on his face. Buck had torn Arnold's bone from the shoulder pit!

The victor rose and staggered back from his defeated enemy. "You said . . . everything went . . . Tutt Arnold," he panted, raising a tired, quivering hand to wipe the perspiration from his eyes, "and I guess . . . you got . . . what was . . . comin' to you." He reached down and, taking hold of Arnold's collar, hauled him slowly to his feet. As he stood there, swaying from side to side, with his twisted right arm dangling from the shoulder, Tutt Arnold was almost a broken man, but not quite. His agony was forgotten in his hate.

"My gun!" he cried in mingled rage and pain. "Somebody give me my gun! Give me a gun!" From behind, someone in the crowd pressed a gun into the twitching fingers of his uninjured left hand.

The thundering crack of a six-gun filled the Silver Dollar Saloon, and a streak of crimson darted along the back of Tutt Arnold's hand as the gun dropped from his nerveless grasp. Through the blue, weaving smoke came

183

a voice. "Put 'em up!" Cash Jordon cried sharply. "'Way up! Come on, you sons-of-bitches, move *pronto*. Keep your hands away from your holsters. There's three of us here, just spoilin' to let daylight through some of you measly scuts. Keep 'em covered, boys!" he called back over his shoulder to Slim Rollins and Big Ike who moved their long, blue .45s in a way that made every rascal in the place think he was the one at whom the black, menacing barrels were leveled.

At the first words, Buck had leaped to the bar and got his guns, and now, he, too, was covering the crowd. "All right, you *hombres*, clear out of here, quick! Scatter! I don't trust you in a bunch." As the crowd filed out, its arms still pointed toward the sky, Buck added: "I don't reckon none on interferin' with your freedom an' you can come and go as you like, but for the time being, mebbe further bloodshed can be prevented if you go out and take the air and cool off some." In a few moments the place was empty, save for the bartender, Tutt Arnold, who slumped, groaning, in a chair, and Buck and his assistants.

"You sure arrived in time, boys." Buck laughed easily. "But I don't understand yet how you got here so quick. Seems like you-all dropped right out of the sky."

"We kinda suspected somethin' might happen your first day out," Cash explained, "so we trailed in this mornin' and have been followin' you around town ever since. When we came in here, you were just layin' your guns on the bar. Bein' as we could still smell smoke, we couldn't understand your move a-tall, so we kinda stuck back in the crowd till we were needed."

184

"An' needed you were," Buck said. "I'm much obliged, boys."

"Aw, it ain't nothin' to thank us fer," Slim Rollins ventured in an abashed way. "We admire to sit in on a game of this kind, don't we, fellows?" The others nodded assent as Cash asked: "What was the shootin' before we come in here?"

Buck explained in a few words what had started the fight with Tutt Arnold.

"Looks like a frame-up to me, to get you with your guns off, an' then put you out of the runnin'," Cash said.

Buck nodded. "I know it. I reckoned it was foolish to let my guns out of my hands, but, when that *hombre* over there dared me to fight, I sorta saw red for a minute. It's a good thing you boys arrived when you did. I guess, after all, I'll have to swear you in as my deputies. From the way things have started out, it looks like we might have a right lively time for a spell an' I may need some assistance. I know you're willin' to help, but it makes it more legal-like in case there's any killings." He hesitated a moment. Then: "Cash Jordon, Slim Rollins, Ike Peters, raise your right hands. Do you swear to carry out my orders and help me to enforce the law to the full extent of your ability?" The three men answered solemnly in the affirmative, "All right," Buck went on, "you are now legally constituted deputies. Mebbe those aren't the right words for the procedure, but they'll do."

"Whoopee!" Slim yelled. "Now, mebbe I'll get some excitement. I'm getting plumb tired of punchin' cows."

"Not so fast, Slim. You'll all have to stay on the ranch, unless I need you." Buck smiled. "Then you can come a-runnin'. I'll send for you when I do."

"Speakin' of the ranch," Cash said, "somebody ran off with fifty head of the white-faced yearlin's last night. You know, the new ones you bought from Trent last month, that we had fenced in. They didn't break through, because if they had, they'd've been around some place, but the fence was down an' they clean disappeared. I didn't take time to look much, but Ramsay and Joe're out lookin' for 'em. We three came right on to town, as we figgered you'd need us more than the cattle did. I guess our hunch was right."

Buck spoke gravely: "That's something we'll have to expect. Let's get out of here, and you can get back to the Circle X." He motioned to Tutt Arnold. "We'll have to get this *hombre* to the doctor. Ordinarily I'd let him shift for himself, but I gotta think of other people's rights. Come on, Arnold."

The man at the table groaned, and his face was white with pain. His left hand was bleeding slowly, but the darkening crimson showed that the wound was congealing. "I can't walk. You'll have to get a wagon to bring me."

"Wagon, hell!" Cash said. "Any man that puts up a fight an' can stand punishment the way you did, can walk a short piece to the doctor." He took him under the arm, and Big Ike took the other side. "Come on, we'll help you." Groaning and protesting, the now-broken Arnold got to his feet.

"Arnold, I could put you behind bars for disturbing the peace," Buck said, "but I won't. Out of respect for that clip you fetched me on the jaw, I'll be square with you. Regardless of what your virtues may or may not be . . . and I reckon you're a pretty mean skunk . . . you can hit like a wild cayuse kicks when you get the chance. It's the first time Buck Thomas ever went down for the count and, in spite of my better reasoning, I can't help but admire you for it."

"Jail or no jail," Cash said, "this galoot ain't goin' to do no harm for some time . . . not with both wings on the bum, he ain't."

As they reached the door, Buck turned to the bartender, who had been watching them, afraid to speak. "Take my advice, barkeep, and clean out your joint regular from now on. There's a bad bunch of *hombres* hangin' out here, an', if you don't watch your step, I'll close you up."

"Yeah" — Slim Rollins put in a parting shot as he hesitated at the door — "you better get religion and get good, barkeep. If you don't, somebody'll be puttin' you to bed with a shovel, an' the minister'll be sayin' slow words over your lifeless corpse."

CHAPTER
TWELVE

For a week all had been peaceful and Buck chafed at the inactivity. He'd had no word from the ranch, so he concluded everything was going all right there and his presence not required. Each day Buck made several tours of the town, but everything seemed quiet and aside from "gentling down" a couple of drunken cowpunchers, Buck might have been in the most effete, cultured city of the East for all the action the job of being sheriff afforded him. Several times he had entered the Silver Dollar Saloon, but the few patrons who were there greeted him with the respect that is born of fear, and not the slightest thing happened to which he could take exception. However, there was an ominous atmosphere about La Roda and Buck had a grim foreboding that all was not right. It was too quiet — like the lull that precedes a terrific storm.

Buck rose early one sultry morning and emerged in search of breakfast from the room that served as his office and living quarters over Houghton's General Store. Seating himself at the rough, board counter in one of the town's restaurants, he ordered coffee and pancakes, and rolled a cigarette to kill time till the food was ready. His eye chanced to light on a copy of the

188

Albuquerque *Evening Times*, and something in the headlines drew his attention. He pulled the paper, which was several days old, in front of him. There, in large black capitals, were the words: **SHERIFF OF OTERO COUNTY MYSTERIOUSLY MURDERED**. Followed the sub-headlines, the date and then the story:

> Citizens of Escalona, Utero County, were awakened at midnight last evening by the sound of shots proceeding from the vicinity of Sheriff Winfield's office. No one thought of the matter, however, as the El Paso & Northeastern Express had pulled in but a short time before, and it was judged that a party of cowmen, returning from Chicago, were indulging in a little hilarity.
>
> Upon investigation this morning, Sheriff Winfield's riddled body was found stretched across his doorway. He had died almost instantly, as any one of several bullets would have proved fatal. No clue was left to show who had committed the dastardly deed, and by the time the body was found the murderer could have been miles away.

The paper had followed newspaper tradition and put the story in the first paragraph for the benefit of those who cared to read no further. Then followed the article in detail. Buck read it through to the end and was about to lay the paper down, when another, smaller headline at the side of the page caught his eye. There, in small black capitals, Buck read: **JAIL DELIVERY AT**

MESCALERO RESERVATION. The article was dated two days before the date of the murder article and went on to say that a party of twenty Apaches had made their escape from the Mescalero Jail by sawing through the bars. How saws were procured was unknown, but it was thought that the jailer, who was being held pending an investigation, was bribed to let them through. Being unarmed, most of the Indians were quickly rounded up by soldiers from the Government Barracks. However, six of the Indians headed by one Kicking Horse had left the main party with a body of white men, the captured Apaches reported, and a further search was instituted that resulted in the finding of the seven Apache bodies at the foot of the Sacramento Mountains, hanging to trees. The bodies were quite cold and had been dead for some time, when found. The paper continued:

It will be remembered that Kicking Horse was the Indian who headed the party that went on the warpath a few months back and killed D. A. Flint, well-known New Mexico cattleman, when he made a brave last stand against them in the desert. Strange to say, the Indians who accompanied Kicking Horse at that time were the ones who were hanged with him.

It was at first suspected that friends of Flint's committed the lynchings out of revenge, but, if so, why were the other Indians allowed to escape, too? It may be that this couldn't be prevented in the rush to get away. The captured Apaches say they know nothing except that the saws were furnished to them by Kicking Horse.

Another supposition has to do with one Bartley Lannon, known as Black Bart, who served a term for cattle stealing in the State Penitentiary of New Mexico some years ago. He it was who was suspected of heading the war party at the time of the Flint killing, but shortly afterward, being taken into custody by the authorities of Austin, Texas, he produced an unshakable alibi.

As nothing could be proved against Lannon at the time, he was released, before a proper investigation could be made. The night of his release, a bank was blown open and a small amount of cash procured. The next day Black Bart could not be found. Perhaps he had something to do with both the jail release and the bank robbery. *¿Quién sabe?*

At this moment the pancakes and coffee arrived and Buck slowly laid the paper down as he started to eat.

He whistled softly to himself as he mused: *It sure looks like Black Bart's work. Sheriff Winfield and Kicking Horse and the other braves . . . the only ones who could prove Black Bart had anything to do with the raid on Escalona when Winfield hid behind the milk cans, or with Dad Flint's death. Too bad Winfield didn't have the nerve to shoot it out with Black Bart that day. Black Bart's sure enough covering up his trail. First he knocks off Kicking Horse, then Winfield. He's traveling west. With Wolf Lannon dead, too, there isn't anyone can prove anything on him, except that Mariposa girl. I sure wish she wasn't a woman.* His gray eyes steeled at the thought of what he'd do if she could be made to talk.

Buck rose and tightened his belt. *Yep, Black Bart Lannon, you're sure travelin' in this direction, an' I hope to get news of you soon,* he said to himself. A sort of holy light gleamed in his eyes at the prospect of a finish fight. He stopped at the doorway of the restaurant and, taking his guns from their scarred and battered holsters, looked carefully over them as he spun the cylinders to see that the mechanism was working smoothly. *Black Bart must have a right smart crowd of badmen with him to get away with anything like that Winfield killing and the Apache hangings. I reckon it would be wise thinking on my part to get Cash into La Roda . . . yes, and Slim and Big Ike, too. I might be needing some help right soon. Now that I think of it, there was a powerful lot of new faces in town yesterday. None of 'em looked very law-abidin', either.*

He emerged from the doorway of the restaurant, and, as he did so, he heard shouts. Glancing back, Buck saw an excited crowd of people hurrying in his direction. They started to talk before they came up to him.

"Well, Sheriff," the foremost man said, "you're kinda sleepin' on your job, ain't ye?"

Buck looked him straight in the eye till the man quailed, as the others gathered around. Then he inquired calmly: "What's excitin' you-all? Somebody tryin' to set our town on fire, or something?"

"Worse than that." — "Murder's been done." — "Lawyer Higgins is dead, an' he ain't died nat'ral." A number of excited voices vouchsafed the information.

Buck started, in spite of himself. For a second he stared unbelievingly into the circle of wide-eyed men. "You're a hell of a sheriff, you are!" somebody at the back of the crowd sneered. The words brought Buck back to normal.

"None of that kind of palaver," he said sternly as his hand dropped to his holster. "Who said that?" No one answered, and Buck continued. "You, Chet Wiggins, you appear to be aching to talk and you're about the only man in the crowd that hasn't been stampeded out of your senses. Tell me about it. Who discovered it?"

"Well," Wiggins said, "I went down to see Higgins this mornin' . . ." He broke off for a moment, then went on confusedly: "You know me an' the missus ain't been pullin' so well in double halter o' late. It all come about over that time I drank some moonshine, an' it made me kinda foolish for a while, I guess . . ."

"I'm not interested in your family troubles at home," Buck interrupted. "Get on with your story and tell me about Higgins."

"Well, when I stopped at Higgins's door I didn't get no answer . . ." Wiggins broke off again, and then went on. "You see, as I explained before, I came home kinda feelin' my oats one night from a jug o' moonshine I'd been soppin' up. Well, the old lady was kinda riled when I come in drunk, because I clean forgot a spool of Number Sixty cotton thread she told me to bring her when I left that mornin' . . . was it Number Sixty, or was it Number Sixteen, I clean forget. Wait a minute." He fished a dirty scrap of paper from an inner pocket and consulted it a minute. "Nope, I was right. It was Number Sixty . . ."

Buck was exasperated. "Never mind about the thread, Wiggins. Get on with your story."

"Well, as I was sayin' before you interrupted me, I rapped at Higgins's door, an' I got no answer, so I turned the knob. You see, Buck, when I left that mornin' the trouble started, Mirandy says to get her this thread I'm tellin' 'bout. Well, I got in early that night, 'bout midnight, I guess, an' I'd clean forgot to buy her thread. She was kinda put out about it, I guess . . . not real mad like sometimes . . . but put out, you know how. Anyway, she breaks our new gilt-and-silver mirror over my head. From then on, we had some words. Not that nothing was said, we talked things over reasonable-like, only it made her kinda peeved when I busted her on the jaw with the alarm clock. Women are like that, ain't they? Get riled at nothin'. Anyway, she ups and says she's goin' to get a *devorce*, an' all because I took a little weeny drink o' moon . . ."

Buck had at first been inclined to let Wiggins tell the story in his own way, but he saw he was losing time. "Wiggins," he said angrily, "I'm not aimin' to hear about your drinking. You've been drinking this morning, or you'd be able to talk sensible."

Wiggins eyed him in wide-eyed indignation. "I ain't had a drink this mornin'. Leastwise, not much. Coupla pints, mebbe."

194

"Get on with your story," Buck roared, "and don't talk about anything else but Higgins."

Wiggins looked at Buck in hurt astonishment. "Well, ain't I tellin' it? Higgins? That's just who I been talkin' 'bout. Well, Mirandy goes to Higgins to get this here *devorce*. I didn't like that none, 'cause she only let me sleep home 'bout three night outta the week, an' the meals weren't ever got reg'lar-like no more, so I promised to let her subscribe reg'lar to the *Fireside Companion* an' we fixed it up thataway. Us men allus have to give in to the weaker sex . . . besides I like to read that there magazine myself. It's got a lot in it about dukes an' earls an' such. Anyways, I goes up to Lawyer Higgins to tell him everything is runnin' smooth as greased wagon wheels again an' to tear up them *devorce* papers . . ."

But Buck had already turned away and was striding furiously down the street in the direction of Higgins's office with the crowd following. Chet Wiggins turned and waddled after him.

"Buck," he said, catching up and hurrying his fat bowlegs over the ground, "don't you want to hear about the murder?" Buck looked straight ahead without speaking as he hurried along the walk. Wiggins said: "As I was sayin', I knocked at Higgins's door, an' I didn't get no answer, so I turned the knob, expectin' him to say . . . 'Come in.' But when I got the door all the way open, they wa'n't no one there. So I closed it again, an' go back along the hall, where I meet Dummy Jack. I ask him where Higgins is, but he doesn't answer me. I plumb forgot he was deef an' dumb. While I was trying to get him to talk, Jim Marvel comes runnin' up the stairs with the doctor an' a lotta people. It was him, Jim Marvel, what had discovered the body. Then, I come out with a lotta people follerin' me, all excited-like about Higgins . . . ain't it funny, Buck, about him and me havin' names that all sounded alike? They was Firkins an' Perkins an' . . . an' . . . I forgot the other. I was sayin' to Mirandy one day, men that have names that sound alike must be all from one big family. Them's the kind, I says to her, that becomes famous an' rich someday. She says to me that she ain't never heard no name that sounded exactly the same to her as mine. I tried to explain, right in this town there's Higgins, but she wasn't convinced. Women is dumb-like, sometimes, ain't they? But Higgins now . . . I knew right away you'd want first-hand information about Higgins's bein' killed, so I hurries right to you. Mebbe now, I wish he hadn't been murdered thataway. Mirandy poured scaldin' coffee on me this mornin' before I left, an' I judge somethin's upset her again. You see" — Wiggins was almost running to keep up with Buck — "when she gets them playful fits, I allus know it's a forerunner to a storm, an' I was thinkin' mebbe it's be a good plan to get that *devorce* paper anyway, an' keep it handy-like, in case she gets real mad some time. But it's too late now, I guess . . ."

CHAPTER
THIRTEEN

When Buck ascended the stairs of the two-story building that held Lawyer Higgins's office, he found a crowd of people around the door. He elbowed his way through the throng and went inside the office, which was empty. From an inner office, Buck heard the sound of voices and he made his way through the door into what had served as Higgins's living quarters. Dr. Waverly, Jim Marvel, a ranch owner, and two citizens of La Roda, were sitting around the body.

The doctor looked up at his entrance and nodded. "Bad business, eh, Sheriff?"

"Sure is. Any idea who did it?"

"No," the doctor answered. "We're leaving the discovery of the murderer to you."

Buck flushed. "Well, I'm not going to leave anything undone to find the coward." He turned to Jim Marvel. "I understand you found the body, Jim. Tell me about it. I tried to get the story out of Chet Wiggins, but that fat-headed numbskull couldn't tell me anything."

"They ain't much to tell," Marvel said. "I came in to see Higgins about a land deal he's handlin' for me, but, when I come into the office, he wasn't there. I was in something of a hurry to get back an', as I was a mite early, I judged that he was still asleep. Lots of times before I came in early like that and I allus went in and waked him up, when the outer door was unlocked, as it generally is. So this mornin', not wantin' to lose any time, I walked right on through, an' there he is a-lyin' on the floor, an' that knife stickin' up between his shoulders. I rushed out and got the doctor, an', when I come back, Chet Wiggins was talkin' to Dummy Jack. He followed me into the room and took one look at the body an' set up a howl of murder, like he was bein' killed himself. I quieted him down and told him to go get you. I suppose he stopped and talked to everybody on the street before he found you."

Buck knelt down and examined the body where it lay before an opened safe. The weapon was of the ordinary variety listed in the Sears-Roebuck catalog under the nomenclature of "Hunting Knives". It was embedded nearly to the hilt in Higgins's body, which lay in a sticky, black pool, telling how thoroughly the knife had done its work.

Buck stretched his hand to the handle of the knife, which quivered under his touch.

"Don't remove that," the doctor warned. "We haven't held the inquest yet."

"I'm not," Buck said. "Just wanted to see how solid it was. It sure took a powerful arm to drive that knife in so solid, at that angle. Big man, too."

He rose and went to the safe. It was clean, not a scrap of paper to be found. "It looks like the killing was done for robbery," Buck said. "I don't understand that, though. Higgins was telling me just the other day that he never kept any money here to amount to anything." He glanced up and back at the door. "Looks to me like Higgins had been kneeling before the safe, putting something away, or taking something out," Buck said slowly, "when the murderer crept in behind him and drove the knife into his body before he had time to turn and put up a fight. There isn't any sign of a struggle."

"That's what I think," the doctor affirmed. "Death was almost instantaneous."

"How long has he been dead?" Buck asked.

"I should judge the murder was committed about midnight. Death occurred probably two or three minutes later. The murderer had plenty of time to get out of town."

"Mebbe so," Buck admitted, "but I got a hunch, Doc, that the man who did it hasn't left town yet."

"What gives you that impression?"

"Don't ask me for a reason, Doc, because I haven't got this thing all worked out in my mind yet. To begin with, though, now that I've been thinking it over a mite, I reckon there's something deeper than just plain robbery back of this killing. If it was just money the murderer was after, he'd have left papers scattered around and only taken the cash. There isn't a bit of paper in sight. That means somebody in this town is a heap interested in somebody else's affairs, an' they're stickin' around to watch developments."

The doctor nodded his head. "Perhaps there is more than a grain of sense in what you say. It's up to you, Sheriff, to help those developments along, and you can't make yourself more solid with the citizens of La

Roda than by doing the developing yourself. The matter is put squarely up to you, Buck Thomas."

"I'm not doing any talking, Doc, about what I aim to do. Time enough to begin talking after the murderer's caught."

"You're right. And now," the doctor said briskly, "I guess it's time that I, in my official capacity of coroner, hold the inquest. Will you go out and bring in twelve citizens of La Roda to serve as coroner's jury, Sheriff?"

Buck left the room and within a few minutes had picked a jury that he brought back with him. The jury looked over the body, turned it over, and examined it from all angles, after the knife had, with some difficulty, been withdrawn. After a few minutes' talk with the doctor in a short time they returned a report that Higgins had "come to his death from a knife wound through the heart, the blow delivered by some person unknown. Motive for murder, also murderer unknown."

"Well, I've got to be getting on my way," the doctor said. "Will one of you men stay with the body till I send the undertaker here?"

"I'll stay, Doc," Buck said. "I'm going to hang around a while, anyway, and look this room over. Mebbe I can uncover something we overlooked."

The doctor hurried out, followed by the other men. In a few seconds, Buck was alone. He looked at the still form now laid out on the couch. As he gazed at the white face, thoughts of the deaths of Jimmie and Dad Flint and Kicking Horse and Sheriff Winfield crept into his mind. Those killings, he was sure, had been the work of Black Bart Lannon. Could Black Bart have

200

anything to do with this murder, too? The thought persisted that he had, but Buck tried to drive it out of his mind. So far as Buck knew, Black Bart had no fight with Higgins. And yet, Black Bart was traveling west . . .

He shook his head doubtfully as he examined the floor, safe, and surrounding walls, but there was nothing to tell Buck what he wanted to know. He examined the knife that had killed Higgins, but there were no marks on it to identify it from any other knife of the same make. He dropped to the floor in search of dusty footprints or anything of the kind, but it was no use. So many men had tramped around the room, that the floor was covered with dusty footprints, no one recognizable from another.

Buck rose and leaned against the doorjamb. His face was furrowed with thought as he sifted some Durham into a wisp of paper. As he rolled the cigarette, he saw, from the corner of his eye, something on the jamb that set his heart thumping like a trip hammer. He turned and there, caught on a rough sliver where the wood was worn, was a heavy woolen thread such as might have been torn from a red serape when its wearer rushed through the door.

CHAPTER
FOURTEEN

Buck examined the red thread closely for a few minutes, and then folded it into his handkerchief and placed it carefully inside his shirt pocket, buttoning down the flap as he did so. Suddenly Buck heard a noise from the other room. So tense were his nerves that, without thinking, his hands flashed to his hips and came up with his .45s ready for action. It was only Chet Wiggins.

"Hey, Buck," he said, "here's the undertaker comin'." Then, noticing the guns: "Don't shoot. What's the matter, Buck?" Wiggins's knees were shaking as he asked the question, but at Buck's grin, as the guns were put away, he forced a sickly smile to his fat face.

"I didn't know who it might be, Chet." Buck laughed. "I wasn't aimin' to take any chances."

In a few minutes the undertaker came in and Buck left the room, followed by Wiggins.

"Did I ever tell you," Wiggins said, " 'bout my brother Peleg killin' a man that way? That was in Nebrasky, afore we come down here. Peleg wandered into the jail one day. They wasn't nobody there when he went in, an' he picks up a gun that was layin' there. Just then the jailer comes runnin' in, an' Peleg gets excited an' pulls the trigger. It comes as a sort o' surprise to the jailer . . . anyways he had a funny, surprised look on his face when they laid him out. I don't think he was lookin' for Peleg himself. You see, Peleg was just escaped from the state asylum for the feebleminded, and folks was lookin' for him. Peleg was allus gettin' out an' doin' suthin' like that, an' folks knew what to expect. That is, ev'rybody but the jailer's family. I allus had an idee they held a grudge against Peleg. O' course, they wa'n't nothin' we could do, but some folks can't never understan' that an accident's an accident. Peleg was allus up to suthin'. I likes to mind the time when he stole the steam roller from the Public Works Department of Lincoln. It was brand new then, an' bein' as Peleg never had no chance to get rides much he gets on the steam roller when the engineer ain't lookin', an' knocks him on the head. Away he goes an' you'd laugh to split to see how horses was bein' chased up on the sidewalks. Folks were kinda indignant 'bout that, too. Seems like some people can't never take a joke."

Wiggins rambled on into Buck's unhearing ears, as he puffed alongside of him. Buck was paying no attention to what Wiggins was saying and finally the garrulous fat man dropped behind. Buck could think of nothing but the red thread that reposed so safely in his pocket. That *was* a clue. Black Bart Lannon must be in La Roda. Buck figured, if he wasn't keeping out of sight, he'd be found at the Silver Dollar Saloon sooner or later.

If I only knew what he looks like, Buck said to himself as he started for the Silver Dollar. *Well, I can mebbe find somebody in town who knows him.*

At that moment he heard the sound of galloping hoofs behind him, and, looking around, Buck saw a young Mexican boy astride a horse, tearing along at a terrific speed. The boy was wild-eyed and his face was the color of ashes. In the rear, whooping and yelling, came a group of riders, their horses' hoofs raising a veritable cloud of dust in the road. As they tore by, Buck could see they were gaining on the boy. He broke into a run, but the riders soon passed him and left the town at the far end where the street spread out into open country. As Buck ran, he tried to keep his eyes on the riders, but they disappeared around a bend of the road in a cloud of dust.

Passing Houghton's General Store, Buck saw a lean cayuse at the hitching post. It took him but a minute to untie the horse, leap into the saddle, and be on his way. Far ahead he heard shouts that boded no good for the young Mexican, and, taking his gray sombrero in his hand, Buck whipped the beast to greater efforts.

As he swung around the bend in the road, he saw a sight that made his heart stand still. There under a tree with a rope around his neck stood the boy, precariously balancing himself on the saddle of one of the horses to which the tips of his toes just reached. The other end of the rope, which had been flung over an overhanging limb of the tree, was tied to the saddle of another horse upon which was seated a man who Buck knew to be one of the regulars among the Silver Dollar patrons. The lynchers were so engrossed in their work that they didn't notice Buck till he was almost on top of them. As he rode into their midst, the horse upon which the young Mexican stood was being slowly led away. As the horse moved from under the tree, the victim fighting for life stretched his toes to the utmost that he might keep the rope from tightening about his neck, thus retaining his slim hold on life. Just as the body was about to swing off into space, Buck's hand darted to his holster.

Crack! Crack! Twice the long blue gun vomited fire and smoke from the muzzle and the boy dropped like a limp rag to the ground, the rope cut in two places. As they pulled the horse back to its haunches, Buck's other gun flashed into his hand.

"I reckon you-all know I mean business," his stentorian tones rang out, "when I ask you not to pull no guns. The first man that makes a break for his holster gets plugged through. I may be new at sheriffing, but you-all know that I'm not new at throwin' lead when I get riled. You're a brave bunch, aren't you?" Buck sneered, "a-pickin' on a poor Mexican. Next thing you know you'll be getting real tough an' murderin' women an' little children."

"Aw, the damn' little skunk had it comin' to him," one of the men growled.

"In your opinion, mebbe," Buck retorted, "but not in mine, nor in the county's that gives me my authority."

"That's a lot of talk, Buck Thomas, but how d'you know you can back it up. What's to prevent us from rushin' you an' takin' you're cannons away an' rubbin' 'em under your nose . . . eh?" another man cried.

"If you take my advice, you won't try it," Buck drawled. "Mebbe you might get me, and then again mebbe you mightn't. If you did, there's the county behind me, an' behind the county's the governor, an' after that . . . well, the U.S. government can clean you out if it has to. I don't reckon this affair'll go any further than me, though," he finished sharply.

A volley of sharp reports blended into a ragged crash and Buck heard the vicious whine of a bullet zipping by his ear, while another tore its harmless way through the crown of his sombrero.

"I told you not to make any breaks," Buck said through the blue smoke that curled from the mouths of his guns, his voice cold with rage. Two of the men were writhing in pain as they nursed the arms through which Buck's bullets had torn. "Another thing . . . you aren't hurt so bad but that a few weeks will put you in shape to hang some more babies. Next time I won't aim so carefully, an' mebbe then your friends will be walking slowly behind you to a lot in the cemetery. I tell you men, right here an' now, these necktie parties have got to stop. I aim to enforce the law, an' the quicker you realize it, the better for you. Mebbe you could string a man up before for running off with a few cattle or stealin' a horse, but the law hasn't told me anything about it yet."

206

Some of the men looked as though they would disobey, but a look at Buck's set face determined them otherwise and in a few minutes they were riding far ahead of Buck and his three prisoners.

CHAPTER
FIFTEEN

"Keep those two galoots locked up," Buck told the jailer, "till their wounds heal. Better get the doctor right away and see how badly they're shot up. I could charge them with shooting with intent to kill, but I won't, bein' as I've got nothing else on 'em. They won't be out for a few weeks yet, an', if anything further against 'em crops up, I got a hunch it'll crop up right soon."

"How about the Mexican?"

"Put him in the cell at the far end. The one with the bed in it. He's only a kid, an' I guess we can afford to treat him a mite better than the two he-buzzards."

Buck followed the boy and the jailer down to the cell in which the young Mexican was to be placed.

"All right, Frank," he said, "you can run along to your other prisoners now. I aim to stay here and talk to this young Mex for a bit. By the way, have somebody return that cayuse to Houghton's store. I don't aim to be accused of horse stealin'."

The jailer nodded and turned to go. Buck shook some tobacco into a paper, rolled, and lighted it. He didn't speak till the cigarette was burned clear down to his lips as he stood and eyed the boy who had sunk down on the bed. Finally Buck tossed the butt of his cigarette out of the iron-grated window.

"Well, Mariposa," he said cheerfully, "you seem to be playing at bein' a man, now. Hair cut off and everything. What's the idea? These clothes might make some people believe you're a man, but not Buck Thomas. I heard you escaped from the Conejo Lures jail. Sawed your way out, didn't you? Plumb funny how people in jails get saws lately."

The girl raised her large black eyes to Buck's, and then dropped them again without answering him.

"Won't talk, eh?" Buck said gently. "All right. We'll let it go for another time. Mebbe you'll tell me how you come to get into that hanging scrap."

The girl looked at Buck again. "Ah, señor," she said, "I did not keel the señor Higgins."

" 'Course you didn't," Buck answered. "But how come they thought you did?"

The girl didn't answer for a while, then as she raised her eyes to Buck's: "I was standing, señor, near a doorway where a big crowd of mens was collected. I did not know eet at the time, but they were waiting for the . . . what you call heem? . . . the undertaker, to bring forth the body of the señor Higgins. When the body had left, the crowd, too, went away. But two mens stay behind. They were ver' dronk, señor. Quick one man seizes my arm. 'Where you come from, boy?' he say. I get, oh, so frighten', señor. I cannot answer. Then the other man say . . . 'Heesa stranger. May-bee he keel Higgins.' I am near perish with fright, señor, when the first man say . . . 'A murderer always ree-turns to the scene of the crime.' Other man come up, then more, and the two mens say that I keel the *señor* Higgins. At first they don't believe, and they ask me, did I keel heem? I take my courage an' I say 'No,' like that, 'no.' Then the first man heets me an' I drop to the ground. When I geet up, the second man say . . . 'Confess that you keel Higgins.' I say . . . 'No!' Then second man knock me to the ground. When I get up, I am, oh, so scare', *señor*, an' the man hurt me terr-rible. Then they tell me again . . . 'Confess . . . ' an' I do not like to be heet again, *señor*, so I say . . . 'Yes, I keel Higgins.'" Throughout the recital of the tale, the girl's eyes flashed dramatically, but when she had finished, she sank down on the bed in tears.

"So that's the way they got the confession. An' then," Buck prompted, "what happened?"

The girl brushed the tears from her eyes and raised her head. "Then somebody say . . . 'String heem up . . . ' and they start to talk weeth big voices, but, when they talk, I see my chance. Then I run an' jump on my horse, but mans come after and catch me. You know the rest, *señor*. Eef you have not arrive in time, Mariposa would be dead." She stopped a moment, and then went on. "You have save my life, *señor*, an' I am thankful. I would do anything for you."

"All right," Buck flashed, "tell me where Black Bart Lannon is."

An inscrutable look veiled the girl's dark eyes. "That I do not know, *señor* Buck."

"You're lying, Mariposa," Buck said sternly. "You do know, but you won't tell. Black Bart Lannon's some place around La Roda. If he wasn't, you wouldn't be here. What are you doing here, anyway?"

"I do not like Conejo Lures, so I come to leeve in La Roda."

"Oh, you've come to live in La Roda, eh? An' in boy's clothes . . . it ain't likely," Buck scoffed dryly.

"But I have not had the time to change, señor. Boy's clothes are so easy for to make the travel."

"Well, you make it sound plausible, Mariposa, but I don't believe you."

"But weel you let me go, Señor Buck?" The girl caught at his hand as she rose from the bed and looked at him with pleading eyes.

"Not till you tell me everything you know about Black Bart Lannon."

"Ah, I should like to, señor, but I cannot . . . I do not know."

"More lies, Mariposa," Buck said. "Well, I'll have to keep you locked up here till you feel more like talking. You'll be more comfortable, anyway." He turned and strode into the street, after locking the door behind him and leaving the key with the jailer.

Buck made his way along the rough boardwalk till he came to the Silver Dollar. As he entered, his eyes met a sight that nearly took his breath away. There were only a few men at the bar, but among them was a tall, dark man. In the reflection of the mirror, Buck noted his high, greasy cheek bones and the beady eyes that were constantly shifting. Across his left shoulder was draped a magnificent red serape!

Buck stared at him several minutes till the man, feeling the scrutiny of the piercing eyes, swung easily around till he faced the doorway where Buck stood. For a second neither moved. Buck was standing with his hands on his hips, waiting for the red-seraped one to make the first move. Suddenly the man made a snake-like movement, but Buck was too quick for him. As if by magic, his guns flashed into his hands, but he didn't shoot.

"You're right fast with them shootin' irons," the man snarled, "an' I don't see no call to be shovin' 'em at me thataway, when a man reaches for his tobacco." He folded his arms across his breast.

"Tobacco, hell," Buck spat back at him. "You were reachin' for your guns."

"Mebbe you think I was." The words came coolly, as if he wasn't greatly concerned.

Buck looked at him, puzzled. *Could this be . . . ?* "Your name, stranger?" Buck's words snapped out like the crack of a whip.

"My name? My name's Bart Lannon, but mostly I get called Black Bart." There was a mocking light in the beady eyes as the name left his lips.

CHAPTER
SIXTEEN

"Black Bart Lannon," Buck said, each word sounding like the report of a pistol, "you're under arrest."

"What's the charge?" The snaky eyes gleamed questions at Buck.

"Several charges. Mostly murders . . . Jimmie Flint, Dad Flint, George Higgins, and some others. There's some robberies against you, too, but I don't reckon you'll ever come to trial for them." Buck spoke the words meaningfully as he slipped one of the guns into a holster and reached into his hip pocket for handcuffs. "Hold out your hands," he ordered. Lannon was at first disinclined to obey, but one look at Buck's determined face and the unwavering muzzle of the long .45 made him change his mind. He held out his arms and the handcuffs were snapped on. "Now, come on," Buck jerked out, "get movin'."

Without further parley, Lannon preceded Buck through the door. He stepped in front of the Silver Dollar for his horse, but Buck prodded him on with his gun.

"You can do without your horse. I haven't got mine, an', anyway, that horse'll be a pre-historic pile of bones by the time you're able to use him again."

213

Straight for the courthouse over the jail Buck walked his prisoner, not once taking his eyes from Lannon or removing the gun where it prodded into the captive's back. Past rows of staring faces they walked, but Buck looked neither to right nor left till the two reached their destination.

When they arrived, Judge Hosmer was asleep in a chair in front of the jail. He was a thin, irascible, domineering man who meant well, but who was continually in fear that somebody would interfere with his authority.

"Wake up, Judge!" Buck cried to the slumbering man.

The judge stirred, and the lids of his eyes fluttered open. He closed and then opened them again, looking up at Buck and his prisoner, in anger at being so rudely awakened.

"No need to yell at me that way, Sheriff," he muttered. "I can hear you. What do you want now?"

"I want to swear out a warrant against Black Bart Lannon," Buck said, motioning to his prisoner. The judge looked at Lannon a moment, and then started for the door. Buck followed with Lannon into the building, but paused at the door leading to the cell-block.

"Just a minute, Judge, till I lock this *hombre* up!" Buck called.

"No, bring him along, Sheriff. I may want to question the man myself."

Swearing under his breath, but knowing it wouldn't further his interests, nor accelerate the working of the law, Buck complied with the judge's order. Turning, he

214

drove Lannon ahead of him up the stairs till they reached the judge's office.

The judge entered and sat down at his desk, took his spectacles out of his pocket, and placed them carefully on his nose. Reaching into his desk, he procured some papers, took the stopper out of the ink bottle, and, pen in hand, turned to Buck.

"Now," he said, "what are the charges against this man?"

"Murder," Buck answered. "The murder of D. A. Flint and James Flint. There's some others . . ."

"Have you proof of this?" Judge Hosmer cut in coldly.

"Plenty of it," Buck answered.

Judge Hosmer turned to Lannon, who hadn't spoken. "Is this true?" he asked.

"It sure ain't," Lannon answered. "Let him furnish his proof."

"In the first place," Buck said, "you murdered Jimmie Flint, then you incited the Apaches to revolt, an' murdered old Dad Flint. I'm plumb sure of those two murders."

"Where's your proof?" Lannon insisted, his eyes sparkling with hate.

"That's right, Sheriff," the judge said, "let's have your proof that this man committed these murders. Besides, if I remember rightly, James Flint was killed in Mexico, and Dad Flint in Otero County. Have you any power from the authorities of those two places to take this action?"

Buck lost his temper. "Damn it, Judge," he shouted, "I've got all the authority I need, and you know it! There's no damn' sense in your holding up the proceedings this way. Fact is, I can lock this man up without no warrant, if I take a notion to."

"There's no sense of getting angry, Sheriff," the judge said pacifyingly, overawed by Buck's tone. "All I want is proof that this man has done what you say."

Buck cooled down as he reviewed the situation. Where was his proof? He was sure he had the right man, but could he convince a jury of that fact? There was but one thing to do. Get Mariposa to tell what she knew.

Black Bart Lannon laughed a short, mean laugh. "I reckon the sheriff is some excited, Judge, but maybe I can help clear up this here situation. Fact is, I reckon he's got me mixed up with my brother Wolf. He's a plumb bad *hombre*, an' mebbe he's the one that done them murders the sheriff tells about."

"You see, Sheriff Thomas, there is a great likelihood of your being mistaken," Judge Hosmer said. "Now, if you could produce some proof . . ." His voice trailed off as he looked to Buck for evidence that Lannon was the murderer.

Buck was in a quandary. "To tell the truth, I haven't got much actual proof, but I'm sure certain I've got the right man."

"Certain," the judge said sarcastically, "certain. That won't go very far as evidence."

Buck pulled his handkerchief from his pocket and spread it out under the judge's nose as he showed him the piece of woolen thread from the red serape.

"There's your evidence!" Buck cried.

The judge looked blankly at the thread. "What's this?" he asked.

"That thread," Buck explained, "was torn from the serape of the man who murdered George Higgins some time last night. I found it sticking on a splinter in Higgins's office where it probably got brushed off when the murderer was running away."

"Even so," Judge Hosmer said, looking at the thread with interest, then up at Buck, "what does that prove against this man?"

"Look for yourself," Buck said impatiently. "Black Bart Lannon wears a red serape . . . he always wears one."

For the fraction of a second, Lannon's face blanched, then he recovered himself as he said nervously: "That don't prove nothin' again' me, Sheriff. They's a lot o' those red serapes worn. I ain't the only man who's got one." He glanced out of the window, near which he was standing. "Look out o' the window, an' you'll see what I mean." Sure enough, there, strolling along the sidewalk on the opposite side of the street, was a man with a red serape. "You see," Lannon said, the color coming back into his face, "these here red serapes don't mean nothin'."

"Nonetheless," Buck said, "the man who killed Lawyer Higgins wore a red serape, an' I'm lockin' you up on suspicion, charging you with the murders I spoke about."

"That's what a man gets for havin' a brother that ain't law-abidin'!" Black Bart cried. "I heerd before that I was accused of committin' some murders that Wolf done. He wears a serape like this, and we look alike, too."

"Don't try to throw the blame on your brother," Buck said sternly. "Wolf's dead, and you know it."

Lannon tried to look. surprised, but he didn't succeed very well as he said hypocritically: "Poor Wolf, I allus knowed he'd come to some bad end. What happened?"

"You know what happened," Buck said sternly, "just as you know what happened to Jimmie Flint, Dad Flint, Sheriff Winfield, Kicking Horse, and Lawyer Higgins. There're probably a lot more things you know about, too."

Black Bart's eyes shifted uneasily. "I don't know nothin' about any o' them names you mentioned."

Buck turned to the judge without answering Lannon. "Judge Hosmer, I aim to lock this galoot up 'n' bring him to trial, whether you want to let me do it or not. I advise you to throw your chips in on my deal. If you don't, I'll put this Lannon where he'll be safe an' I can keep an eye on him. Then, I take this business up with somebody bigger'n you. Mebbe after I play my cards, you won't be feelin' so pert. Are you with me, or against me?" Buck finished in threatening tones.

The words took all the fight out of Judge Hosmer. "Why, certainly, Sheriff Thomas," he replied quickly, "I shall be glad to do anything to further the prompt enforcement of the law. What do you wish to be done?"

"I'm lockin' this *hombre* up, downstairs," Buck snapped, "an' it's up to you to draw up all the necessary papers to hold him. I don't know what they are . . . that's your business . . . but I don't want any loopholes left for Lannon to wiggle through. Mebbe, you don't think so, but I'm plumb certain I've got the right man an' I'm going to prove it before many more days go by." Without giving the judge time to answer, he turned to Lannon. "Come on," he said, "you're sleeping behind locked doors tonight." Then he added: "An' for a good many nights to come, too."

"I kin prove," Lannon began, "that I ain't been nowhere near the place any o' them murders was committed . . ."

"Haven't been near the places, eh?" Buck flashed at him. "Then, Black Bart Lannon," he said, chopping every word out short, "how come you know where those places are? You said a mite back that you didn't know anything about any of those murders!"

Lannon saw he had said too much. "What I meant," he began, "is that . . ."

Buck cut him short. "I know what you mean, Lannon, but you're not puttin' it in the right words, an' I'm not aimin' to hear any more of your lies. Get on downstairs, now, you measly hyena, before I kick you down. I get plumb excited every time I look at you an' think of your slimy ways. Get goin'." Lannon turned and stumbled down the stairs with Buck behind him.

As the cell door clanged behind Lannon, he held out his hands to Buck. "Ain'tcha goin' to take these here handcuffs off?" he asked.

"Handcuffs off, hell," Buck said through the grating. "You're lucky you aren't swingin' from a tree this minute without your wantin' those bracelets off your wrists." He turned to the jailer. "Keep an eye on that snake, Frank. He's liable to be kind of slippery, an' he an' his friends have a bad habit of using saws liberal-like."

In spite of his confident manner, Buck knew that something more would have to turn up to furnish the proof that Lannon was the right man. He'd said something about being able to prove he wasn't near the scene of the murders. After all, it might be difficult to convince a jury of Lannon's peers that he *was* guilty. *Well*, Buck said to himself, *Lannon's in a right tight hole now, anyway.*

Buck emerged from the jail door and swung into the street. The rays of the afternoon sun were spreading their golden light over La Roda as he headed in the direction of his office.

"Cripes, what a day," he muttered, his brow furrowed with thought. "A murder in the morning, a necktie party at noon, and Black Bart Lannon in jail by evening. I feel like I've lived a year in the last few hours."

CHAPTER
SEVENTEEN

Buck spent the following day searching La Roda for evidence that might more surely fasten the murder of Higgins on Black Bart, but his efforts were without avail. He talked to Mariposa again but could get no information from the girl. The following morning, remembering that Cash Jordon had mentioned some cattle being stolen, Buck decided to ride over to the Circle X and see if they had been recovered, or if anything had been uncovered that might give a clue to the identity of the rustlers. Buck felt sure that they were all members of Black Bart Lannon's gang. He saddled his horse and within a couple of hours the Circle X hove in view.

As he rode down past the ranch house and around to the bunkhouse, a series of yells and hoots from the direction of the corral greeted his ears. He swung his horse's head around and was just in time to see Big Ike pitching, head foremost, off a frenzied bronco. The tall cowpuncher sailed through the air like a bird and came down sprawling on all fours, digging up the dirt with his nose, as Slim ran out and caught the still-plunging horse. The row of cowpunchers seated on the fence laughed till their merriment nearly caused them to fall off while Big Ike painfully picked himself from the ground, rubbing his shoulder.

The horse was a long, lean, sinewy beast with a snake-like head. "Drat it all," Big Ike said ruefully, "that there Rattler horse throws me every time."

"Lemme show you how to ride 'im." Slim laughed. Big Ike removed his saddle and Slim ran to the fence and pulled down his own saddle. While two of the cowpunchers held Rattler's nose, Slim slipped the saddle on the sweating back and tightened the straps till the horse grunted. Then, with a flying leap, he vaulted onto the horse's back and slid his feet into the stirrups.

"All right. Let 'im go."

There came a squealing, mingled with the roars of the cowpunchers. Slim, on the back of the pitching, squalling, kicking tornado, swung his huge sombrero in defiance of the coiled, steel spring in horse flesh. Swinging with every movement of the horse, he was never in danger of being thrown, even in Rattler's sun-fishiest jumps and stiff-legged pitches. Suddenly Slim settled his hat on his head and, darting his hand into a pocket, produced tobacco and papers. He let the reins drop for a moment to spill the tobacco into the paper, but the trick was too difficult, and, as the paper and tobacco slipped to the ground, his hand fell forward to the saddle.

"Yeah! He pulled leather!" — "You pulled leather!" — came the shouts of derision as Slim slipped out of the saddle and came to the fence.

"Dang it," Slim said, "I can ride Rattler all day long, but just the minute I begin to roll a cigarette, I had to

222

pull leather to keep from bein' throwed. I'll ride 'im yet, you can bet a mess o' lizards on that."

Buck had sat his horse, smiling, while the riding was in process. This was just like the old, happy days when Dad Flint was alive. Cash Jordon turned, and, as he did so, he spied Buck.

"Hello, Buck!" he called. "We've just been gentlin' down them new bronc's you got from Trent. We got 'em all licked but Rattler. He's one tough baby."

Buck answered his greeting and spoke to the rest of the crowd, then turned again to Cash, who had vaulted the fence and come up at his side.

"Cash," he said in low tones, "I got Black Bart . . ."

"No! Did'cha?" Cash said, his eyes wide with astonishment. "Where'd you get him?"

"I walked into the Silver Dollar," Buck said, "an' there he was standin' at the bar, like he didn't have a care in the world. I got the drop on him, slipped the handcuffs on, an' took him over to the jail. Judge Hosmer had one of his meddlin' fits an' he held up the proceedings for a time, but I finally put Black Bart behind the bars."

"Whoopee!" Cash yelled. "I'm mighty glad t'hear it, Buck. So'll the boys be. What comes next?"

"I'm not sure about it, Cash. Lannon denies everything, of course, says he can prove he hasn't been near where the murders took place. He doesn't seem to be worried none, either, an' that bothers me. Of course, we haven't got any real proof . . ." Buck broke off to tell him that Higgins had been killed and about finding the red thread from the serape. He also told him about

223

Kicking Horse and Sheriff Winfield having been murdered.

Cash whistled under his breath. "Yeah, I know about Higgins," he said. "A rider from the Crazy X come by this mornin' an' told us."

"Did you ever locate those cows that were run off, Cash?" Buck said next.

"Yeah. What was left of 'em, leastwise. They were run off by some pikin' hideskinners that ain't got the guts to steal a cow outright 'n' sell them. When the boys found 'em, there was nothin' left but the skinned carcasses. The hides were plumb gone. We couldn't find the ones that did it, though."

"Where'd you find the cattle?" Buck asked.

"Down near the cabin, just the other side of the creek. That's why the boys didn't catch anybody. We never figgered they'd go in that direction. From the looks of things, the gang that run them cattle off has been livin' in the cabin for some days, just waitin' their chance to pull somethin'."

"Get your horse and we'll ride down there and look the place over," Buck said.

In a few minutes, the two men were loping off across the range in the direction of the foothills that dot the approach to the Pinoso Mountains. They rode silently, giving their horses full headway and within an hour and a half swung around north of the Brias Mesas, where they passed a clump of scrub oaks that grew at the bottom of the foothills. Turning to the left, they began a gradual ascent, the horses shouldering their way through a tangled timber wood that ceased suddenly and gave way to a stretch of hardpan. As the two riders moved on, the ground became more stony and the region took on a mountainous aspect. Huge boulders were passed as the ascent became steeper. Suddenly they came to a stop at the edge of a high bluff that descended swiftly till it became the bed of a small stream that twisted its way between rock-strewn banks.

"Down this way it's easier goin'," Cash said, as he turned his horse to the right and started on the downgrade. The horse picked its way carefully, followed by Buck's horse. In a few minutes they passed through a tangle of brushwood and then emerged into an open space of pebbly ground, with here and there a sparse bit of sagebrush springing up. At the edge of the stream, resting on long timbers, stood a small log cabin. Across the creek about half a mile up and surrounded with rock country a patch of meadow gleamed green against the purple mountains.

"I wonder," Cash said as they dismounted, "Why old Dad bought this stretch of land. It's no good for raisin' cattle."

"I asked him that one day," Buck answered, "an' he said he liked it because it was pretty country. He and Missus Flint used to come down here when Jimmie was a baby. He didn't own it then, but, after Missus Flint died, he added it to the ranch land. Dad used to come down here and go fishin'. I think he caught a fish once, too. I guess mostly he kept the land because of his memories."

225

"I saw him down here one day with a pick and shovel," Cash said. "Probably tryin' to scratch some worms out of these rocks to fish with."

They turned and went into the cabin. Everywhere was found evidence of its recent occupancy. An empty tomato can was thrown into one corner and in the middle of the floor, resting upon the dead embers of what had once been a cook stove, was a frying pan holding a few scraps of burned bacon.

"I reckon whoever was here was pretty careful about leavin' tracks," Cash said.

Buck nodded. "Yeah, outside of the fact that we know somebody's been here, we haven't found anything else. Well, let's see what we can find outside."

As they stepped through the door of the cabin, they noticed simultaneously a huge rattlesnake stretched on a flat stone at the edge of the stream, warming itself in the sun. Both men drew their guns and the two reports sounded almost as one. In a second, a headless body was coiling and writhing on the stone, till it slipped off the rock into the stream. They watched it as it floated along, still wiggling, in the swiftly running waters.

"Wonder which of us took the head off." Cash laughed.

"I rather reckon," Buck said, "that we both had a hand in it."

They mounted their horses and forded the stream to the other side, then rode down to the meadowlands. Aside from the blackening carcasses of the cattle, which the skinners had left, they could find nothing to throw light on their search. All afternoon they rode up and down the river in search of tracks, but with no success. It was dusk when they returned to the cabin. They dismounted and went in for a last look. As he crossed the threshold of the door, Buck's eye glanced down to the ground. There, lying in the hollow made by a boot heel, was the butt of a partly finished cigarette. He stooped and picked it up.

"What'd you find?" Cash looked at him curiously.

"Cash, somebody's been here while we were gone. What kind of cigarette papers d'you use?"

"Just the ordinary sort, like everybody does."

Buck opened his hand and showed Cash the butt. "Well, this isn't the ordinary sort." The paper, around the tobacco, was brown, of the wheat-straw variety.

Cash opened his eyes as he gazed at it. "That's one of them 'Mexican Blanket' papers, they calls 'em," he said.

"Yes, sir. Somebody's sure been here."

The two men went out around to the side of the cabin and began to look closely over the ground.

"Here's tracks," Buck said. "We weren't around this way . . ."

A vicious whiz sounded in his ear and a bullet imbedded itself in the side of the cabin as the crack of a rifle was heard overhead. Looking up, they saw a row of evil faces looking down at them from the top of the bank that reared itself high above the cabin roof. Cash and Buck emptied their Colts at the faces as they ran for the shelter of the cabin. It took them but an instant to get there, but a perfect fusillade of bullets spattered around them as they ran.

Cash, being the nearest, reached the cabin first, and, as Buck dashed in close on the heels of the other man, Cash slammed and barred the door.

"Whew," he said, "that was close. Did you get hit?"

"You're sayin' somethin'. No. Did you?"

"No. I don't see how we escaped it, though. We were lucky." They reloaded their guns as they talked.

"Wonder what they'll do next?" Buck said.

"I sure hope they don't take a notion to push this cabin into the stream," Cash replied. "It ain't any too solid built to them timbers."

They looked around at the interior of the cabin. There were two windows, one facing on the stream and the other in the front, near the door, and looking upstream.

"Wish they'd built a window on the hillside," Cash grumbled. "We might be able to get a shot at them galoots."

"Yeah, an' they could get a shot at us, too. We couldn't watch three windows."

They listened, but all was silent outside of the cabin. Suddenly they heard a crashing through the brush on the hill.

"They've been down an' took our horses," Cash said. "Mebbe we can get a shot at 'em before they get to the top of the hill." Buck unbarred the door, and Cash, six-gun in hand, cautiously stuck his nose out. He jerked his head back as a bullet tore its way into the doorjamb.

"They're watchin' us close," Cash said as the door was re-barred.

"I've been thinkin'," said Buck, "that the best thing for us to do is to wait a couple of hours till it gets dark enough to make a break for the open. Mebbe we can get away from 'em in the shadows before the moon comes up bright."

Cash nodded. "We can try it, if they let us alone till then."

For the next two hours the men said little. Their nerves were tense and the strain of waiting became almost unbearable. By the time it was dark enough to make a break for the open, the light of the rising moon had begun to cast its silver light over the hilltops.

Buck looked at the shadowy figure, watching at the other window. "Appears kind of funny to me," he said, "that they don't come down the hill an' try to get a shot at us."

"Guess they's kinda 'fraid of our lead," Cash drawled. "Who d'you think they are?"

"I don't think there're two ways about that," Buck's voice came through the darkness. "It's Lannon's crowd, or I'm a hoot owl. Easy to see Lannon isn't with 'em, or they'd've attacked long ago."

"I crave action," Cash said. "If we wait much longer, the moon will be up full. This here waitin' around is kinda hard on my nerves. Whadda you say, Buck, will we make a break for it?"

Buck nodded and, then remembering that Cash couldn't see him in the gloom of the cabin, said: "Come on, we'll try it."

They slowly unbarred the door, but as they did so, the tip of the moon rose above the hills and flooded the ground in front of the cabin with light. As the two men emerged, a report sounded and a bullet kicked up dust at their feet. They turned and ran back into the cabin. As they closed the door, they could feel a hail of bullets striking all around the cabin.

"Those snakes were sure waitin' for us," Cash panted.

"Yeah," Buck replied, "we'd've been dead men if we tried to make it."

"I've been thinkin'," Cash said, "that mebbe they figure on starvin' us out."

"Well, they got a right smart wait ahead, then," Buck said.

"I don't know," Cash said dryly. "It's been a long stretch since breakfast. I'd sooner be shot than starved."

"Me, too," Buck said, "but we aren't in any immediate danger of starving."

They stood watching, for an hour, speaking only at intervals and waiting for something to happen. Once Buck rose and started to open the door, but a crash of lead warned him back. The moon was high in the heavens by this time and it was almost as light as day, as the light streaming through the two windows showed the tense faces of the men standing near in the shadow.

Suddenly Buck said: "I smell smoke. Did you drop your cigarette into anything?"

Cash sniffed the air for a moment. "No, I allus put my cigarettes out with my heel." At that moment a crackling sound was heard at the back of the cabin.

"The snakes are burnin' us out!" Buck cried. "That's their game. That's what they were waitin' for."

Cash moved over to the corner of the cabin. "Yep, I kin smell the smoke plain. Looks like they got it all their own way, now, Buck. Bright as day outside, an' then, when we come out of the door, they'll pick us off as easy as pie."

"We might've known one of 'em would slip down and set the place on fire," Buck said, "but I guess I'm kinda dumb sometimes. I never thought of that."

"Me, neither," Cash said.

The cabin began to fill with the curling smoke. They could hear the breeze outside, fanning the flames to greater fury.

"Flop down on your face," Buck cried, "it's easier to breathe near the floor."

Suddenly the crackling increased and from between the logs in the corner of the room a small tongue of flame licked forth. It disappeared and was followed by a curling drift of smoke. Then another flame appeared, larger and more fierce than the first. At another spot more flames burst into the room and in a moment the corner of the cabin was ablaze, lighting up the interior with its red light. Hotter and hotter it grew till the place seemed a raging inferno and the two men stretched out on the floor could scarcely breathe, as the scorching heat beat down on their defenseless heads.

CHAPTER
EIGHTEEN

"Cash," Buck gasped, "it's gettin' too hot to be comfortable here. Let's get movin'."

"Right you are," Cash answered, his voice coming in short jerks. "We can only die once. Let's go."

They rose, the flames behind licking out as if to catch them, and staggered over to the door that Buck unbarred. One moment they paused to clasp hands, and then, as Cash commenced to swing open the door, Buck said: "Listen!"

Above the crackling and roaring of the flames, there burst from the top of the hill an uproar that carried down to the two waiting men — crashing shots, screams, yells, howls of dismay and cries of triumph. But this time there were no shots fired in the direction of the cabin.

"Appears to me like I hear Big Ike's voice," Cash said, cupping his hand around his ear as they emerged from the burning cabin.

"Slim's, too," Buck answered, as they started for the hill.

"Wow! Yippee!" Cash yelled, breaking into a run. "Come on, Buck."

The two men scrambled up the hill, but before they reached the top, the noise had subsided. When they did get to level ground, a sight awaited them that made their eyes stick out.

There, in the bright moonlight, surrounded by Circle X riders, was a group of about twenty men on foot. Guns lay scattered all over the ground and from the men in the circle of riders came an occasional groan that showed some of the Circle X bullets had found a mark.

As Buck and Cash approached on the run, Slim looked up and saw them.

"Yea-a-a-a, Buck," he sang out, "what'd you think of our roundup?"

"Looks plenty welcome to me," Buck said laughingly.

Cash put in: "Regular old-time shootin' battle, eh, Slim?"

"Not much of a battle," Slim said scornfully. "These here coyotes ain't got no guts to fight. They were all interested waitin' for you to come out o' the fire an' we rode down on them 'fore they seen us. We all hollered like wild-cats and come ridin' in, shootin' and yellin'. I guess they like to think the whole county was after 'em, so they didn't put up no fight. None. I guess we got the whole caboodle of 'em, too, We hit a few of 'em, but nobody ain't hurt bad enough to keep 'em from servin' a jail sentence. Mebbe to make sure, we better string them to a tree right now."

"No," Buck ordered, "some of you tie those scourings up, an' we'll take 'em to La Roda in the morning. How did you know we needed you, Slim?"

"Dude Timmens was out lookin' for a couple of strays in the afternoon, an' he got 'way out, over near the Brias Mesas. He hears a coupla shots, but just then . . ."

"That must've been when we killed that rattler, Buck," Cash broke in.

"Don't interrupt your savior, Cash," Slim said, and then continued: "Well, anyway, jest about the time Timmens heard the shots, he spied the strays, an', while he was roundin' 'em up, he plumb forgets the shots till he gets back to the bunkhouse. Then he thinks it over a while, an' finally tells me. I didn't know what was stirrin', but knowin' you were headed in that direction, I thought mebbe it'd bear lookin' into, so I rounded up the boys an' . . . well, here we are. You know the rest."

"You were sure usin' your good-for-nothin' noodle, Slim." Cash laughed affectionately.

"A-ah! I was doin' it for Buck," Slim retorted. "For all I give a damn, you could've been croaked, then mebbe I'd get your job." He playfully pushed Cash in the face as he spoke the words. These two had been together so long, they were like brothers.

"Well, you've done a good piece of work, Slim." Buck laughed at the two as they scrapped. "Tie those *hombres* in the saddle while Cash an' I find our horses, an' we'll be moseying back."

With the captives tied to their saddles, the Circle X men got under way and within a few hours were back at the bunkhouse. The prisoners were locked in one of the sheds till morning.

After breakfast, the prisoners were brought in, two at a time, to the ranch house, where they were questioned by Cash and Buck. They were a motley array of half-breeds, Mexicans, and good-for-nothing cowpunchers gone wrong. However, nothing could be learned from them. All refused to talk and would not say what they had been doing at the cabin. So far as Buck could learn, they had no particular leader except a huge half-breed to whom they admitted they looked for orders, but he was more stolid than the rest and would not even answer when Buck questioned him. His companion, a shifty-eyed, cringing individual, appeared to be ready to weaken several times, but a snaky glance from the half-breed's eyes silenced him.

While they were talking to the two, Slim came in and informed Buck there was a man waiting to see him.

"Who is it, Slim?" Buck asked.

"You got me. I never seen him before. Says his name is Treharne. He's got them funny ridin' pants on, an', when I seen him comin' in the gate, he was bouncin' up an' down in the saddle like he was tryin' to bend over and bite the horse's ear. He don't ride like no 'puncher a-tall. An' his saddle . . ." Slim paused to give full weight to the scorn in his voice. "His saddle is one of them postage-stamp kind. Just a little, flat piece of leather on the horse's back."

"All right, Slim, tell him I'll be out in a minute." Buck turned to Cash. "Take them back, Cash," he said, motioning to the captives. "I'll talk to them later, especially Shifty-Eyes there."

He turned and left the room. As Buck stepped out on the verandah, a large man in riding clothes rose to greet him. From the moment he cast eyes on him, Buck didn't like his looks.

"Mister Treharne?" he said.

"Yes, are you Mister Thomas?" Treharne thrust out his hand, but Buck pretended not to notice the gesture.

"What can I do for you? I'm asking you to make it quick because I find myself powerful busy this mornin'."

Treharne flushed as Buck refused to take his hand. His smooth manner dropped as he said: "My business will take but a few minutes. I just rode out to ask you when you contemplate vacating my property!"

Buck stared at him, astounded. "Your property?" he finally managed to stammer out.

"Certainly," Treharne said in short, crisp tones. "The Circle X belongs to me. You know that."

Buck recovered himself with an effort. "You know damned well, stranger, that I don't know anything of the kind. I can't see where you have any call to claim the Circle X, anyway. You must be mixed up."

"I have a bill of sale," Treharne said, "that shows the ranch to be my property."

"I think you're plumb loco," Buck said savagely, "an' I want a look at that bill of sale. Dad Flint willed this ranch to me a few days before he died."

"If he did," Treharne said, "he must have been crazy."

Buck advanced a step toward Treharne, his fists clenched, then he got himself under control. "There

236

wasn't a saner man ever lived than Dad Flint," he said steadily. "The Circle X was willed to me, an' there's papers to prove it."

"That may well be," Treharne said, and his tone was confident, "but I doubt that you have any such papers. If so, produce them."

"I can produce them plenty quick," Buck said. "I . . ." He stopped as the thought broke in upon his consciousness that he couldn't produce them. The papers that showed the Circle X to be Buck's had been in Lawyer Higgins's safe. At the time of the murder they had disappeared, together with other papers, when the safe was cleaned out. Until now he hadn't given the matter a thought, but now the idea began to dawn on him that the murder of Higgins was all a part of the move to get Buck off the ranch. But why? There were other ranches in the county, fully as good as the Circle X. A thousand thoughts flashed through his brain, as he sparred for time.

"Well," Treharne broke in impatiently, "if you have any papers to show that the Circle X is your property, I'd like to have a look at them."

"There's papers, all right," Buck said, "but I'm . . . I don't have 'em with me right now. I aim to see that bill of sale you mentioned a few minutes back."

"If you give me your word of honor not to damage it in any way," Treharne was saying slowly, as he reached into an inner pocket, when Buck broke in: " 'Course I won't damage it."

"All right." Treharne produced a paper, unfolded it, and handed it to Buck. To Buck's amazement, he saw a bill of sale, dated six months before, made out properly and signed with the crabbed signature of *D. A. Flint*. Buck looked more closely at the signature. It was Dad's writing, and yet it wasn't. "It's a forgery, nothin' but a forgery!" Buck cried angrily. "And you better clear out *pronto*, Treharne, before I kick you out."

"You refuse to leave the ranch, then?" Treharne said in a rage.

"I not only refuse to leave the ranch, but I'll hang onto this forged bill of sale," Buck said coolly. "I promised not to damage it, an' I won't, but I'm figurin' on keeping it till this affair's settled."

Treharne suddenly withdrew his hand from his coat pocket. In it glittered a revolver and Buck found himself looking down its black muzzle. "You'll return that bill of sale," Treharne roared. "It's genuine, and will hold in any court. If you won't get off the ranch, I'll get out an injunction and keep you off by force, if necessary."

"As I said before," Buck said without a quiver in his voice, "I'm going to hang onto this bill of sale, and you can get out injunctions till hell freezes over, but you won't budge me off the Circle X. I've got a dozen fightin' 'punchers back of me, too, so you better think twice before you do anythin' rash. An' now, *Mister* Treharne," he finished with a sneer in every word, "you can go ahead an' shoot, an' to hell with you!"

CHAPTER
NINETEEN

The two men stood glaring at each other in the tense silence that followed Buck's words. Treharne's finger quivered nervously on the trigger, and Buck expected every minute to see the menacing black muzzle belch fire and death. He was just gathering himself for a spring.

"It's all right, Buck. I got this city-bred snake covered," Cash Jordon's cool drawl came around the corner of the door. "I've been listenin' in, an' I thought he might pull something, so I was plumb ready for him." In a bound, Buck reached Treharne and wrested the gun from his hand.

"Treharne," he said, his tones ringing on the morning air, "you're under arrest for threatening an officer . . . and maybe some more things. Bring him along, Cash. I just had a sudden notion we can use this *hombre*. I feel plumb ashamed for lettin' that pavement lizard get the drop on me, though, an' I don't know as I'll have respect for myself till a few things are cleared up." He made his way out to the bunkhouse, called the cowpunchers around him, and explained what he wanted. "We'll see what a bluff can do," he finished.

In a few minutes the prisoners were brought out of the shed where they could see Treharne with Cash holding a gun over him. Half a dozen of the cowpunchers got their horses and, going to the crowd of prisoners, two of them singled out Shifty-Eyes and, picking him up between them with a hand under each arm, galloped to where Buck stood waiting. As they reached the spot, they let go of their captive and he sprawled at Buck's feet as the two horses dashed to either side.

Buck reached down and hauled the cringing wretch to his feet. "Look here, you buzzard," he said to the man, while the others watched them from a distance, "you're going to talk, an' talk plenty, or you're liable to leave this earth right sudden."

"I don't know nothin'," the man said sullenly. "I told you before . . ."

"Mebbe, then, you'd like to know that Black Bart Lannon is behind bars," Buck cut in on him.

The shot went home. The man started, but said nothing.

"Furthermore," Buck continued, "he's confessed everything."

"That ain't nothin' to me," the man said, regaining a grip on himself. "I don't know nobody by the name of Lannon."

"You lie," Buck said. "You see that *hombre* over there?" He pointed to Treharne as the man turned his shifty eyes to the spot where Cash stood guarding his prisoner. "I suppose you don't know him, either. He's been doing some confessin', too."

240

"What'd you want outta me, then?"

"There's a few details that aren't quite clear yet. You might just as well furnish them, because, when your trial comes up, it'll go a lot easier with you. Now, are you going to talk, or aren't you?"

Shifty-Eyes started to speak, but changed his mind. "No," he said stubbornly, "I don't know nothin'."

"All right." Buck straightened up impatiently. "There's more'n one way to make a man talk." He motioned, and six cowpunchers rode out, swinging their ropes. As they trotted up, six circles of flying rope sailed through the air and settled gracefully around the captive's body, tightening as they fell.

"When I count three," Buck ordered the cowpunchers, "you six ride away in different directions, hangin' on tight to your ropes. We'll see if we can't squeeze a few words outta this stubborn mule."

"Aw, you can't do that, Buck," Slim called from behind, carrying out the bluff, "that'd be murder!"

"Oh, I can't, eh?" Buck said. "I reckon I'm boss here, an', if you don't like it, you can get out." His tone was savage, but, as he turned to Slim with a wink, he was grinning broadly. He swung back to Shifty-Eyes. "I'm going to begin counting now. One! Are you going to talk?"

The man shook his head defiantly. "No, an' you don't dare do nothin' to me."

"Two!" Buck's voice was inexorable, and the ropes tightened a little.

"I'll talk . . . I'll talk!" the man yelled. "Whaddya want to know?"

"That's better," Buck said. "First, who's head of this gang?"

"Black Bart."

Buck nodded, but said nothing. His first surmise was correct. Then he went on questioning and probing. The man talked freely. When Buck was through with him, he took the other captives, one by one, and, when they learned that Shifty-Eyes had confessed, they were more than eager to tell what they knew in the hope that their jail sentence might be made lighter. In a short time, Buck had nearly the whole story.

As he went back to the ranch house, followed by Cash Jordon with Treharne, Cash said: "What'd you learn, Buck?"

"Enough to convict this whole gang, Treharne and Black Bart Lanon included," Buck answered. "Bring Treharne into the house and tie him up. I'll tell you the whole story." They entered, and Cash began roping Treharne to a chair.

"You, Treharne, mebbe you'll feel like supplying some details to this story as I go along," Buck said. Treharne didn't answer, so Buck turned to Cash.

"In the first place," he began, "with the capture of that bunch of skunks out there, we break up Black Bart Lannon's gang, an' they told just about everything we want to know. It was Black Bart Lannon who killed Jimmie and he was at the head of the Apaches when Dad Flint was killed. It was Black Bart Lannon's gang that strung up Kicking Horse and his braves, an' it was the same gang that killed Winfield. Also, it was Black Bart Lannon who murdered Lawyer Higgins, an' it was

242

Lannon that sent his gang down to the cabin to get me, knowing sooner or later I'd come down to look for those stolen cattle."

"What did he have against Higgins?" Cash asked.

"Higgins had the papers that proved that Dad Flint willed the Circle X to me. This Treharne paid Black Bart Lannon to put Jimmie and Dad out of the way, so's he and Lannon could claim the ranch."

"That's a lie," Treharne broke in. "I don't know this Lannon you speak of." He scowled at Buck, but was agitated and his eyes blinked nervously.

"Well, there's plenty say you do," Buck said dryly. "From what I hear, you an' Black Bart Lannon have been right chummy the last several months." Without waiting for an answer, he went on with the story. "You see," he explained, "they figured with Dad and Jimmie out of the way, they'd have clear sailing. Jimmie going to Conejo Lures made it all the easier for Lannon to get him. Where they fell down was on not knowin' Dad had willed the ranch to me."

"What I don't understand," Cash said, "is what they want the Circle X so almighty bad for. They're lots of other ranches, some of them better situated."

"That's something I don't savvy no-wise," Buck said. "Treharne, it's up to you. Why are you so keen on getting the Circle X?"

"I don't know what you've been talking about," Treharne answered. "I wanted the Circle X as an investment. I'm interested in cattle raising and I bought the ranch from Flint. I paid a good price for it, too."

"Well," Buck replied, "why did you take so long about claimin' it? This bill of sale you produced is dated six months back. Probably you just wrote it yourself a couple of days back."

"The reason," Treharne said, thinking fast, "that I didn't claim the ranch before is because I have just returned from a hunting trip in southern Texas."

"Yeah! Some huntin' trip," Cash said scornfully. "Huntin' trips don't last six months . . . leastwise in Texas."

"Previous to that," Treharne continued lamely, "I was taken ill right after concluding the sale of the ranch with Flint and spent over five months in the hospital."

"What hospital?" Buck shot at him. "Quick, answer."

Treharne hesitated a minute before he replied: "I don't remember."

"That sounds likely," Buck scoffed. "Well, it'll all come out at the trial, an' we'll find out all about those hunting trips an' hospitals, then. When you and Black Bart Lannon begin telling the jury all about it, we'll see whether those stories'll hold water or not. With the evidence we've got right now, none of Black Bart Lannon's gang stands to get off. We get the murderers, cattle rustlers, skinners, all of 'em."

At that moment a sound was heard at the door and Chet Wiggins came in, panting. "Oh, there you are, Buck. I gotta letter for you that a big *hombre* in one o' them red serapes give me to give you. He says as how it was bad news for you, an' you'd be anxious to get it. Did I ever tell you, Buck, about the time my brother Peleg had a letter to deliver . . . ?"

244

But Buck had no time to hear the story. He jerked the greasy envelope from Wiggins's hand and ripped it open and read:

Buck Thomas
    I'm headin' fur Conejo Lures. Ef yu want me, yu kin come end git me.
                                        Black Bart Lannon

For an instant Buck's senses swam. Then his mind leaped into action. "Cash," he said, "run like hell an' get our horses saddled. Take Treharne out and turn him over to Slim. Tell Slim and the rest of the boys to bring the whole gang down to the La Roda jail. You and me're goin' to La Roda right off, an' we aren't stopping to pick no daisies on the way."

Cash hurried Treharne out of the door almost before Buck could hear him urging Treharne to greater efforts as they passed the window of the ranch house: "And you better hustle now, if you never hustled before," Cash was saying, " 'cause, if you don't move right *pronto*, I aim to split your head open with the barrel of this six-gun. Come on, shuffle them dogs, this ain't no hop-toad race you're in . . ."

Cash's voice died away as the two passed out of Buck's hearing. Buck turned to Wiggins. "When did you get this letter, Chet?"

Chet rolled his eyes to the ceiling and appeared to concentrate. "Was it this mornin'?" he asked himself. "No, 'course it wasn't. It was yestiddy forenoon . . . or afternoon . . . I disremembers which. Le's see. It was yestiddy afternoon, long 'bout five o'clock. I 'member now, 'cause Mirandy kept me t'hum to do the washin' in the forenoon. Funny thing about Mirandy, she's allus washin'. I 'member the last time she washed. It was durin' that rainy spell we had that time . . ."

Buck cut him short. "I don't care anything about your family affairs like I told you more than once before. Get this straight, Chet, and answer my questions. You said you got this letter yesterday afternoon. Where was the *hombre* that gave it to you?"

"I was walkin' along peaceful-like when this big geezer with the red serappy, like I told you before, comes gallopin' down the road. Just as he gets up to me, he pulls in the hoss an' gives me the letter, tellin' me like I told you. He drawed a gun an' said if I didn't deliver it *pronto*, he'd come back and shoot me full of holes. Jest to show him that no man kin talk to Chester Wiggins thataway, I went an' got a coupla drinks first an then I kinda fergot the letter till this mornin'. I 'member oncet when Peleg had a letter to deliver . . ."

In his haste to get out the door, Buck nearly swept the fat man off his feet. He tore down the steps of the verandah, and a few moments later Cash came tearing around the corner, leading Buck's horse. He didn't slow up, and, as Buck caught the bridle and swung himself into the saddle of the galloping horse, Cash yelled to him: "What's all the rush about, Buck? You seem kinda in a hurry to get to La Roda."

"Rush is right!" Buck shouted back. "Black Bart Lannon's outta jail, an', if he isn't put back right quick, there'll probably be some hell a-poppin'."

CHAPTER
TWENTY

As the foam-flecked horses dashed through the center of La Roda, they left behind them a cloud of dust that well-nigh choked the astonished citizens as they turned to gaze after the two riders. Straight for the jail they rode, and, as they pulled up short before the door, Buck and Cash threw the reins over the horses' heads and hurried inside and up the stairs to the judge's office. As usual the judge was sleeping. With little ceremony, Buck took him by the collar and jerked him awake.

"Here, here, Sheriff," Judge Hosmer cried as he struggled to get out of Buck's grasp, "what does all this mean?" He rubbed his eyes and peered at Buck indignantly.

"Where's Black Bart Lannon?" Buck roared at him.

"Lannon? He's around town some place, I guess," the judge said.

"What's he doing around town? I told you to hang onto him. How did he get out?"

"He gave bail," the judge said. "He produced an alibi and I couldn't do anything but let him go when your evidence was so slim. He'll be here for the trial, all right. He promised me, personally, that he would."

"Promised, hell," Buck said. "He headed for Conejo Lures yesterday an' you'll have a sweet time getting him back. What kind of an alibi did he produce?"

"A man by the name of Treharne came here yesterday and he took an oath that Lannon had been acting as a guide for him over in southern Texas on a hunting trip for some time past . . ."

"Heh-heh," snickered Cash, "some more o' them six-month huntin' trips."

"You chuck-headed fool," Buck cried, "an' did you let him go on that?"

"Certainly, why not?" the judge queried. "Treharne is a responsible man, and he had good credentials. He's a big banker over in Austin."

"How do you know he is?" Buck asked. He was cooler now that his first rage was wearing off.

"Why . . . why . . . ," the judge stammered, "I don't know . . . I guess . . . well, he told me he was."

"You meddlin' old woman," Buck said. "Those credentials were forgeries. Mebbe you'll be interested to learn that if it wasn't for this Treharne *hombre*, Lawyer Higgins an' some others, too, would be alive today. We captured Treharne and a bunch of Lannon's gang that were sent down to the Circle X to kill me an' run off cattle. Oh, yeah, there's plenty of evidence to prove that Treharne's crooked."

"Well . . . well," Judge Hosmer said weakly, "Treharne furnished bail for Lannon, anyway."

"How much did he furnish?" Buck asked.

"Two . . . two hundred dollars," Judge Hosmer squeaked confusedly.

"Two hundred dollars?" Buck roared. "Didn't you have any more sense than to let a murderer go on two hundred dollars' bail?"

"Well, you see, Sheriff, Treharne said he was all right, and I thought perhaps you were mistaken. Maybe you'd better go after Lannon right away, if that's the case. Good gracious, I hope I haven't done wrong in letting him go. It might go hard with me if this gets out." The judge was by now thoroughly frightened, and, as he sank back into his chair, his face was ashen and his hands trembled as though he had the palsy. Buck began to feel sorry for him.

"That's all right, Judge," he said quietly. "I'll do what I can to straighten things out. Slim Rollins is on his way here now with Treharne and the Lannon gang. Don't let any of them out under any consideration without seeing me first."

"I won't, Sheriff, I won't," he promised earnestly.

As they were descending the stairs, Buck said: "Now I know why Lannon was so cocky that day. He knew Treharne was coming and would get him out. He probably figured he'd get off clean in a trial, too, with Treharne swearing to his alibi. If we hadn't got that gang at the cabin and made them confess, he'd probably have got away with it, too."

Cash nodded as they emerged from the door, got into saddles, and rode slowly side-by-side to Buck's office. "Yeah, he sent that gang down to wait for you, knowin' that you'd go down to investigate the stealin' of them cattle, an' then they'd pump you full of lead. Meanwhile, he stays in La Roda and he can prove he ain't had nothin' to do with your murder. Yes, sir," Cash said slowly, "it was sure lucky for us that we caught the coyotes."

"I don't understand Lannon headin' back for Conejo Lures," Buck said, "and leavin' the whole scheme flat."

"I've been thinkin' of that," Cash said, "an' the way I got it figured out is that he just wrote that note to throw you off the track an' didn't go to Conejo Lures a-tall. Then, probably thinking you would give up the chase, he headed for the cabin an' got there just in time to find his gang bein' rounded up by Slim and the boys. That bein' the case, he turned around and dug out before anybody saw him. Mebbe he's gone to Conejo Lures now, though. I don't think he'd hang around this neck of the woods. The thing for him to do would be to beat it out of U.S. territory. Conejo Lures is the closest place to here over the border, an' he might've gone there to lay low till he sees what happens."

"That sounds right plausible, Cash," Buck said slowly, "an' the more I think on it, the more certain I am that you're right." As he finished speaking, they drew rein before Buck's office and, after tying the horses, went inside.

As they passed through the door, which was unlocked, a man rose from Buck's chair.

"Is this Sheriff Thomas?" he said.

"You've called the turn," Buck answered shortly. "What can I do for you?"

"I'd like to talk to you for a few minutes. My name is Charles Sinclair. I'm from the Assayer's Office in Albuquerque. I came to La Roda to see D. A. Flint, who formerly owned the Circle X Ranch. Then, I learned at the bank that he is dead and you are the owner. If I may have a few minutes of your time, perhaps I can tell you something that will be to your advantage."

"This is Cash Jordon, my foreman," Buck introduced, "an' he can hear anything you've got to say." The man shook hands, and then sat down.

"To begin with," Sinclair said, lighting a cigar, which was a mate to the ones Cash and Buck were lighting, "did you ever hear of a man by the name of Wilkens, Homer H. Wilkens?"

"You're plumb tootin' I did," Buck said. "He made a nuisance of himself tryin' to buy the Circle X from me."

Sinclair nodded. "At one time Wilkens worked in the Assayer's Office. Some months back, Mister Flint came to see us with two unusually high-grade samples of silver ore, which he had uncovered on his ranch. Leaving the samples, he asked us to put them to test and see how they came out. We were to write him an account of our report. We had just finished the report when Wilkens absconded from the office with a sum of money, the report, and the samples. When he left, he took several other papers with him and affairs were in such confusion that it has taken us some time to get them straightened out."

"You say there's silver on the Circle X?" Buck asked blankly. Sinclair nodded as Buck continued: "Mebbe you're right, but there isn't any silver land around there that I know of."

"Sure," Cash broke in, "down near the cabin. There might be silver in any of those hills. I bet that's what Dad was doin' there that day I saw him with the pick and shovel. I thought he was huntin' for worms to fish with an' I didn't give it no more thought. Dad never said nothin' about lookin' for silver, did he, Buck?"

Buck shook his head. "He wouldn't anyway. Dad never said much about anything unless he was sure." He turned to Sinclair. "Are *you* sure they's silver on the Circle X?"

"Just as certain as I am that I'm alive," Sinclair answered. "But I'll get on with my story. When affairs were in such confusion, we wrote Mister Flint, telling him how things stood, and not knowing that the samples of ore were gone, that we'd send him a report of the analysis just as soon as we got straightened out. We didn't hear from him after that and I supposed he was waiting for us to write. Meanwhile, we were searching for Wilkens. A few days ago, he was caught in El Paso. Upon his capture, he confessed he had stolen the report with the intention of going into partnership with one Treharne. Treharne has been mixed up in more than one crooked deal in various parts of the country, and the police of several states are looking for him at present. Anyway, Wilkens and Treharne formed the partnership and they set out to get the Circle X Ranch. I imagine it took them some little time to get busy, because Wilkens said the police were following so closely on their trail they couldn't work back to this part of the country. You say Wilkens has already approached you on the subject of buying the ranch?"

Buck nodded. "Yeah. He and Treharne both have been to see me," he said grimly. "Not being able to get the ranch any other way, they hired a killer to put the rightful owners out of the way, an' then forged a bill of sale after murderin' the lawyer who had the papers and the will, showing the Circle X belongs to me."

Sinclair whistled under his breath. "I didn't think they'd go to such lengths. They couldn't have paid you for the ranch, unless they got the money in some crooked way. From what I hear, Treharne is pretty bad . . ."

"He won't be any longer," Buck broke in, and then he told Sinclair the whole story from start to finish. "And now I know," Buck finished, "why they were so anxious to get the Circle X. You say those samples you spoke of show up rich?"

Sinclair reached down into his traveling bag and produced two samples of ore that he laid on the table. "Wilkens had these with him at the time of his capture," he said. "I'll be glad to leave them here, because they're too heavy to carry around with me, I've found. You can see for yourself" — tracing with his pencil the wide, white streaks that ran across the cross-section of the rock — "that it looks pretty good."

"No, I'm not saying that I can," Buck answered. "What I don't know about silver ore would make a right big book."

"Well, according to the figures that Wilkens had with him, the analysis shows that the value will prove up pretty high to the ton . . . right now, I dislike to state the exact amount. When we have had the opportunity to verify Wilkens's figures, I'll have something definite to say. We'll send two or three men down within a few days to look over the land and bring back some large pieces of the ore. Then we'll know exactly where we stand. But I'm positive, Mister Thomas, that there isn't the slightest doubt in the world but that you have in your hills one of the biggest things ever uncovered in New Mexico. I advise, however, that you take immediate steps to prove your ownership to the ranch. It may cause some confusion and no little trouble unless you get that matter straightened out. Well, I must be going. I hope everything turns out OK." Sinclair shook hands with the two men and, after some few words, left.

CHAPTER
TWENTY-ONE

"Well, there's just one thing to be done," Cash was saying, after Sinclair had gone, "and that's to get the papers an' the will that Dad left."

Buck slowly nodded his head. "You're right, Cash, providing those papers are still in existence. It'd be just like Treharne to tear them up."

Cash shook his head. "I don't know, Buck. He might've tore up the will, but I reckon he'd hold onto the deeds to the land. He would have needed them."

Buck thought deeply for a few moments before replying. "Mebbe you're shootin' straight, Cash. I'm goin' to mosey over to the jail and talk to Treharne. Mebbe he'll let somethin' slip that'll give me a tip where those papers are. You wait here an' see if anything turns up." He settled his sombrero on his head and passed through the door.

Buck had nearly reached the jail, when he met Slim coming along the street. "Did you get your prisoners put behind bars?" he asked.

"You're shootin' I did," Slim replied. "Every one of those bastards is restin' graceful in his cage, right this minute. That old gran'ma of a Judge Hosmer nearly blew up when he saw Treharne. You know all about it,

256

don't you, about Treharne bailin' out Black Bart Lannon and everythin'?" Buck nodded, and Slim went on: "After he talked to Hosmer for a while, Treharne broke down an' said he'd confess everything, so Hosmer quick gets a man to write it out an' he was takin' down every word Treharne said when I left. The boys was getting' kinda thirsty, so I told them to go and sluice down while I came here to see you."

"I'm on my way to see Treharne now. Cash's waitin' in the office. Go on down and see him. He can tell you some more things that'll clear up a heap of questions."

When Buck entered the jail, Judge Hosmer was waiting for him with the confession. It was practically complete, even to Treharne's acknowledging that he had it fixed with Lannon to get Dad Flint and the others put out of the way. Tutt Arnold was also implicated. He it was who was expected to shoot Buck the day of their fight, and it was only through the intercession of Cash and the other cowpunchers that such a fate had been averted.

"Now, if you can only get this Black Bart Lannon," Judge Hosmer said, as Buck finished reading the confession, "you'll be doing the country a real service, Sheriff."

"We had him once," Buck said meaningfully, and swung on his heel out of the room.

A few minutes later, he was in Treharne's cell. "Well, Treharne, seems like you got yourself in a mess."

"I know it, Sheriff . . . Mister Thomas," Treharne answered, "but I'm hoping through my confession to get a lighter sentence."

"I don't know about that," Buck answered dubiously. "There wasn't much you could tell that we didn't already know before you started to talk."

"Well, I want to do anything I can to help matters along now," Treharne said. "If there is anything else you'd like to know . . ." He hesitated as Buck cut in.

"There are a couple of things, Treharne, but first I'll tell you something. I notice you didn't say anything in your confession about why you wanted to get the Circle X. Now, I know why. Wilkens was arrested in El Paso a few days ago, and he had one of these confession spells, too. So that part's cleaned up, and you can't figure on gettin' the silver after you get out of jail."

Treharne blanched. "That was something I forgot to tell," he muttered.

"Forgot, hell!" Buck said. "Now, I want to know where Black Bart Lannon is."

Treharne looked him straight in the eyes. "That is something I can't tell you," he said. "I thought he was going to stay around La Roda after I bailed him out and . . . and . . ."

"And shoot me," Buck supplied.

Treharne nodded weakly.

"Well, he's gone," Buck said, "and what I want to know is . . . where are those papers and the will that proves the ranch is mine. No, I know you haven't got them" — as Treharne started to speak — "I asked at the office before I came in here and I know they weren't found when you were searched. Now, where are they?"

"I gave them to Lannon to keep, while I went out to the ranch to see you. I was afraid there might be some trouble and I didn't want to have the papers on me."

"I guess you're speaking the truth," Buck said, "and, if you aren't, God help you if I find it out." With that, he left the cell. As the door clanged after him, the thought came to Buck that perhaps Mariposa might tell him something that would help.

As he entered the cell, the girl was busily engaged in trying to decipher the English words in a Bible she held on her lap. As she laid the Bible down, a wave of pity swept over Buck. She was such a child, and despite her former life perhaps something could be done to save her.

"Mariposa," he said, "Black Bart Lannon's gang is broken up, but Lannon's got away. Will you tell me where I can find him?"

"I do not know, *señor*."

"But you must know something about him. You followed him up here to La Roda."

"*Señor* Thomas," the girl said with sudden decision, "eet is true I followed Black Bart here, but he did not know I was here. I came . . . oh, bad woman that I am . . . to keel Lannon."

"To kill Lannon," Buck said in surprise. "Didn't Lannon help you to escape from the Conejo Lures jail? What'd you want to kill him for?"

"Because I loved Wolf Lannon, an' Wolf Lannon was just a young boy, but he tried to be bad like his brother. If eet was not for Black Bart, we could have been happy. I, too, have been verra wicked, but eet was for

Wolf. Now, I am sorry, *señor*. Eet was my own friends that help me make the escape."

"But, jumpin' lizards, Mariposa, why didn't you tell me that before, when I asked you where Black Bart Lannon was?"

"I was afraid, *Señor* Thomas, that you would lock Black Bart up before I could kill heem. Now, I know it would not be right for Mariposa to do that. If I get out of jail, I will be, oh, so good, *señor*."

"Mariposa, I am going to Conejo Lures to see if I can find Black Bart. When I get back, I am going to be married. How would you like to come out to the ranch an' live with us? Mebbe we could find some work for you to do."

"Oh, *señor*, that would be gr-rand," she said, tears welling into her eyes. "I would work so hard, and I . . ."

Buck cut short her thanks as he turned to go. Then she caught his hand and said: "If you look for Black Bart in Conejo Lures, *señor*, seek him at the Calientas *cantina*."

"Calientas *cantina?*" Buck repeated. "Why?"

"*Sí, señor*. That is where he always goes when he is in Conejo Lures. They do not like heem, nobuddy in Conejo Lures like heem, but they are afraid to speak when he is present." Mariposa brushed the tears from her eyes. "May you have much of the good luck, *señor*. *Adiós*."

"*Adiós*," Buck said, and was gone.

He returned to the office and found Cash waiting for him. "I told Slim an' the rest of the boys to head back for the Circle X," Cash said. Buck explained in a few words what he had learned from Mariposa and Treharne.

"But what are you goin' to do about those papers?" Cash asked.

"I'm pullin' out for Conejo Lures tomorrow an' see if I can find Lannon," Buck answered, "and, if possible, I'm going to bring him back here alive. If not . . . mebbe he'll get me. *¿Quién sabe?* Because of that I'm riding out to see Helen Fanning this afternoon. I expect we'll be married after this ruckus is all settled down. I don't aim to tell her where I'm going tomorrow, so don't say anything to anybody."

Cash nodded. "I get you. Mebbe I'd better go along to Conejo Lures with you."

"No," Buck said, "I'd like to have you with me, Cash, but Lannon's my meat. Besides, if anythin' does happen . . . well, you'll have to kind of be around to handle things. Another thing. Mebbe Lannon isn't in Conejo Lures. Keep your eye peeled. He might be in this neck of the woods yet."

"Yeah, but I don't think so," Cash said. "Oh, I forgot to tell you. Slim was plumb excited about the silver mine an' he wants me to ask you if he can have enough silver to make a pair of spurs with."

"He sure can, an' a lotta other things." Buck laughed, then he grew serious. "It's going to take me a long time to square up with all you boys, after the way you've backed me the last few months, Cash."

"Aw, it ain't nothin'," Cash said, abashed. He stood silently for a few moments, then: "Well, guess I'll be

261

trailin' along." He stuck out his hand and Buck seized it.

"S'long, Cash."

"S'long, see you some more," Cash answered. He turned and in a minute had passed through the door. Thus did these two men part, perhaps never to meet again, but the strong clasp of their hands told more than could be put into words.

CHAPTER
TWENTY-TWO

The afternoon sun was painting the adobe houses a brilliant orange when Buck rode into Conejo Lures the next day. From the low, flat-topped buildings the inhabitants were emerging, yawning, from their afternoon *siestas*. They glanced idly at Buck as he loped into town. It made them weary, just to see him moving so fast. A shrug of tired shoulders, or a muttered imprecation on the ambition of all *gringos*, and their minds relapsed to the tedious business of existence.

Straight for the Calientas *cantina* Buck rode. Arriving there, he tied his horse in front at the water trough and entered into the coolness of the dim interior. As his tall form shadowed the door, some Mexicans drinking at the bar turned and looked idly at him for a few moments, before returning to their tequila. Buck tossed some silver on the bar and, after sluicing down his alkali-caked throat with copious droughts of acrid water, turned to the bartender and asked where he could find Black Bart Lannon.

For a moment the man stared and his mouth slowly opened as if to speak. Then fear overcame him and he shook his head. Buck questioned the men at the bar, but, after hastily swallowing their tequila, they, too, shook their heads, and left hurriedly. Nothing was to be learned in the place, so Buck turned and went out. As he emerged from the doorway, something on the horse's back caught his eye. Transfixed to the saddle with a long knife was a piece of cloth that had been cut from a red serape. Black Bart Lannon had been there while Buck was in the *cantina!*

The rest of the afternoon and far into the night Buck haunted the town's three saloons, but without finding trace of his enemy. Once, as he entered the dance hall where Jimmie had been shot, a fleeting glance was had of a man with a red serape as he disappeared around the corner of a door in the far wall. Buck, gun in hand, reached the door before it slammed shut. When he looked out, there was nothing to be seen but the bare runway between two buildings.

Gradually, as midnight passed, the noises of the town subsided, and Buck commenced a ceaseless patrol of the single street, which was now deserted. From somewhere on the outskirts of the gray line of adobe buildings the cool breeze carried down to Buck the faint tinkling of a mandolin and he could hear a soft, tenor voice raised in an old Spanish serenade. Occasionally, back in the hills, a coyote's howl split the night, and then far to the right from another point would come the answer. Other coyotes would take up the cry and the howls resounded as they gathered in volume and rolled across the hills, to die slowly away in low, murmuring echoes. Then all was silence again.

The stars grew less distinct and the pallid light from the ghostly moon, as it swung low to the hilltops, cast weird shadows across the lonely street. Along the eastern horizon a faint gray was beginning to tinge the sky. Buck, standing in the sheltered dark near a small shop, was waiting with every nerve tense and his hearing strained to the utmost. Trying to keep an outlook on all sides, he expected every moment to hear a gun flare out and to feel cruel lead rip into his body. Once, something came sneaking along the road, and his hands flew instinctively to the holsters. There was a slow expelling of breath when he saw it was only a prowling dog.

Suddenly, across the street, a form moved in the shadow between two houses. As his eyes focused to the darkness, Buck made out Black Bart Lannon, a gun raised in his hand. At that instant Lannon fired, and Buck felt something hit his shoulder with a staggering smash. The impact of the bullet whirled him sidewise as his hands darted to his hips. His right arm, benumbed by the shot, refused to act, but from his left hand ran a stream of fire. Black Bart's gun flew through the air as he spun half around, hands tearing at his body, and crumpled into the dust. Through the blue haze of drifting smoke, Buck could see Lannon, struggling to right himself as he groped at the holster for his other gun. As Buck came running up, Lannon got to his knees. Bracing himself with one outspread hand, his gun flashed up and a bullet tore viciously along the loose bandanna at Buck's neck. By this time the numbness had left Buck's right arm and the black grip of the long .45 seemed to leap eagerly into his hand as fire and lead thundered from its muzzle. Lannon's head went back with a jerk, then sank slowly forward as he pitched on his face in the dust. For a minute he twisted snakily, then a compulsive shudder ran through his body, and he lay still.

Buck bent, swaying, over the fallen man, as he returned the smoking guns to their holsters. Then, stooping at Black Bart Lannon's side, his hand fumbled a moment in the bullet-riddled shirt and came forth holding some bloodspotted papers. As they were spread out, Buck saw, in the gray light, that he held the will.

To this day the natives of Conejo Lures tell of that fight. They heard the shots, but so greatly was Black Bart Lannon feared that, for a time, no one dared venture out to see which was the victor. Finally, when all was silent again, an aged *mestizo* woman crept timidly forth. A second she gazed down at the stiffening figure, while underneath a crimson pool blended slowly into the red serape. Next, her head lifted to Buck. There was a grateful light in her old eyes as she bound up his shoulder. Then he walked slowly back to the waiting horse and wearily hauled a tired body into the saddle.

The morning was half gone when Buck met Cash and Slim on the trail to the Circle X as they rode, whooping, to meet him.